A Cardinal Odyssey

Written by:

William Mowat

CROWN & ANCHOR PUBLISHING

crownandanchorpublishing@gmail.com

Copyright © 2025, William Mowat, Author
Published in Canada by Crown and Anchor Publishing,
Welland, Ontario L3B 3H9
ISBN 978-1-7380796-67

Table of Contents

"It is not the strongest or the most intelligent who will survive but those who can best manage change."

-- Charles Darwin

Chapter 1 - The Hunt

Grant Cardinal stealthily led his young son Cody through northern Labrador's dense, dying spruce forest. Both had their hand-carved wooden bows drawn and were ready to take down their prey. Heavy snow swirled down from the overcast skies as they stalked silently between the trees. They were careful and deliberate with their steps, avoiding the loud crunches that might alert the nearby caribou. Along the ridgeline, they crept, focusing on a large bull male.

Cody spotted the bull caribou, glanced at his father, and pointed toward the valley. Grant placed his gloved index finger to his lips. The caribou emitted a series of grunts and bugles to signal to his nearby herd, yet the bull still failed to notice the hunters. Grant and Cody moved through the thicket to get a closer shot. The wind masked their human scent, and their bodies blended with the dark hues of their clothing among the browning coniferous forest.

With rosy cheeks and chapped lips, Grant nodded to his son as they crept into position thirty metres from the massive bull. Now was the moment. They both drew their bows, steadied their nerves, aimed, and released their homemade arrows. Thwack, thwack. Both arrows soared through the air and struck the bull in the ribs. Startled, the buck reared up, kicked his front hooves in the air, and uttered an unsettling cry.

"Got him!" Cody said.

"Me too!" Grant said, smiling at his son.

The buck ran about ten steps and then dropped to the snowy forest floor.

Grant smiled and turned to his son, warning, "Remember Cody, he's still dangerous, even when lying down."

"Come on!" Cody said as he slid down the rocky formation into the open valley.

The caribou buck was no longer breathing when Grant and Cody arrived at the body. This hunt would ensure a month of sustenance for their family, providing them with food, clothing, and tools during the harsh winter months ahead.

Grant fashioned a stretcher from twine and tree branches to enable the two men to drag the carcass out of the bush before predators discovered it. He understood the need for speed in processing, as darkness would descend soon, and the big cats and packs of dogs would be on the prowl before long.

The two men carefully rolled the animal onto the stretcher, secured it, and began the arduous task of dragging the 400-pound beast home. Grant and Cody took a rein, slung it over their shoulders, and set off through the deep snow.

The father and son said very little to each other on the journey home, as they were both on high alert. Dusk was prime feeding time, so they remained vigilant for big cats, bears, and wolves. If one or more were nearby, they would certainly have to surrender the buck.

After a strenuous trek through the snow, they arrived home after dark, drenched in sweat and parched. Cody smiled at the smoke billowing from their stone chimney as he caught the enticing aroma of delicious cooking. The home was the heart of the Cardinal family's world, symbolizing warmth and comfort amid the cold, barren emptiness.

Grant opened the door to the processing shed and dragged the snowy, half-frozen buck inside. The log shed had a dirt floor and a massive, handcrafted worktable with old iron tools hanging everywhere. These traps, augers, axes, chains, knives, and other instruments enabled the Cardinals to forge a livelihood in such a harsh world.

As he had done a hundred times before, Grant threw a rope over the centre beam, tied the buck's hooves down, and lifted it off the ground.

Meanwhile, Cody had started a fire in the small stone fireplace at the far end of the shed. Processing the caribou buck would take all night, and the boys needed heat to prevent it from freezing and to ensure a comfortable working environment. After hanging the buck and getting the fire blazing, Cody and Grant stepped out of the shed, latching it behind them, and made their way into the main log cabin.

The Cardinal cabin stood grey with age and weathering. It featured a large wooden door and two small windows at the front, with smoke billowing from the chimney. Though it was only one storey, it offered adequate space for the family.

Cody jumped onto the snowy front porch and opened the front door to a dimly lit cabin. Warmth welcomed the cold, exhausted boys, especially Cody, who was only twelve. Growing quickly, it was challenging for him to gain weight and retain body fat, so he felt the chill more than most. He walked straight to the large stone hearth, sat on a small stool, and warmed his hands.

"Claire? Brooklyn?" Grant called as he stamped off his boots.

No response led Grant to assume they were still hunting ptarmigan together. The small white birds were common in

Labrador and made for a delicious delicacy. Grant headed to the kitchen and uncovered a pot of stew left on the back burner of the wrought-iron stove from the early 1900s. The meat and potato stew wafted steam into Grant's face, filling his nose and making his mouth water. After a long day, he had built up a tremendous appetite.

"Your mom left us some stew, Cody," Grant announced.

"I'm starving," Cody replied, jumping to his feet.

Grant used a hand-carved wooden ladle to scoop out a couple of bowls and handed one to his son. "Remember to chew your food and enjoy it," Grant said with a smile.

"I will," Cody responded, taking the bowl and sitting back by the fire.

Both men began eating the warm meal when Claire and Brooklyn came through the cabin door, each carrying a few dead, white-feathered ptarmigan.

"Look, Dad!" Brooklyn exclaimed excitedly. "I got three!"

"Nice shooting, peanut," Grant said, taking another spoonful of stew. "It's cold out there, isn't it?"

"This is the coldest, whitest September so far," Claire remarked with a frown.

"I know," Grant replied, taking another bite. "You'll be happy to hear we bagged a 400-pound buck today. Cody and I dragged it back. It's hanging inside the shed, thawing out."

Claire smiled at her husband.

"I want to see it!" Brooklyn jumped up and rushed outside to check out the freshly caught caribou.

"Wait for me!" Cody shouted as he dashed out after her.

Claire and Grant shared a warm hug and a kiss in their cozy cabin. Life was growing increasingly challenging year after year: the number of animals was decreasing, trees were dying, and the growing season was nearly nonexistent, making it challenging for the family after ten years in northern Labrador. Despite the hardships, today's caribou was a significant victory and source of relief. Soon, all the large game animals would migrate south, and the trapping season would begin.

"Congratulations on the buck, my dear," Claire said with a smile.

The small cabin was adorned with animal skins from various creatures the Cardinal family hunted. Rabbit furs, beaver pelts, caribou hides, bear skins, and mink furs decorated the walls. Much of their clothing was made from these hides, including their winter boots, jackets, gloves, and hats.

"We'll have to stretch the hide tomorrow," Grant said, pulling Claire close.

Claire originally hailed from Laval and married Grant Cardinal 15 years ago in a charming little church on the east side of Montréal. At one time, Grant held a stable position as an engineer with the Québec government's Ministry of Transportation. The two young adults first met at a small diner Grant often visited for lunch. Claire worked there as a waitress and initiated a flirtatious conversation one afternoon, and the rest was history.

"I look forward to it," Claire replied, kissing him.

Over the past ten years in Labrador, Claire had mastered the skills of trapping, sewing, woodcarving, and homesteading. She had come a long way from her previous life as a waitress, serving toasted BLT's, runny eggs, and stale coffee.

"Our ancestors would be proud of you," Grant said, sliding his hands down the small of her back.

Grant's parents had moved to Churchill Falls, Labrador, to work on the massive hydroelectric dam in the 1960s. His engineer father built the cabin with friends during their time off the dam project. For young Grant, the cabin became a magical gathering place where he observed local Cree trappers, dam workers, and old-timers making snares, stretching hides, and sharing stories of the far north.

Grant developed his interest in engineering from his father, enriched by cherished memories of their time spent outdoors in northern Labrador. He vividly recalled the image of his father in a red flannel shirt at the lake near their cabin. Grant's father also took him to see the massive Churchill Falls when they first dammed the river and guided it into the spillway for the enormous turbines. It was such a striking memory that he couldn't help but smile every time he thought of it.

"Your father would be proud of you," Claire said as they embraced and swayed by the fireplace. Grant's parents endeavoured to teach him the traditional ways of hunting and trapping in Labrador. The family secured the property's hunting rights and trapline licenses, providing an ideal classroom for young Grant. The lush evergreen forests, freshwater streams, and expansive lakes formed the perfect environment for big game hunting, traplines, and monster freshwater fishing.

Unfortunately, Grant lost his father a few years after the hydroelectric plant was finished and his mother soon thereafter. His parents left him the secluded cabin as part of his inheritance, which included everything inside—pots, pans, utensils, tools, snare wire, and even linens. In the years following his parents' passing, he and Claire began their family in Montréal, which hindered them from visiting Labrador frequently. Even though he had steady, well-paying work at the Ministry of Transportation, and Montréal felt like home, Grant and Claire still managed to make the drive about once a year. It wasn't ideal, as the journey took roughly 17 hours. Maintaining the cabin while living in Montréal was also inconvenient because it was a significant trek from the nearest town, so bringing supplies in was tough. Having young kids at the cabin was also challenging, as they required constant supervision in the harsh wilderness.

"How did you like the stew?" Claire asked.

"It was perfect," Grant replied with a big smile.

"Grant, I'm worried about this winter," Claire said, abruptly shifting the conversation.

"We will manage; we always do. That buck and the spring catch should sustain us. We'll be prudent and modest with our rations," Grant stated.

"I know, I know, but this land is becoming more barren and inhospitable every month. We hardly saw any warmth this growing season, and the lakes are already frozen, and its only mid-September," Claire said as she moved to the kitchen and began plucking the white feathers from the birds. "How long before this entire area turns into a frozen wasteland?"

"Perhaps it's a good time then," Grant said, taking another spoonful of stew.

Claire spun around to look at Grant. "A good time for what?" she questioned.

"To tell them."

Brooklyn and Cody came barging in through the door.

"It's huge, Dad!" Brooklyn said. "The rack is massive."

"All three of us are going to process it tonight, and we'll start the smokehouse in the morning," Grant said. "Sound good?"

"Yeah!" Brooklyn yelled.

After the birds were plucked and the bowls of stew devoured, Grant and his two children entered the shed and latched the door behind them. Grant had added extra provisions on the shed this past summer because a black bear had made its way inside and tore the place apart. Luckily, the bear didn't destroy anything that couldn't be repaired.

Once inside the shed, Brooklyn and Cody lit several small lanterns, and the three began processing the caribou buck.

Both children had done this dozens of times and were perfectly comfortable in performing the various bloody, gruesome tasks. Grant was proud of his little cubs. They sharpened their knives and drained the blood from the hanging caribou into a bucket. Nothing would go to waste. They removed the head and skinned the buck, eventually quartering the animal. Once more manageable pieces were separated, they could start cutting hundreds of strips of meat for the smokehouse in the morning.

The children enjoyed working with animals. It was kinesthetic, educational, and rewarding. Grant and Claire taught them the basics of biology, the functions of organs, the proper way to cut and process, the tastiest cuts, toolmaking, and everything else that served a purpose. The main lesson was never to waste any part of the animal. In the coming months, even the scraps would be used as bait in the traps.

"I'm going to get a couple buckets of water," Grant said, his hands-stained red. "Be careful and watch what you're doing. I don't want any injuries this winter."

The temperature had plummeted below zero. Arctic winds made any venture outside challenging. Grant tied up his winter rabbit fur hat, grabbed his axe, and left to brave the elements. Once outside, he was reminded that this was the most dangerous time to be outdoors. Animals were prowling, and things were generally unpredictable. He could encounter a mountain lion or a pack of wolves. Either way, he remained mindful as he journeyed to the water's edge.

A significant winter task was opening and maintaining a hole in the ice. The strategy was to check on it daily and keep it exposed throughout the winter months for easy access. Water was essential and needed for the survival of their family of four.

Grant scanned the horizon across the frozen lake, searching for anything that appeared out of the ordinary. He carefully assessed the treelines, looking for any shadows or sudden movements. Last winter, he had seen a pack of about 30 wolves crossing the bay in front of the cabin. He knew that animals were becoming as desperate as he and his family. This winter, he had promised to set twice as many snares along his traplines to help keep the wolf population down. Wolves had been killing more and more caribou and had driven out the white-tailed deer entirely. Wolves had become increasingly at ease with Grant and his family, and he wanted to change their passivity and comfort with humans.

Grant took a few mighty swings with his axe and broke the two-inch-thick ice into chunks. He glanced up again and scanned the area. He plunged the two buckets into the water, hung them on his axe, and carried them back to the shed. He kicked the door with his hands full, and Brooklyn opened it for her father. Both Brooklyn and Cody's leather aprons were covered in blood as they finished cutting the hindquarters of the caribou.

"Remember to wash and scrub everything well, including your hands," Grant said. "We don't want to spread any bacteria or disease. The last thing we need right now is for one of us to get sick. Wash those aprons well, too."

"Yes, Father," both children replied.

Grant poured a bucket of water into a large pot and placed it on the small stove to warm for cleaning. It had been a long but very productive and rewarding day for everyone.

"I'll stock the smoker with wood and chop more kindling for tomorrow. Remember what I told you," Grant said.

"Yes, Father," they said again.

Exiting the shed with his axe, Grant stepped into the frigid darkness and began chopping wood on the massive tree stump near the woodshed. Claire and Grant had loaded the structure earlier in the summer, anticipating another long, cold winter.

As he chopped away, he pondered whether to share the ultimate truth with Brooklyn and Cody: the turmoil, the monumental journey, and the many sacrifices he and Claire had faced in a world that had grown harsh, cruel, and unkind.

Deep down, Grant never wanted his children to know the truth about what happened ten years ago. He wished to shield them from the corrupt nature of man, their indelible desire for something more, and the horrors they were capable of inflicting. If it were up to him, he would stay here forever, safe in the embrace of family and homesteading.

The kids emerged from the shed after finishing processing the caribou buck.

"All done?" Grant asked.

"Yes, Father," Brooklyn replied. "My hands are sore."

"Let's bring the meat inside for tenderizing," Grant said. "But first, let's haul this wood inside."

"Yes, Father," the children chorused.

After Grant and the children moved the wood and brought the meat indoors, the family prepared for bed. They stoked the fires, shared a few stories, and before long, Brooklyn and Cody were sound asleep in their bunks.

Claire and Grant eventually sat down together in front of the living room fireplace, enjoying warm cups of mint tea.

Claire felt gratitude for everything she had, but tonight, she began to reflect on the reality of their situation. She struggled to grow much around the cabin; deep down, she knew their family could not stay here forever.

"I was thinking about what you said," Grant told his wife.

"You were?" Claire responded.

"I think we should head to Goose Bay with the kids to show them everything," Grant suggested.

"Everything?" Claire asked.

"Well, at the very least, we'll learn what's transpired over the past ten years. Maybe take them to a library? Show them maps and pictures of humanity, you know. They're eager for knowledge. I can see it. I'd love to share a few books with them and help them understand Labrador's history and the world." Grant was deep in thought.

"We've sheltered them for a long time," Claire agreed, nodding. "We've done our best to protect them, but it might be time. They're both so strong, Grant. It's going to be a long, cold journey. We'll need shelter and provisions."

"The way I see it, it would take about three weeks to get there," Grant stated.

"Three weeks is a long time in minus-fifty-degree weather," Claire replied.

"We could travel much faster along the frozen rivers and lakes," Grant suggested.

"The Churchill River?" Claire asked, disbelief evident in her voice.

"Yes, and I think we'll also need a buckskin tipi. So, we'll have to stitch something together," Grant added.

"I have a few ideas," Claire said. "We might need more leather cordage for a project of that size, though."

The husband and wife gazed into the fire, captivated by the challenges of travelling hundreds of miles across the frozen wasteland. While Claire and Grant had confidence in their children's abilities, they recognized that it was time for them to come of age. With rosy cheeks and mesmerized by the flickering light, they sat and reflected on what might lie ahead in such uncertain times.

Chapter 2 - Preparations

In the early morning, the Cardinal children awoke to another dark, overcast, frigid day. Despite the chilly conditions, Brooklyn and Cody were eager to get the smokehouse fired up and slowly smoulder the caribou they had processed the night before. They dressed excitedly in their winter gear. Claire had been hand-stitching clothing since they arrived at the cabin ten years prior. She crafted hand-stitched moccasins, pants, shirts, and jackets for the family from the various animals they had hunted and trapped. It was a skill she had nearly perfected. Though the kids often complained about being too warm, it was certainly better than the alternative.

Grant and Claire were awake and chatting at the dining room table, enjoying cups of tea, when the kids emerged from their room, fully dressed to brave the elements. "Good morning, little cubs," Claire greeted them.

"Good morning," both kids replied.

"Ready already?" Claire asked, surprised. "Very responsible."

"You betcha!" Cody grinned.

"Big day ahead," Grant said. "We're going to smoke that tenderized caribou, and we also need to make ourselves a sled.

"A sled for what?" Cody inquired.

"A sled big enough to carry a tipi and supplies," Grant answered. "It'll need to withstand a long, rugged journey."

"What do we need a tipi for?" Brooklyn asked.

"We're going on an adventure to the edge of the world," Grant replied with gravitas.

"All four of us will need it to sleep in during our adventure," Claire added.

"Why are we going on this adventure?" Brooklyn asked.

"We are going to travel further than we have ever travelled before. Hundreds of miles through snowy, uneven terrain," the determined Grant said. "We will travel across the tundra, the forests, and the mighty rivers of Labrador."

"But why?" Brooklyn persisted.

"We are in search of knowledge and a long-lost past that we believe to be on the edge of the world," Claire explained.

"I still don't understand." Brooklyn was interested but growing frustrated with the line of conversation.

"Never mind now," Claire said. "You two go and get that smokehouse started; there is much to do before the deep freeze of winter."

The two young, bewildered pre-teens donned their rabbit-fur hats and buckskin mittens and ventured outside into the blowing, sub-zero conditions.

Both parents recognized that their children were entering adulthood and an entirely new phase of life; they would become more disobedient. Confrontational and questioning everything, the innocent, kind-hearted, youthful spirits would drift into fierce independence, craving the company of friends while experiencing emotional volatility. Grant and Claire understood that their children would begin to question the world around them, eventually requiring them to reveal the truth about their surroundings and the motives that had guided them for the past decade.

Cody and Brooklyn had to shovel the foot of freshly fallen snow blocking the smokehouse door. Once inside, they set up a fire, and Brooklyn lit it with the flint rod she wore around her neck. The grass bundle caught fire with a few sparks, and soon, smoke began to billow from the small chimney above the racks.

"Good job, now let's get the meat," Brooklyn said.

Cody closed the smokehouse door to let it heat up and fill with smoke while Brooklyn went inside to grab the first load of caribou meat. Cody was puzzled by his parents' desire to build a new sled. They already had a perfectly good sled for hauling game and firewood. It was also intriguing that the new sled needed to carry a tipi and poles. Although he couldn't remember sleeping anywhere but the cabin, the prospect of adventure excited him. He would face off against wolves and bears, see new mountains and horizons, and fish in unknown lakes and rivers. Whatever obstacles or challenges arose, he would confront them head-on.

Brooklyn emerged with a big pot of seasoned caribou meat. "Could you open the door?" she asked.

Cody opened the smokehouse door, and they laid the strips of red meat on the wire racks inside. Smoke billowed into their young faces, but they didn't seem to mind.

Claire came outside to check on the children's progress and was pleasantly surprised by their hard work and attention to detail. Smoked meats were the primary food source for the Cardinal family during the winter months. The Cardinals had embraced ancient Cree preservation traditions for years. Salmon, trout, pike, caribou, bear, and wolf—anything could be smoked and preserved during the brutal winters. Claire also occasionally rehydrated some meats to enhance broths and stews. Different woods imparted unique smoky flavours, and the longer things were smoked, the longer they lasted on the shelves in the Cardinal kitchen. The smokehouse was central to a healthy, balanced, and flavourful diet in such a harsh part of the world.

Claire stepped aside while Cody and Brooklyn packed the smokehouse, watching her kids with pride. She smiled as her little cubs took on more responsibility around the cabin.

"Ok, shut the door and keep an eye on the sky," Claire said. "Why don't the two of you go set some snares along the trapline?"

"Sounds good," Brooklyn said.

"You can work on the sled with your father when you get back," Claire said to both children.

"Ok, mom. Keep an eye on the smokehouse. You might have to add a couple of logs," Brooklyn responsibly said.

"No problem, have fun," Claire said.

"Come on, I'll grab the snare wire," Cody told Brooklyn as the two kids approached the shed.

Lately, Claire had felt uneasy about her future and her family's safety. The dramatic, shifting climate was at the heart of her anxiety. She had observed and carefully measured the lengthening winters, the shorter growing season, and the vanishing game animals. This past summer, a midsummer frost had wiped out most of her garden, leaving only a few patches of root vegetables. Deep down, she knew they would need to adapt to the changing conditions, or it would cost them everything. Claire and Grant were both aware nothing could be done to stop the northern hemisphere from becoming a cold tundra as frozen as it was 12,000 years ago.

Grant emerged from the cabin into the snowy outdoors and saw his wife sitting on a log near the water's edge. He walked down and sat beside her, sensing that something was off.

"Hi, snowflake," Grant said.

"Hi."

"What are you doing down here?"

"I'm just at a crossroads. This winter is already harsher than last, and I can't seem to focus," Claire replied. "Our children are growing up fast and are almost independent adults."

"They still have a long way to go. We have nothing to fear, snowflake," Grant said, wrapping his arm around Claire. "We've got food, shelter, the wilderness, and most importantly, each other."

It was rare for Claire to be this vulnerable. She was tough, resilient, and had persevered through her years. Sometimes, she became so wrapped up in thoughts of the future, her children, their sustenance, and approaching winters, that she felt waves of sadness and depression wash over her. She reminisced about her childhood, the sounds of her mother cooking in their kitchen, and her father building furniture in the garage of their tiny wartime home in the suburbs of Montréal. She longed for a simpler world where her children could learn, grow, and start their own families.

"So, we travel to Goose Bay, then what?" Claire asked.

Goose Bay lay hundreds of miles to the east, where the North Atlantic Ocean met the rocky shores of Labrador. It was a military town that went radio silent, only weeks after the outbreak of global chaos, ten years prior.

"Well, we'll show them the library, the docks, the military base, the airport. We'll tell them what happened, how the world used to be," Grant said, looking at his wife, "It might take a month to get there. The uneven terrain, overgrown trails, and deep snow will slow us down, but I think it's time we take that chance."

In many ways, Grant shared Claire's concerns; he worried about their children's future, the coming winters, and the lack of food in the area. It seemed a good time to travel and explore, as the snow made transportation more manageable for their sled, and the cold wasn't as severe as mid-winter.

"Come on, Claire, let's boil some water for spruce bending. There's a lot to do."

"Okay," she replied, rising to her feet. Claire felt a bit more optimistic and motivated.

The two proud parents went to the work-shed, stoked the fire, and began boiling a large pot of water. The spruce wood they would use to build the sled was still relatively green, making it ideal for bending. They needed to bend the top rails, footboards, a cargo bed, a handle, runners, and stanchions. The project would take about a week to complete, but it would be mandatory for the journey into northern Labrador's cold, unforgiving, snowy tundra.

After Claire finished debarking some pieces of spruce, she returned to the main cabin to plan and build the tipi where the family would sleep during their adventure. They had a canvas tent they'd used before, but this tipi needed to be warm, well-insulated, easy to set up and take down, lightweight, and able to fit on the sled. It would take time to make, as she had to stitch a liner, a cover, and a smoke flap, in addition to carving poles, lacing pins, and pegs to stabilize the structure.

Over the years, the Cardinal family had harvested dozens of animals: deer, caribou, bear, fox, beaver, and wolf. They had enough hides to construct the tipi, but she needed to make at least ten metres of rope and ten metres of leather cordage to stitch the hides together. Claire knew she had to use all the deer and caribou hides they had because they were waterproof and insulated well; the rest would be utilized as blankets and for extra insulation. The entire project was massive, but it kept Claire focused and determined to move forward, steering clear of any feelings of depression or anxiety.

Cody and Brooklyn worked hard on the traplines that spanned around the small lake where they lived. The trapline crossed rocky meadows, evergreen thickets, and small streams where the game would often gather and graze. They carefully disguised each snare with strategically placed sticks to help funnel the unsuspecting prey toward the traps. Year after year, the trapline proved successful. They might trap snowshoe hares, mink, squirrels, or even the occasional fox, using rotten fish or decomposing animal organs in some areas to entice the animals to follow their intended path. Brooklyn and Cody, though still in their pre-teens, had become excellent trappers and small game skinners. Cody learned to stretch perfect pelts, and Brooklyn became a brilliant seamstress, just like her mother. Brooklyn had made moccasins, mittens, hats, and clothing for herself and the rest of the family.

Once the two children finished their tasks on the trapline, they returned home and entered the shed where their father had begun bending the runners on the sled. Cody threw down his gear and looked at his father, who worked slowly and meticulously, warping the wood along their workbench.

"Wow, this sled is going to be huge," Cody said, looking over his father's shoulder.

"I need you two to start processing some pine tar," Grant said, locking the spruce runner in place. "We'll need a lot for the lodge poles and the sled. Do you remember how to do it?"

"Yep," Cody replied.

"Make sure to crush that charcoal as finely as possible," Grant suggested.

"Got it," Brooklyn responded. "Hey, where's Mom?"

"She's inside, starting on the tipi for our journey. Brooklyn, why don't you ask if she needs any help?" Grant asked.

"Sure thing," Brooklyn replied without hesitation.

"I'll go get the pine resin we collected," Cody said, leaving the shed.

Grant needed to concentrate and ushered the kids inside. "Thanks, kiddos," he said as they exited through the shed door.

Hour after hour, day after day, their designs became a reality. The gigantic tipi was stitched and ready for transport, the lodge poles were smooth and weather-treated with pine tar, and the sled was sturdy, looking slick and prepared for a cross-country adventure. Brooklyn worked diligently on the bedding and the liner while Cody cleaned, skinned, and smoked plenty of fish, rabbit, and squirrel for the weeks they'd be away from home.

As time passed and September turned to October, the days grew shorter, and temperatures plummeted into the minus fifties. October had been in the minus forties the previous year and negative thirties the year before that. Their corner of the world was getting colder, but Claire and Grant couldn't be sure about what was happening in the rest of the world.

Despite the frigid temperatures, the Cardinals were extremely well-dressed and ready for the cold. They were completely confident in their abilities and in one another. The family even practiced setting up the tipi, taking it down, and sleeping in it for consecutive nights to test its capabilities.

The tests had been successful. The central fire inside was warm enough and the animal skins insulated well. North-westerly winds had blown against the tipi at over 50 miles per hour on those nights, and everything held together perfectly. The sled was equally durable and successful in its testing. They had fastened harnesses to the front runners and rear handlebars to help tow the sled through the deep snow and rough terrain. The sled's four-metre length would accommodate the long lodge poles, the tent, and all the other supplies they were taking along for the journey.

Grant recalled a conversation with one of his father's friends at the cabin, who spoke of his Cree ancestors and their nomadic ways in the vast expanse of Labrador. These forebears would traverse the land, following caribou herds and adapting to seasonal changes. The Inuit and Cree nations constantly moved, seeking fresh water and bountiful fishing grounds. He painted a picture of a time before 'new-world' problems emerged - a time free from addictions, health issues, and governmental interference. He described how his people found true contentment in their nomadic lifestyle, exploring new territories and living in harmony with nature. This account resonated deeply with Grant, who recognized the potential for sustained happiness in a life of constant movement.

That evening, the Cardinal family went over everything and anything that they might encounter on the trail to Goose Bay in the coming weeks. They would each carry packs filled with extra food, dry clothes, and various tools. Grant was also insistent that they would each have a weapon of some sort, along with their bow and arrows. There was a good chance they would encounter large predators on the journey, and Grant wanted everyone to be as safe as possible.

On most occasions, Grant would be on the front harness carrying most of the sled's weight, while Claire would be the one to push from the rear. Brooklyn and Cody would lead in finding the most suitable and least treacherous path while the sled followed behind. They packed fishing gear, an axe and saw, plenty of provisions, a few tools, and dry firewood for the first night. The Cardinals would need to collect firewood daily to heat the long, cold nights. This certainly wasn't a leisurely trip; it would be challenging, formidable, and wrought with hard work and danger.

The Cardinal family made sure to secure absolutely everything around the homestead. They had boarded up the windows, any food they were not taking was put into cold storage in the basement crawl space, tools were hidden, and they stoked the cabin with firewood for their return.

Excitement was starting to build as they felt more confident about leaving the homestead. The family sat by the fire and played crazy eights with a twenty-year-old, beat-up, ragged deck of Bicycle playing cards.

"Pick up two!" Brooklyn told her father as she laid down the two of hearts.

"How could you?" Grant said with a frown.

"Kids, we are leaving early, long before first light," Claire said to Brooklyn and Cody.

"Ok, Mom," Cody said.

"Where exactly are we going again?" Brooklyn asked.

"We are going to a place that is called Goose Bay. A spot that Grandma and Grandpa Cardinal used to go to a long time ago," Grant said.

"What are we looking for?" Brooklyn followed up her line of questioning.

"We are looking for clues as to the changing weather patterns and animal migrations to see if we need to move from this area permanently," Claire said, looking over to Grant. "Animals are becoming scarce, and the cold is worsening yearly."

"Well, kids, it is time for bed; we have a long day ahead," Grant said.

"Go get under the blankets, and we'll read you a story," Claire added.

The kids shuffled off to bed while Claire and Grant gathered the cards and wiped the tables. A few minutes later, Grant entered Cody and Brooklyn's small bedroom. The space had a hand-crafted wooden bunk bed, some hooks to hang clothes and gear, a nightstand, and it was filled with various feathers, skulls, and mementoes the kids had procured over the years.

Grant sat on the edge of the bed and recalled an old tale he had recently remembered from childhood. "Long ago, in a place far across the ocean, when the world and humanity were young and fragile, a man named 'Noah' received a message from his ancestors. Noah and his family loved all living things, and God saw his passion. God gave Noah a warning that a massive flood was coming to cleanse the Earth of all its wickedness. But Noah was a righteous man, so he was chosen to build a great ark to save his family."

"What's an ark?" Brooklyn asked.

"It's a big boat," Grant answered. "Then, after being asked to build an ark, God asked Noah to bring aboard a pair of every kind of animal on earth."

"There's no way that two of every animal could fit onto a boat," Cody said, putting his hands behind his head and looking at the ceiling. "Think of the smell. Yuck."

Brooklyn gave a little laugh. "Imagine the domestic fights."

Grant continued the story without acknowledging his son and daughter's silly comments. "Noah gathered his daughter and son, and they began to build the ark together. It was massive, unlike anything the world had ever seen. They worked tirelessly, day after day, gathering wood and supplies, and constructing the ark exactly as they had been instructed."

"Instructed by who? God?" Brooklyn asked.

Grant continued. "Noah was mocked, people laughed at him, and he was considered insane for building a huge boat on dry land. But his faith in his ancestors and the Great Spirit fueled him. The ark was finally complete. Noah and his family boarded the ark, along with all the different animals, including the lions, the elephants, the horses, and all the rest. Then, the heavens opened up, and rain poured like never before. It continued to fall for 40 days and 40 nights, flooding the entire Earth. But Noah and his family were safe and dry as a bone inside the ark."

"This sounds made up," Cody said. "Why have I never seen or spoken to this God or Great Spirit?"

"After the floodwaters receded, Noah sent a lone dove to find dry land. When the dove returned with an olive branch in its beak, Noah knew the Earth was ready to be inhabited again. Noah and his family emerged from the ark and thanked the Great Spirit in the sky for their safety. So, Noah and his family began a new chapter in the history of the world. They were ever so grateful for the chance to start afresh and live harmoniously with all living creatures. Now, close your eyes and drift off to sleep, and count all the different animals, two by two."

"So, who was cleaning up all the crap on the boat?" Cody joked.

"Did the bears eat the deer?" Brooklyn said, laughing.

"Did Noah bring birds on the boat?" Cody asked.

"Goodnight, my darlings," Grant said. "Children, have faith in the Great Spirit, and most of all, our ancestors."

Claire stuck her head in the doorway. "Come on, Mr. Cardinal, let's go to bed," she said with a smile.

Grant kissed the foreheads of a reluctant Brooklyn and Cody and went off to bed.

Chapter 3 - Into The Void

Claire awoke before sunrise, gave her husband a gentle shake, and his eyes opened. He looked at his wife and smiled. "Well, good morning," he said, smiling and kissing her forehead.

"Good morning. Ready to get moving?" Claire asked.

"Yes, let's pack the sled before we wake the children," Grant said.

"Sounds like a plan," Claire said, sitting up. "I'm going to miss this bed; I just know it."

Grant and Claire got up, changed and prepared for the day ahead. They packed the sled with every provision they had planned leading up to this day. They did their best to minimize the weight they needed to pull; then, finally, they woke the children.

Once the kids were awake and everyone had something to eat, Grant did a final lap around the cabin, checking for anything they missed. The cabin cooled as the fireplaces died out, and the chimney stopped billowing. Brooklyn, Cody, Claire, and Grant put on their handcrafted wooden snowshoes and bundled up in their winter gear. They were eventually ready to disembark on their long journey.

Claire and Grant had done the math repeatedly, and judging by their calculations, Goose Bay was about 300 miles southeast. If they set a good pace and went about 20 miles a day, it would take about 15 days to arrive. While they didn't know the exact route, they would travel due south until they hit the formidable Churchill River and followed it east into Goose Bay.

They boarded up the front door with old lumber and rusty nails and said their final goodbyes to the cabin. Grant thought it might be the last time he would ever see the cabin his parents had built. He thought about his father and how proud he would have been that he carried on the old trapping ways, snowshoeing along traplines, skinning pelts, and doing everything the hard way without snowmobiles or modern machinery.

Grant's father, Sam Cardinal had won many awards with his furs. He sold most of them to the Hudson Bay Company in the 1960s and 70s. He would come home with all the money and complain it was "too heavy", and the cash was "weighing him down." Everyone always got a good laugh from Sam. The nostalgia of leaving the cabin and his family's legacy was sad, but it also instilled great pride in Grant.

Grant threw the sled harness around his shoulders, took a deep breath, and glanced one more time at the boarded-up cabin.

"We're ready, Dad!" Brooklyn said.

"Okay, sweetie." Grant looked at his bundled-up family and smiled. "Let's get moving."

"Yes!" Cody yelled.

Cody and Brooklyn were both in good spirits and overly excited to explore beyond the reaches of the cabin. They were in great anticipation of seeing the mighty Churchill River and the town of Goose Bay, as both places seemed so alien to their imaginations.

After putting on her snowshoes, Claire stood up from the porch and looked at Grant, staring at the cabin. "We're all going to miss it," she said.

"OK, let's get moving. Snowflake, are you ready?" Grant asked.

"Ready as I'll ever be," Claire answered as she walked over to the rear of the sled and grabbed the freshly crafted handles.

"Forward, ho!" Grant yelled as the sled started to move.

The sled was smooth along the snow. It was a freshly waxed machine, and Grant wasn't having any problems as the Cardinal team pulled the sled out of the homestead valley. They marched until they reached the ridgeline a few miles from their cabin. They had a general vantage point from the ridge of the terrain before them.

The early morning was frigid as the cold winds numbed their faces, and their eyes began to water. It was a slow, methodical pace. Cody and Brooklyn led the convoy, packing the snow down for the sled behind them. The sled was awkward initially, as Grant constantly had to adjust the leather straps around his shoulders until they eventually felt comfortable. Before long, he had warmed up and felt more willing and able to guide the spruce sled without making fewer awkward adjustments.

The Cardinals were familiar with the area, as they had been hunting the forests and ravines for years. Northern Labrador was millions of years old. Through the eras, the mountains had been worn down into rolling hills made of igneous rock, which made traversing the terrain relatively easy. The dying forests were also thinning out, so finding walkable routes was painless. The clouds were grey and thick overhead as the morning light appeared. It had been years since the sun shone on Labrador, so the morning was nothing unusual. Grant and Claire knew the world was drastically changing; they knew clouds were getting thicker, air thinner, and global temperatures were dropping.

Cody and Brooklyn were coming of age and embraced the scouting role they were given. They would look back at their parents every few minutes to ensure they were still on course. They scanned the horizon lines for predators and always took the paths of least resistance.

Everyone's legs started burning as they had travelled 10 miles before noon. Grant knew this was a great pace, but could they maintain it for a few weeks? They stopped momentarily for a rest and a quick bite, as their spirits were still very high.

"Are we going to have to cross any mountains?" Brooklyn asked.

"The whole journey is going to be like today," Grant answered. "Lots of hills, some streams, maybe a lake or two, but we need to keep alert; there's still a lot of danger out there."

"How are your feet and your snowshoes?" Claire asked the children.

"So far, so good," Cody answered.

"Mine are good too," Brooklyn added.

The snow on the ground was relatively compact, so they didn't sink very deep with each step. The sled was working with ease, especially on the downward slopes. Everything was going perfectly.

"Do you want to try pulling the sled?" Grant asked Claire.

"Sure, I'll give it my best," Claire happily agreed.

The Arctic winds were strong as the four prepared to continue. Claire slung the straps over her shoulders, and Grant grabbed the rear handles. Cody and Brooklyn, once again, started ahead.

"Remember to look for a good spot to set up the tipi!" Grant yelled.

"OK, Dad!" Brooklyn yelled back.

"We need a spot protected from the winds," Cody said to Brooklyn as they marched on.

"It needs to be flat, too," Brooklyn added.

The Cardinals continued the trek amongst the thinning evergreen forest, weaving around rock formations and thickets of dead spruce and pine. By late afternoon, the family was ready to quit. Cody and Brooklyn found a nice clearing covered by a small rocky outcropping that would divert the northwesterly wind.

As a team, the Cardinal family assembled the tipi. The tripod went up first, then the rest of the poles. They tied the liner on the poles, assembled the smoke flap, and finally laced the pins, tying everything together. With all the practice from the previous week, the tipi was up quickly, and before long, the liner and furs were spread on the ground inside, and they had started a fire in the small pan they brought to contain the coals. They spiked their snowshoes in the snow and went inside the spacious home away from home.

The tipi warmed quickly; before long, everyone could peel away their winter jackets. They boiled some water for tea and shared some smoked caribou and trout. That night, the food tasted especially good. The air seemed extra sweet, and the tipi got toasty warm as darkness settled over Labrador. As the children drifted off to sleep under their bearskin blankets, Claire and Grant cuddled together and listened to the outside winds and the crackle of the fire. Grant threw a couple more pieces of wood on the fire as his ears perked up to the sound of howling wolves in the distance.

"They are miles away, sounds like a dozen or more," Claire said.

It didn't worry either Claire or Grant as they knew the canines would scatter at the sight of humans. Before long, Claire and Grant, utterly exhausted, cuddled close and fell sound asleep in the eerie depths of the wilderness.

The morning came quickly. Grant was the first to rise. He got dressed and went outside to find everything covered in a layer of freshly fallen snow. He brushed off the sled and found all the snowshoes disguised under the blanket of snow. He took the saw and axe from the sled into the thicket, cut down a few dead-standing spruce trees, sawed them, and began bringing them to the sled. It was essential to have wood ready for the next night, to quickly get things warm without scrambling around at night after exhausting days.

Upon Grant's return from the nearby thicket with an armload of wood, he noticed that Claire and the kids had already begun breaking down the tipi. Claire smiled at her husband as he carefully packed the freshly sawed wood on the sled.

"Ready for another long day?" Claire asked Grant.

"I certainly am. How did you sleep, everyone?" Grant asked.

"Like a rock," Claire said.

"Isn't that a Bob Seger song?" Grant joked.

"Who is Bob Seger?" Brooklyn asked.

"Grandpa's oldest fishing buddy," Grant quickly responded.

"Morning came so fast," Cody said as he removed the buckskin smoke flap and folded it carefully.

"I was so hot," Brooklyn said.

As it was good to hear, given the frigid, sub-zero temperatures, Claire smiled.

"Me too," Cody added.

Once all the furs, the liner, and the cover were folded and packed away, Grant and Claire took down the poles and untied the tripod as the kids put their snowshoes on.

"Hey Brooklyn, how are your feet?" Cody asked.

"Pretty sore, but I'm sure they'll get better as the days go on."

The first day and night were a tremendous success. The Cardinal's confidence grew as they started to feel that this trip wouldn't be as daunting or intimidating as they initially thought. Despite the bitter winds and the minus 50-degree weather, they were in good spirits.

The second and third days were very much the same: the same weather, the same types of terrain, the same lunch breaks, and very similar teamwork in setting up and breaking down the tipi and camp. They carefully crossed frozen lakes and streams and caught marvellous views atop hills. Their endurance grew over 72 hours, so the Churchill River was getting closer, and Grant and Claire were on the lookout. Once discovered, the Cardinals could use it as a guide to Goose Bay.

On the fourth day, the Cardinals started early, hoping to make the Churchill River by nightfall. Once again, Cody and Brooklyn began ahead, and Grant and Claire followed with the sled.

By the afternoon, Cody and Brooklyn emerged from a forest, stopped at the edge of a treeline, and looked around. Grant and Claire looked confused as they approached their stationary children on the path ahead. Both Cody and Brooklyn looked back at their parents with confusion. As they caught up with the children, Grant and Claire immediately recognized the Trans-Labrador Highway, or Highway #500. Though desolate, overgrown, and completely covered in snow, it was still a visible man-made sightline that carried on for miles into each horizon.

Cody lowered the scarf around his face. "What is this, Dad?" Cody asked. "Is this a huge game trail or trap-line?"

There were no visible street signs or signs of life anywhere except for the sparse animal tracks dotted along the snowy highway.

"No, son, this is a highway for cars. They used this to travel between towns, so they could go fast without going around trees and lakes. The old-timers cleared thousands of trees and laid down miles of stones and gravel to allow the vehicles to travel." Grant tried to explain the old world in ways Brooklyn and Cody might understand.

"There must have been a lot of vehicles," Brooklyn said.

"There were many vehicles a long time ago," Claire said.

"I wonder where all the vehicles are now?" Grant asked, looking at Claire with concern.

"Where are all the people that drove those cars?" Brooklyn inquisitively asked.

"The oncoming winters from the past 10 years probably drove them to leave and migrate south," Grant answered. "Maybe we are the only ones left. People from the past hated the cold, and this is one of the coldest places on earth." Grant smiled at his curious children.

"They must have been crazy," Brooklyn said.

"Something like that," Claire responded.

This was the first trace of civilization the two young kids had seen outside their home, and Grant and Claire were coming to grips with the task ahead of them. There would be long lines of questioning, different frequencies of emotion, and circumstances that would be out of parental control.

Brooklyn and Cody were both going through the motions of comprehending civilization and the fact that thousands of people once lived in the area.

"How many people lived on earth?" Cody asked.

"Well, at one point, billions. Now, I'm not quite sure," Claire answered.

"Come now, it is too cold to stand still. Let's get moving and set up near the river," Grant said, pointing across the highway. "It should be just over that ridge and at the bottom of the ravine."

"Well, what are we waiting for?" Brooklyn said as everyone shared a laugh.

The family moved across the barren highway and back into the forested terrain. Grant had steadily noticed the sparsity of trees and the abundance of standing deadwood in the area, a sign that life was receding in this part of the world. The extra space made travelling easier, but it was undoubtedly disconcerting as it reinforced the purpose of their journey.

Claire had been noticing the actions and reactions of her children to the news of the old world. She recognized their disbelief, curiosity, grief, and the way they were taking everything in stride.

Claire and Grant hid the tragic elements and global conflict that had engulfed the entire earth. After the radio silence in the first few months, things became more normalized at the Labrador cabin. Year after year, they built a functioning homestead and never encountered another human being.

When Claire and Grant were alone throughout the years, they might talk about missing bagels or Mr. and Mrs. Dumont, their old neighbours, but never around the children. They didn't speak of Montréal, their past, friends, restaurants, stores, schools, jobs, or anything else that might spark panic or concern in their little ones. No books, paper, pens, or even magazines were at the cabin when Grant and Claire arrived with Brooklyn and Cody on their backs. They taught the children the alphabet using charcoal from the fireplace, but they only knew the cabin and its surrounding nature.

As concerned, doting parents Grant and Claire were more concerned with raising their children to be tough, resourceful, and desensitized to a world fraught with danger. They hoped that one day, Cody and Brooklyn might be strong enough to cope with the horrors of reality, the truth about the chaos and fallout in the surrounding world. So far, Grant and Claire were content with how Brooklyn and Cody had been handling things and pulling their weight without complaint or reservation.

The Cardinals reached the ridge top and could see the massive frozen Churchill River below. Grant and Claire carefully guided the sled down the steep hill into the ravine, making sure it was a path they could get out of. At the bottom, Grant tied a bright rope around a tree to indicate where they entered the frozen river to ensure they could find their way back.

The Cardinal family was exhausted after an extra long day. They needed to melt some snow for water, rest their feet, and have a hot meal. After days of putting up the tipi, the family had become quick and efficient at the task. They were tying the braces and starting a fire inside the structure in only a few minutes.

The light faded into darkness as Grant chopped wood and Claire made soup with their packed dried goods. Brooklyn watched her mother's careful techniques and attention to detail.

"Mom, did you ever meet the people on the highway?" Brooklyn asked.

Cody overheard the question, and his ears perked up to hear the answer.

"Well, not on the highway," Claire answered. "Me and your father, when we were only a little bit older than you, knew some people from Labrador and Goose Bay."

"What were they like?" Brooklyn continued her line of questioning.

"Well, some were nice, some were happy, some were sad, some angry, some were old, and some young," Claire said. "Most of these people panicked and were not able to help themselves like we were able to do. When these harsh winters began, most people left, and we inherited all this land to ourselves, but things are getting colder and less accommodating. Soon, it will be nothing but ice around here."

"Mom, what did people do?" Cody asked.

"Well, people worked at stores, factories, and schools. Your Grandpa worked in Churchill Falls at the power plant," Claire answered. "But everyone left because of the cold and the lack of resources."

Grant came into the tipi with an armful of freshly sawed wood.

"So that's why we left the cabin? Because soon, it will be too cold for us?" Cody asked.

"Kids, these past few months have been tough for your mother and me," Grant said, putting the wood down. "This year that has just passed has almost been entirely winter weather. There have only been a few days above zero. Since you two were babies on our backs, the sun has hidden itself behind the clouds for the past ten years. Trees are dying, birds and animals are leaving, and we are forced to survive in frigid temperatures year-round; we are setting out to find a better way of life."

"Why is the sun behind the clouds? Why can't we see it?" Brooklyn asked.

Grant and Claire looked at each other.

"What happened?" Cody asked.

This was the ultimate question that Claire and Grant knew they would have to confront. It was layered, complicated, and tragic.

"Well, ten years ago," Grant began, "in a place called the Cascadia subduction zone, off the west coast of North America, far, far away, there was a major disruption and convergence between the Pacific and the Juan De Fuca tectonic plates."

"What are tectonic plates?" Brooklyn quickly questioned.

"They are the moving land masses below the earth that help build our world's continents." Grant swallowed and continued. "From the early details we received from the CBC radio broadcasts, this megathrust unleashed a string of earthquakes that crumbled towns and sent tsunamis crashing around the Pacific rim. Millions of people died within 24 hours. Vancouver was wiped out, as was Seattle and most of California, Japan, and Indonesia. Months later, after the dust settled and the waters receded, there was a massive build-up of magma 30 miles below the earth's crust."

"What's magma?" Cody asked.

"It's red-hot, liquid rock," Grant explained. "This unleashed a series of horrific volcanoes around the Pacific Ring of Fire."

The children were stunned silent as Grant told the story of the beginning of the end.

"The San Andreas fault-line exposed itself in California, just as scientists had worried about for decades. Mount St. Helens, Mount Baker, Three Sisters, Crater Lake and all the volcano belts from Mexico to British Columbia opened up, spewing billions of tons of rock, ash and particulates into the atmosphere. Great Mother Earth showed her mighty wrath during those early days. But that wasn't the worst part of 2028."

"How could things get worse?" Brooklyn asked.

"Well, there's a place called Yellowstone, a national park in Wyoming and Montana. A massive super volcano lay dormant for thousands of years until it was triggered into a series of eruptions and covered almost all of North America in ash. This ash and dust has ushered in a mini-ice age. It killed crops, livestock, and forests, and drove people to migrate away from the carnage." Grant was doing his best.

"How did you two survive?" Cody asked, in a state of bewilderment.

Claire and Grant were immediately thrown into memories of the panic-stricken streets of urban Montréal. Images of rioting, looting, and reckless abandon flashed in their minds. It was a terrible, anxiety-ridden stretch of time that both parents would have liked to have forgotten.

"We saw the infrastructure of things crumbling. Marshall law was implemented across the continent. People were panicking, and chaos exploded. Your Mom and I decided to act quickly. We loaded up and drove towards Grandpa's cabin to try and wait it out," Grant explained. "So, we drove and drove, ran out of gas, and started hiking the rest of the way."

Claire interjected: "It has been ten years without the sun. Most of the world has been lost to starvation, war, and sickness. Animals suffocated, forests burned, and people were starved to death."

"Are we the last people on earth?" Brooklyn asked.

"I certainly hope not," Claire said. "I would bet there's more out there. We just don't know where."

"Your mother and I travelled here with both of you strapped to our backs. We had a few weeks of food, a few tools, and everything your Grandma and Grandpa left behind at the cabin."

Brooklyn and Cody were astonished by the conversation. The revelation left them silent and wanting to know so much more. They each had hundreds of questions running through their heads.

Grant continued doing his best. "We left the big city when the new laws came into effect and were being broadcast on the CBC. Having lived through the Covid-19 pandemic, we knew what people were capable of and that things would never be the same. Luckily, we had gas in our car, food in our cupboards, and our health to get out of Montréal. We drove our little SUV from Montréal to Labrador. When our car ran out of gasoline, we ditched it and walked the rest of the way with you two smiling on our backs."

"What is gasoline?" Cody asked.

"It is the refined liquid you put inside an engine to make it go. It's kind of like food for people; machines need gas, we need food," Claire said with a smile.

"So, when we ran out of gas, we hiked for several days to the cabin your Grandparents built," Grant said. "About 50 years ago, your Grandma and Grandpa moved here to work on the great Churchill Falls power dam. The water generated power and electricity sent through great wires that help illuminate and give electricity to big cities and industry."

"What's electricity?" Brooklyn asked. She had heard her parents say the word before but had never really questioned its definition.

"That is a complex question," Grant said, smiling. "To put it short, electricity powers lights and machines through currents created by generators or turbines. You've seen lightning before; it's like that, but it travels through wires."

Cody and Brooklyn both pondered the thought of lightning travelling through a wire and how unbelievable that sounded.

"Your Grandpa Cardinal worked to get Churchill Falls generating power, and he built the cabin throughout his years here. After he passed away, he left the cabin to us," Grant said.

"What was Grandpa like?" Cody asked.

"Well, he was strong, incredibly strong. He skinned all sorts of animals. He chopped down trees and cut all his own firewood, but most of all, he was funny. He was a local legend, owner of prize-winning pelts, and an expert fisherman. The locals called him the 'Codfather' because he caught so many gigantic fish." Grant was beginning to tear up. "None of us would be here without him, and I thank him every day."

"Brooklyn, you would have loved Grandma and Grandpa Cardinal," Claire said.

"Tell me about Grandma," Brooklyn asked.

"Well, Grandma and Grandpa met at a local dance in Churchill Falls when he came here in 1969 to begin working on the dam. Grandma got a job working in the massive kitchen that would feed the 6000 coming workers. Grandpa always said it was 'love at first sight.' They eventually got an apartment, saved some money, and built the trapping cabin when they weren't working in town or on the dam."

"Is the dam still producing electricity?" Cody inquisitively asked.

"I do not know, but we will find out tomorrow. If we follow this river, we will eventually come across the great Churchill dam and see all the hard work that your Grandpa put into it." Grant remembered the last time he saw the dam; it was a marvel. Though the thundering waters were ominous and eerie, the dam was enlightening, mesmerizing, and transporting.

"Ten years ago, when darkness took hold, farms collapsed, people starved, and eventually panicked. They turned against themselves and lost their faith in God. Riots, looting, and eventually martial law resulted while we were here in Labrador," Claire said, clearly being delicate about the conversation. "Then the radios fell silent…"

"The CBC went silent?" Cody asked.

"Yes, CBC was the only station we could pick up here. Grandpa had a radio with a small crank generator that we would listen to in the first weeks. After about a month, it went silent, and there was nothing but static," Grant explained.

"After the radios fell silent, we sat and waited. We periodically checked the radio for signs but eventually lost hope. Year after year, the winters got colder, and food became scarce. Luckily, we could sustain and raise you amid such chaos," Claire added.

"And you both have thrived in Labrador," Grant said to his children.

Cody and Brooklyn could only look on with shock and awe. They realized that they grew up in the wake of a global catastrophe.

"How many people were there, Papa?" Brooklyn asked.

"There were around ten billion people in 2028. Now, who knows," Grant answered.

"That's a lot of people," Brooklyn responded.

"Do you think they're all dead?" Cody asked.

"I think a lot have died. Without food, people can not survive," Grant said, pondering the horrific nature of starving or freezing to death. "But if we survived, there must be others."

"We are going to travel along the Churchill River to Goose Bay for signs of civilization," Claire said. "We lost contact a long time ago. So, we are looking for any sign of life."

"Are we going to starve?" Brooklyn asked, as her eyes started to well up with tears.

"No, pumpkin, we are not going to starve. We have plenty of food for a long while. We need to keep moving and work hard," Claire responded as she wrapped her arms around her daughter.

"There are people out there, Brooklyn; we just need to find them." Grant was a realist and knew they could only sustain themselves for so long without milder temperatures.

Both parents were relieved that the difficult part of the conversation was over. It was something they had been dreading for a long time. Brooklyn and Cody took the news rather well, considering they had just discovered the world was destroyed. Their resilience and strength made Grant and Claire very proud. It reaffirmed that they made the correct choice in waiting to tell their children about the state of things.

"Come on, let's get some sleep. We are walking along the great Churchill River tomorrow," Grant said.

The winds howled, and the temperature dropped to minus 60, but the Cardinal family was warm in their caribou-hide tipi and bear-skin blankets. Cody and Brooklyn's minds were racing with wonder and intrigue as they battled the fatigue from the day's long journey. They thought about what other children might be like; pondered electricity, war, volcanoes, and their next few weeks. Before long, exhaustion had taken over, and they were both sound asleep.

Grant carefully put a piece of wood on the small central fire as a large pack of wolves could be heard in the distance.

"They sound close, Grant," Claire said.

"Maybe five miles away," Grant answered. "We will keep on high alert tomorrow. Keep the kids close."

"Are we doing the right thing?" Claire asked.

"Of course, snowflake. Now, let's get some sleep. It's going to be a much easier day tomorrow."

They were both relieved to be travelling on the smooth surface of the river in the morning. Grant and Claire watched their sleeping children drift off to sleep, listening to the whistling wind and howling wolves.

Volcanic Activity

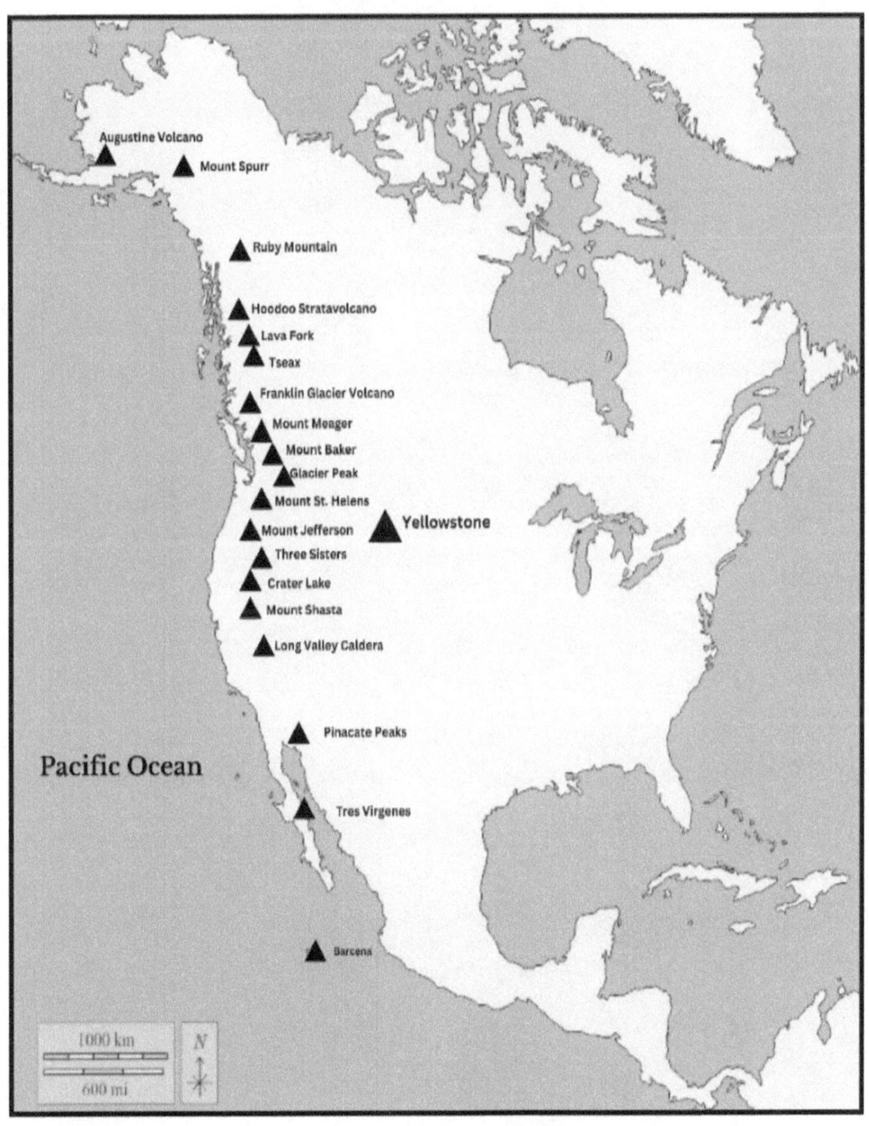

Chapter 4 - The River

The Cardinals rose just before sunrise and quickly devoured a meal of smoked trout and warm fish broth as they broke down the tipi and packed the sled. Claire paced around camp and spotted wolf tracks atop the riverbank.

"Grant, wolf tracks. It looks like a pack of about twenty," Claire said, bent over and examining the tracks.

"Okay, kids, stay close today. Wolves are on the prowl. Keep your eyes wide open," Grant warned.

Cody and Brooklyn had encountered and trapped wolves before and were more thrilled at the anticipation of eating a wolf than being attacked by one.

Their gear packed, snowshoes affixed, and weapons ready, the Cardinals set out on the frozen Churchill River. The ice was about two feet thick, and they had assured themselves they would not fall through. It was much easier work for Grant and Claire to move the sled along the flat ice than the uneven, rocky terrain. It was a nice change of pace as they didn't need to keep staring down, watching for tree branches, rocks, and sinkholes.

Grant had calculated they would come across the Churchill dam, its intakes and the small town in the afternoon at some point. He remembered the town from when he came here with his parents in his childhood and knew it was close by; they just needed to follow the river. The town buildings were all single-storey, and there was a small airstrip that would be used to transport materials to help build the mega project in the late 1900s and early 2000s.

They marched on as the frigid winds funnelled up the river valley, chilling their faces. Everyone tilted their hoods and pulled their scarves over their faces to block the drifting snow and freezing wind. The sharp, biting gales chilled the Cardinals to the bone, but they endured, mile after mile.

"You're doing great!" Grant yelled to his children.

After some time, Brooklyn's pace began to slow. She seemed to struggle as she fell behind her parents for the first time. The cold and her deep thoughts about the world a decade ago slowed her steps and motivation. Millions of other little girls and boys her age must have played and hunted together; they must have shared food and told each other stories. As the thoughts swirled in her mind, she felt a sudden surge of competitiveness. She returned to the front of the sled and eventually caught up with her brother.

"What do you think the kids did a decade ago?" Brooklyn asked her brother.

"I was just thinking about that. Maybe they went fishing or farmed together; I don't know," Cody responded.

"I heard Mom and Dad talking about a school once where children sat together and learned about math, science, and history," Brooklyn said.

"That sounds boring," Cody said.

Grant continued pulling the packed sled until they saw a building in the distance. He could barely make it out with the snow and wind in his face.

"Cody, Brooklyn!" Grant yelled. "Look!" he said, pointing to the building near the river's shore.

Both kids looked up against the wind and noticed the building. Brooklyn threw up her hands and waved to her parents. "We see it!" she yelled back against the gusting wind.

As they approached the building, they realized it was a part of the intake structure for the two gigantic tubes sucking water from the bottom of the river. Because the river was frozen, at least two feet and up to 4 feet in some places, the Cardinals couldn't tell if the intake tubes were still taking on water. Grant pondered the capabilities of the structure; the dykes were holding, and the intake building was still standing. Grant's father had taught him that the power plant gave hydro to millions of people in Newfoundland, Nova Scotia and Québec. He wondered if it could still operate and what it might take to get it working again.

The four weary travellers made their way off the river ice and up the bank towards the intake building. Grant approached the steel door, which was covered in ice. He realized there was no way to get inside, as it would take hours to chip the ice away, and they didn't know if the door was locked.

"There's no way inside," Grant yelled to his family.

"Dad, look, there's a road," Brooklyn said, pointing up the ravine.

Grant strapped the sled back on his shoulder. "Come on, let's go up the road and see what we can find," he said, departing.

They all started up the winding road, looking for signs of civilization. Brooklyn and Cody were relieved to be out of the hard ravine wind, allowing their faces to warm up. Step after step, they reached the top of the ravine and were looking at the small, crumbling, frozen town of Churchill Falls.

In the distance, Cody and Brooklyn couldn't believe their eyes. The community of Churchill Falls revealed itself through the blowing, drifting snow. It was the first town that Cody and Brooklyn remembered ever seeing. Dozens of single-storey boarded-up homes dotted the street. Cody was having trouble processing that so many people could live so close together. He wondered how they could set traps or hunt when there was so much potential for noise and commotion.

Brooklyn was equally intrigued by the town. Though there were no signs of life, she couldn't help the energy rush flowing through her.

"Beautiful Churchill Falls," Claire announced.

"There were hundreds of people living here?" Brooklyn asked.

"Yeah, but they are long gone now," her father answered.

The wooden telephone poles had begun to rot and fall along the streets, and most of the wires had snapped throughout the years of neglect. All the copper, aluminum, and other metals were an exciting notion for Grant, as he had lived without metal for so long, and it would be easy to engineer almost anything with a crucible and proper tools.

Churchill Falls only had a few streets, mainly bungalows; some had collapsed, and others were left standing despite a decade of abandonment, brutal weather, and erosion. Snow drifted to the rooftops of some buildings and others covered in solid ice.

The family walked towards the centre of town and found the large Churchill Falls Community Centre. Its doors and sparse windows were boarded up with decaying plywood. Overall, the building looked in relatively good condition.

As a boy, Grant remembered his mother and father taking him here. There was a hockey arena, swimming pool, gymnasium, and workout room. His mother and father spent many hours at the arena skating, playing various sports, and attending community functions. Grant remembered jumping off his father's shoulders into the highly chlorinated pool as a toddler. Though it was over 35 years ago, it felt familiar to him, almost like a dream.

"Man, it has been long since I saw this place," Claire said.

"No kidding. It hasn't changed a bit," Grant added.

"Let's go inside!" Cody yelled.

"Okay, Cody, but we need to be careful," Claire warned.

There were no signs of human life, only the odd animal tracks. Grant and Claire pulled the sled up near the front entrance and started to dig out the front door. They used their small shovel and walking spears to start plugging away. Piece by piece, the ice chipped away, and eventually, Grant could remove the plywood, using the shovel as leverage. Once the door was finally propped open, they realized there was hardly any light inside except for the windows overhead in the lobby and corridors. It wasn't much, but just enough for them to see around and in front of them. Grant pulled himself through the door and into the lobby.

"It looks okay!" Grant yelled from within.

"Okay, we are coming in," Claire said.

Cody and Brooklyn both stepped through the door to the amazement of such a massive structure. It immediately made them feel small and meagre. It was eerily silent throughout the vacant corridor. A few papers were scattered about, but besides the odd flier, it was relatively clean and in good condition.

Claire shut the door behind them. "No wind, thank God!" she said. "It's so clean. No signs of struggle."

Brooklyn looked at the various children's art pieces still tacked to the corkboard in the lobby. She was amazed to see such vibrant colours on large pieces of paper. She had used charcoal on different surfaces but never such bright colours on vivid white paper.

"Look, Dad! What is this?" Brooklyn asked.

"That is a painting of a sunflower," Grant answered. "It's a giant flower that produces hundreds of seeds. You can eat them or mash and strain them to make cooking oil."

"It's so pretty." Brooklyn was truly admiring the brightness and uniqueness of the flower. Her gaze moved to a painting of an airplane flying above a city. "What the heck is this?" she said with a puzzled look.

Clare stood beside her daughter and smiled at Brooklyn's curiosity. "That, my dear, is an airplane," she said with a smile. "And those are apartment buildings. Lots of little homes inside each one of the structures."

"You're telling me people flew in the sky like birds?" Brooklyn asked.

"A long time ago," Grant answered.

"How?" she asked.

"Well, planes were powered by engines that propelled them into the air. People travelled all around the world."

"I can't believe it," Brooklyn said in awe.

"Hey, Brooklyn! Come take a look at this!" Cody yelled from the end of the corridor.

Brooklyn went down the hall to see Cody standing before a gumball machine.

"What is this?" Brooklyn asked.

"I don't know, but it is heavy and quite colourful," Cody answered.

"That's a gumball machine!" Grant yelled at the other end of the corridor.

"Gumball machine?" Cody and Brooklyn both said, looking at each other.

Grant walked over and pried the lid off the machine, reached in, and grabbed a fist full of the multicoloured gumballs.

"Here, you chew it. Careful not to bite down too hard," he said, handing his children the sweet, chewable candy.

Brooklyn and Cody put a gumball in their mouth, and their faces immediately squinted at the sharp sweetness of the foreign substance. After a few loud crunches and nearly shattering their teeth, Brooklyn and Cody's eyes lit up and began chewing uncontrollably.

"Don't swallow it. It is meant to be savoured," Claire warned.

"This is crazy," Cody said, smacking the gum loudly.

"It feels like my teeth are going to fall out," Brooklyn added.

"The gum will lose its flavour after a while, then you spit it out," Grant said.

"Make sure not to swallow it. It takes up to seven years to digest gum," Claire cheekily added.

"Seven years?" Brooklyn was flabbergasted.

"Yeah, it just sits in your gut," Claire added.

Grant laughed and slowly moved into the nearby reception office, which had been completely torn apart. All the filing cabinets were empty, and the closet only had a few clothes hangers and a broken umbrella. He was looking for any sign of the last survivors at Churchill Falls.

The fax machine atop one of the desks had a few papers scattered around it, which sparked Grant's curiosity. One of the pieces of paper had a Canadian Military letterhead that showed an Ottawa address. It read:

URGENT

TO WHOM IT MAY CONCERN:

ALL CHURCHILL FALLS CITIZENS AND MILITARY PERSONAL ARE RECALLED TO HAPPY VALLEY/GOOSE BAY FOR THEIR SAFETY AND SECURITY. THIS IS EMERGENCY PROTOCOL DISPATCHED BY THE CANADIAN GOVERNMENT AND ITS MILITARY FORCES. SHUTTLE BUSES ARE AVAILABLE FOR THOSE WITHOUT VEHICLES. THE LAST SHUTTLE LEAVES MONDAY, JUNE 17TH, AT 7:00 AM.

ALL RESIDENTS ARE BEING ASKED TO BRING ONLY WHAT YOU CAN CARRY. NON-PERISHABLE FOOD ITEMS ARE ENCOURAGED. ESSENTIAL ITEMS ONLY. MEALS, SHELTER, AND BEDS WILL BE PROVIDED UPON YOUR ARRIVAL AT GOOSE BAY. CHECK IN AND REGISTER AT MILITARY BASE HEADQUARTERS. GODSPEED CHURCHILL FALLS.

AIR FORCE COMMANDER - GENERAL GEORGE R. BIGGS, JUNE 2028

Grant vaguely remembered the summer of 2028. He sat on a rusted-out office chair and tried remembering what happened during that frantic, hazy time. At that time, the world was in darkness, literally and figuratively. Half of North America was buried in ash, and the other half ran for their lives. War had erupted and swept across Europe, Africa, and Asia as the ash clouds spread around the globe. Countries fought one another and themselves for food and supplies as the planet was falling into drought. Tanks rolled into urban areas, rioting began, armies mobilized as communications failed, and starvation began to take hold. That was the last thing he remembered: bombs starting to drop.

Grant stared at the letter from General George R. Biggs and thought about how quickly the world turned on itself. It only took a few months for all forms of government to collapse. Law and order were non-existent, and every man, woman, and child would need to fight for themselves. Though it saddened him to reflect on the chaos and doom in the world, he was thankful for all he had: the skills his mother and father had taught him, his resilient children, and his strong, beautiful wife.

As he stared at the letter, he realized why everything was in such good condition without any signs of struggle. The residents of Churchill Falls were given extremely short notice to evacuate and told to bring only what they could carry. That meant that houses in the town might be filled with food and supplies.

Claire and the kids were still fixated on the crumbling, fading artwork on the bulletin board. Grant wasn't sure if he and Claire had done the right thing. They hid the ugly real world and the awful truth about society's devastation from their children. They grew up knowing nothing besides the bush, the cabin, hunting, and fishing. They were just now being exposed to the proof and existence of a collapsed civilization.

Other artwork captivated the Cardinal children's young minds. Brooklyn and Cody stood, chewing and smacking gum and admiring the artists' techniques. Grant peered through the office doorway at his children and contemplated if Brooklyn and Cody might be vengeful or spiteful considering they had hidden the truth for so long.

Grant glanced again at the date on the letter and realized he and his family would have arrived at the cabin around this time. Were all towns being evacuated to military installations? Were there survivors at Goose Bay, he wondered. It had been ten years; to his best recollection, it was 2038.

Claire came into the office.

"Like leading the lambs to slaughter," Grant said. "Look, one of the last letters recalling all residents to Goose Bay."

"Like those forest fires in 2024, remember?" Claire asked.

"That's right. They did recall Churchill Falls residents to Goose Bay. It wouldn't have been out of the ordinary for the people," Grant remembered.

Claire scanned the document and looked at Grant. "So, what does this mean?"

"It means the last effort of a national unified government was to recall everyone to military installations. I'm sure all Newfoundlanders were called to either Goose Bay or Gander, but I can't be sure."

"So, what are you saying? Do you think there are survivors at Goose Bay?" Claire asked.

"The last thing I remember, after the Yellowstone eruption, the storms, and martial law, were the riots. Remember how food became scarce, and everyone panicked? As the threat loomed, and crops began to fail, so did people's sanity and morality." Grant stood up from the chair. "I do know that we won't find anyone here. We'll set up the tipi for the night, and we can check around town tomorrow. Maybe we can find some supplies. If all goes well, we should be able to head to Goose Bay in a couple days."

"Do you think Goose Bay got hit? Do you think this whole trip has been for nothing?" Claire asked.

"This trip is already giving us plenty of information; we know the river is still here, and it freezes in the winter now, and the dam and surrounding dikes are still holding. As for Goose Bay, I don't know, but if there are answers, they're going to be there," Grant said. "It took us a week to travel here; it will take two more to get to Goose Bay."

Brooklyn came into the office. "What's this place?" she asked.

"It's called an office, where people would type on computers and talk on the phone," Claire said.

Brooklyn tugged at her mom's hand and led her back into the corridor and to the gymnasium. "Look what we found!"

Claire entered the doors to find Cody running around on a large basketball court's warped, cracking, hardwood floor.

"What is this place, Mom?" Brooklyn asked.

"This is a gymnasium, sweetie," Claire said, looking around.

"What are those?" Cody asked, pointing at the backboards and steel rims.

"Those are basketball nets. You try to shoot a ball inside," Claire said, mimicking a basketball shot.

"Like this?" Cody said, taking a shot with a frozen tennis ball he had found.

The ball clunked off the rim.

"Nice try!" Claire said. "Just like that, but the ball was bigger and had a lot of bounce."

"What are those?" Cody said, pointing at the black and red lines on the court.

"Those are the boundary lines in basketball and volleyball. If you stepped on the line, you were out, and the other team would get the ball," Claire answered.

"This place is so much fun," Brooklyn said. "Did lots of little kids play here?"

"Oh, yes, honey. Hundreds of kids came here," Claire said, holding back the tears. "We are going to stay here tonight, so we need to go help Dad put up the tipi."

Claire, Cody, and Brooklyn rendezvoused with Grant, put up the tipi, made dinner, and settled in for the night. The community centre sheltered them from the frigid Arctic winds and the falling snow, making the night much warmer and more comfortable than they were used to.

Grant and Claire looked at their rosy-cheeked children and gazed at the small fire crackling. The children fought hard to stay awake and asked as many questions as possible, but before long, they couldn't fight it any longer and were both sound asleep.

"I hope this isn't too much for them," Grant said.

"We did the right thing, Grant. We knew this day would come, and it would only be a matter of time," Claire replied.

"I hope that Goose Bay has some more answers. This town is completely deserted. It looks like everyone just disappeared." Grant was frustrated as he reflected on the situation in front of them.

"Stay positive, snowflake. We are on the right path, and humanity would be proud," Claire said. "Plus, we'll have a good look around town tomorrow."

One thing I do know is there that there are plenty of building materials within all of these homes; perfectly dried wood, nails, screws, and I'm going to assume plenty of tools," Grant said as he looked toward the billowing smoke funnelling out the top of the tipi.

Town of Churchill Falls

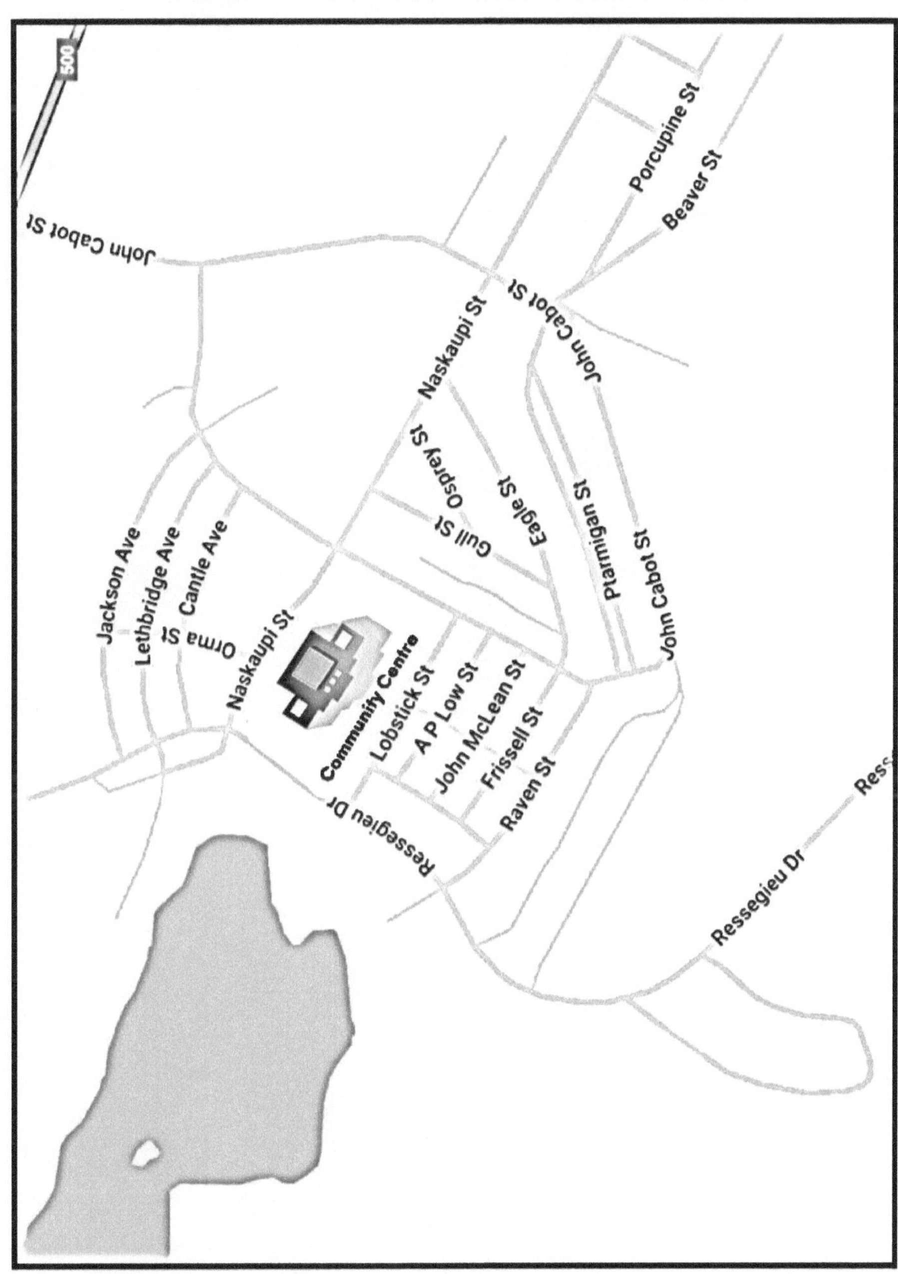

Chapter 5 - Ghosts

Early the following day, the Cardinals journeyed back onto the snowy, frigid roads of Churchill Falls. The town was full of ghosts, and Claire could sense them. The town was haunting, but it did not affect Brooklyn or Cody, as they were fascinated with their first glimpses of a civilization gone by. They each had so many questions as they meandered the town.

The streets were lined with bungalows and single-car garages covered in snow and ice. Most homes were boarded up, with an occasional one collapsed due to broken windows and open exposure.

Churchill Falls was a tiny village. It only had a few streets, some abandoned commercial spaces, and one rundown gas station. The Cardinals also passed the airstrip, which still seemed usable. After a quick lap of the town, they came to a baby blue house with boarded-up windows. Grant removed the plywood from the side window, slid the frame up, and crawled through the small opening.

"Come on," Grant said, sticking his head out the window. "It's all clear."

One by one, the Cardinals all made their way inside the small bungalow. The modernity of the home struck the children right away.

"Look at this kitchen," Brooklyn said. "What is this?" she said, pointing at the stove.

"That's an old stove, but new to your eyes, I guess," Claire said, "People used to cook on them when power and electricity ran to homes."

"They cooked without fire?" Cody asked.

"The falls out there used to produce power for communities all over Canada. They didn't need wood to cook their meals. Power charged portable batteries, powered tools, lit-up rooms, and anything else you could plug in." Grant was doing his best. "You see this?" he said, pointing to the fan and light above. "This would light up the room, move the air around, and keep you cool in the warm months."

Claire smiled at Grant as she turned to their kids. "Families like ours used to live in these kinds of homes. It was a very convenient time for people, and overnight, it was gone. The comfort, luxury, and accessibility all disappeared."

"I don't think I would want to live here," Brooklyn said, looking around. "I like our cabin much better. This place smells."

"Come on, Brooklyn, let's look around," Cody said, grabbing Brooklyn's hand.

As the kids began exploring the house, Grant looked through the drawers and cabinets of the kitchen. As he suspected, everything remained in the house: silverware, plates, pots, pans, and even a few cans of expired beans left under the sink. He found a can-opener and showed Claire with a big smile.

Despite the scattered mouse-droppings, Grant and Claire were delighted to find extra rations for their journey to Goose

Bay, even though most were long expired and frozen solid. They could only hope each house had similar gifts.

"Should we stockpile everything we find in one central location?" Claire asked.

"That's a great idea. Let's find a suitable house with a basement and a useable fireplace." Grant was feeling better now that they were developing a contingency plan.

"We don't need to rush things," Claire said. "The ghosts seem to be welcoming us."

"You're absolutely right. Goose Bay can wait a few days." Grant dropped the can opener on the floor, grabbed Claire around her waist, pulled her close, and kissed her. "I haven't felt this good in a long time."

"This town does feel like a warm blanket," Claire said, hugging Grant tightly.

The Cardinals spent the day meandering through the ghostly Churchill homes, finding anything of use: food, tools, medicine, and building materials. Eventually, they found a house they would use as a stache. It was similar to all the other homes in town, but it had two big fireplaces: one on the main floor and one in the basement. Brooklyn lit fires in both fireplaces and, with the others, began making trips to individual houses.

Grant found padlocks and mounted them to the outside doors. He held onto one set of keys and carefully hid the other set. He also found a modern compound bow and a set of 12 arrows. He was shocked at the power he could draw from the weapon. Grant was also on the lookout for a gun and ammunition; anything that could shoot, he thought.

Claire was a little more practical in her searches. She discovered brand-new thermal underwear and balaclavas for the family. It was different from what they were used to wearing, but it was waterproof and did a better job of securing their body heat.

Claire had found a sewing set in one house with all types of needles and thread. She had struggled with only a few needles over the past decade and was happy to find such a fully stocked collection of thread, buttons, zippers, thimbles, and needles. Claire had been productive throughout the days and gained confidence as their resources grew and they fortified their future.

Cody found his first Swiss army knife and shifted through the different options in amazement. He also found an ice auger in a garage, and while initially puzzled by its unique shape, he soon figured it out with a little trial and error.

Brooklyn was fascinated by the clothes and toys other children left behind. She discovered dolls, building blocks, board games, stuffed animals, dresses, rubber boots, and colourful sweaters. She tried on shoes and jackets, looked at toys with playful curiosity, and admired the artwork left hanging on the peeling walls. It was an exciting day, sifting through each home. However, she knew she couldn't carry everything she wanted, but she held onto a special little troll doll with bright fluorescent green hair.

The house got warmer throughout the day, with fires blazing from the wood they had gathered. Each member of the Cardinal family would pop in and out throughout the day, individually dropping off food, supplies, gear, and anything else they thought might be valuable in the coming days. With each hour, the basement began to fill with cans of food, bags of flour and sugar, fishing gear, carpentry tools, screws, nails, and a tacklebox full of seeds Claire had found in a nearby garage. The tackle box held peas, beans, corn, tomato seeds, and almost every fruit or vegetable seed they could think of. Though it seemed useless, it still brought an element of optimism to Claire's heart.

Grant brought in a load of wood for the basement fireplace and found Claire stacking cans of food on a nearby shelf.

"Hello," Grant said, off-loading his armful of wood onto the hearth.

"I found a whole pantry full of beans and corn," Claire said.

"Let's call this place Solace 2," Grant said. "Like we are astronauts. Solace 2 is in orbit," he joked.

"Love it," Claire said, kissing Grant. "Very cute."

Solace 2 had become like a home over the next few days. They stockpiled an entire basement full of non-perishables, tools and firewood. The Cardinal family had worked hard building their home away from home. They had tried sleeping in separate beds but found sleeping on the floor in front of the fire was much more comfortable. They sprawled on bear skins and caribou hides and cuddled close to one another in the warm space.

That evening, Claire boiled some water and made some ten-year-old hot chocolate she found at the back of a Lazy-Susan. She and Grant looked on as their children tried the sweet drink for the first time. They both pursed their lips and fluttered their eyelashes.

"This place is great; I don't want to leave," Brooklyn said, taking a second sip from her cup.

"This is amazing," Cody said, smiling.

"This is the first time you've had processed sugar," Claire said. "It is not good for you."

"It's okay to have once in a while," Grant added.

"I want to stay here forever," Cody said.

"Soon, this entire place will be covered in ice, the animals will be gone, and this house will disintegrate into the Arctic tundra." We are lucky it is still standing, Grant thought. "We will need to keep moving; there's lots more to explore," Grant said, smiling at his children.

It felt like the Christmas mornings for Brooklyn and Cody they never had. They discovered toys, artwork, candy, and everything that lit up children's eyes on those special holiday mornings.

After finishing her hot chocolate, Brooklyn slowly dozed off with her new troll doll clutched in her arms. It had been a long day for Cody, too. He struggled to keep his eyes open while shifting through the Swiss army knife options. The fire hypnotized the family as the warmth permeated the space. Claire and Grant reminisced about the old days on warm, isolated beaches without a care in the world. They recalled the warm beds, the fridges full of food, the hot showers, and nothing to do except play and enjoy life under the sun.

Though they spoke about better days gone by, they still understood the unspoken truths of staying motivated for the journey that lay before them. Claire and Grant realized that even though their new surroundings were warm, comfortable, and inviting, they could not be permanent.

Their next goal was to reach Goose Bay and find any information they could about the status of the world. Had anyone survived? Was the military still operating? Was there a migration destination? They had not seen or heard from a soul in ten years, not even the Inuit people who had lived and travelled here in Northern Labrador for thousands of years.

Goose Bay was another two weeks away on foot. Temperatures were still plunging, and they needed to find motivation after what seemed like a vacation at Solace 2.

"This town has ghosts; I can feel them," Claire said.

"Me too, snowflake," Grant responded.

"They're in the walls, all around," Claire added.

"They have been rather kind to us. We've been gifted much here by those apparitions," Grant said with a smirk. "I mean, they did give me a new bow and arrows."

"Funny," Claire said, smirking back.

"We'll board this house and lock it down. I'll pack the sled at first light, and we will depart for Goose Bay. Though this town's ghosts surround us, I feel they are rooting for us." Grant rolled onto his side and looked at Claire. "Sleep well, my love. We have a long trek ahead of us."

"Sweet dreams," Claire said as she closed her eyes and contemplated the challenging days to come.

Chapter 6 - Goose Bay

The following day, the Cardinals awoke sprawled across the living room floor in Solace 2. It had gotten so hot during the night that they had thrown the blankets off to stay moderated. Sweat was something they were not accustomed to.

Claire was the first to wake up and got a chuckle at the sight of her family lying all over with their mouths wide open. It was strange for Claire to sleep in this modern house. It was something so foreign to her after a decade of the same bed and surroundings of the log cabin. It retained heat well and was spacious and comfortable, but something about it was still strange and unknown.

As the family began to stir, Claire went outside and filled two pots full of snow, one for bathing and one for morning tea. She had scavenged an assortment of different exotic teas throughout Churchill Falls.

Grant rose and looked around at the chaos of blankets and animal hides throughout the room. "What the hell happened last night?" Grant joked. "Did a bomb go off?"

"A little too much wood on the fire last night," Claire said, kicking the snow off her boots. "I woke up in a pool of sweat."

As the children awoke and Grant and Claire shared some apple-cinnamon tea, the dull, hazy morning light crept in through the cracks of the windows. Grant gathered his things and began packing the sled with all the necessary provisions to get to Goose Bay and back. Meanwhile, Claire and the kids cleaned up the space and prepared for the long trek.

Once all the fires had died down and the space was cleaned up, they battened down the hatches and secured the padlocks on all the doors. Solace 2 would be sturdy and safe until their return.

The Cardinals put their newfound titanium snowshoes on, and Grant threw a new reinforced sled harness around his shoulders. Claire double-checked everything was secure, and they made their way out of Churchill Falls and back down the ravine to the frozen river. They would hike east until they reached Muskrat Falls, another smaller hydroelectric dam along the Churchill River. Just beyond Muskrat Falls was Happy Valley-Goose Bay, one of the largest towns in Labrador.

Goose Bay was far away, and they travelled day and night. Days were getting shorter, so they kept moving despite the darkness. The tipi was tricky to set up in the evening hours, but they managed without much confusion or agitation. They ate smoked meats and beans for dinners along the frozen river and found themselves energized by the beans, even though they had expired about eight years ago.

After several days on the river, they reached Muskrat Falls, another massive, multi-billion-dollar concrete and steel dam project. The lower Churchill River widened as the Cardinals moved toward the power generating station. Water still surged through the six massive tubes along the dike walls. They carefully made their way alongside the river and marvelled at the power of the water that raged out of the structure.

"Your Grandpa helped build this dam," Grant said to his rosy-cheeked children.

"This is another power station?" Cody asked.

"Yes, it is. The force of the water turns the turbines and creates a charge within the stainless-steel core." Grant knew the dam looked like business as usual, but the core of the turbines would eventually corrode without maintenance. "This place created power for millions, just like Churchill Falls did."

"I can't believe humans made this," Brooklyn said.

"It is marvellous," Claire said as she put her arm around her daughter. "Humans are capable of many great things when they work together." Grant could hear the irony in her voice as she spoke of a time when humans worked with one another instead of against each other in a time of panic, uncertainty, and barbarism.

"Come on, it's only a couple more kilometres to Goose Bay," Grant said, straightening the straps on his sled harness.

They moved down along the banks of the river, all the way around the hydro dam and eventually back down to the flat river. After around an hour, the Cardinals saw a road leading up to Happy Valley-Goose Bay.

Grant had spent tons of time in Goose Bay as a child and remembered the sports fields, the playgrounds, and the burger stand where he and his father would get cheeseburgers and root beer. Grant was excited to show his kids all the fun things he once did. There were museums, restaurants, stores and a giant military base in the town centre, where he hoped to get answers.

The military was the biggest employer in town and made up nearly a third of the population. It had a considerable airstrip, barracks, field training structures, government buildings, and housed hundreds of families. NORAD (North American Aerospace Defence Command) was also stationed there. At one time, NORAD was in charge of protecting any incoming threats over North America. Goose Bay was, strategically, one of the most important towns in North America, should there be any threat of war.

Goose Bay was the last major town that Claire and Grant would stop at before going to the cabin. Claire didn't remember much except for the gas stations, the Tim Hortons, the Co-ops, and the pubs. Though she remembered very little, Grant had spoken of it often, so it didn't seem too remote or alien.

It was only a few more feet over the ridge to the town, and they were all in great anticipation of a city, a potential civilization, and any information about the ongoings in the world. They hoped to find survivors that might form some notion of community, something to plant a seed of hope for the Cardinals' future.

Cody and Brooklyn had been super resourceful throughout the trip so far. They had travelled nearly 300 kilometres on foot. Both Claire and Grant were extraordinarily proud of their grit and determination.

"Only a few more steps!" Grant yelled.

"Thank goodness, my feet need a rest," Brooklyn said.

They marched up the final stretch and reached the top of the ridge overlooking Goose Bay. Brooklyn and Cody arrived on snowshoes first and froze in awe of what lay before them. Grant and Claire struggled with the sled and finally arrived at the ridge beside the children.

The sight sank the hearts of the winded Cardinals. A 30-mile crater spanned the horizon of where Goose Bay once rested. There were no remnants. No airport, no buildings, no houses, only the massive crater of what they assumed to be a nuclear blast. Saplings and snow-covered shrubbery were starting to grow in the middle of the crater, which signalled this disaster had happened long ago, most likely at the outbreak of chaos.

"My God," Claire said, staring at the carnage. "What happened?"

"Looks like a nuclear weapon," Grant responded.

"Who the hell would attack Newfoundland or Labrador?" Claire rhetorically asked.

Grant potentially knew why Goose Bay was attacked. NORAD was strategic in protecting the U.S. and Canada. Goose Bay would be a calculated, shrewd first strike if foreign powers wanted to attack. Goose Bay's destruction would leave cities defenceless and militaries in the dark.

Was this a foreign power? A rogue group? Mercenaries? Artificial intelligence? Grant could only laugh to himself as he covered the emotions of frustration, anger, sadness, and self-defeat as he looked at the crater.

"What's a nuclear weapon?" Cody asked.

"A giant bomb, Cody," Grant answered. "Sheer hellfire."

"Oh," Cody said, surprised that man could create such weapons.

"Well, what do you think?" Claire asked.

"I think we need to go back to Solace 2 at Churchill Falls," Grant said. "There's nowhere else to go. This is the end of the line."

Grant and Claire both had sullen feelings of defeat. They had spent months preparing for this moment, which had become anticlimactic. Grant put his arm around Claire, and she rested her head on his shoulder.

Chapter 7 - A New Horizon

A long, cold, gruelling 13 days later, the Cardinals finally returned to Solace 2 in Churchill Falls. They were glad to spend a few days in the warmth after the bitter, disappointing journey to Goose Bay. Though disappointing, it did answer some lingering questions. No one was alive in Goose Bay, and likely, nowhere in Northern Canada either. The disappearance of the Inuit was probably a result of the nuclear blast as they moved west across the Arctic tundra. It also answered the reason for the radio silence. All communications were obliterated, and satellites were incapable of communicating.

Throughout the trip back, Grant brainstormed ways to get to the ocean, the one place that might be able to sustain them. Claire suggested building a boat to sail down the Churchill River when the ice broke up. At first, he dismissed the idea because the window was so narrow between thawing and freezing. After thinking things through, he realized the Churchill River could carry them right into the Atlantic Ocean if their timing and navigation were accurate. The river could carry them to the ocean, and with sails, they could travel even further.

Inside Solace 2, Claire started a fire and immediately put a massive pot of snow on the fire to melt. The entire family needed a bath, as it had almost been two weeks without substantial cleaning. She also started a basic soup broth that the family would enjoy later.

Grant was in the basement and had been gone for a couple of hours while the kids were upstairs in the kitchen, piecing together a dinosaur puzzle they had found in a nearby house.

"Where's dad?" Brooklyn asked her brother.

"I think he's downstairs," Cody answered.

"What's he doing down there?" Claire asked her kids.

"I don't know," Cody responded.

Grant came blasting through the basement door. "I've got it!" he announced.

"Got what?" Claire answered.

"A boat, a big boat," he said.

"A boat for what?" Claire asked.

"A sailboat to take us to the ocean. Look, I've made some basic plans. Now, let's take the Churchill River from here, head downriver, take the boat out at Muskrat Falls, bypass the dam, row past Goose Bay, navigate Lake Melville, maneuver through the tributaries, and head into the Atlantic Ocean. We might have a safe passage south. Once on the coast, we can install the boat's keel, raise the mainsail, and head south toward warmer waters where food and supplies are hopefully abundant."

"Sounds good, but where are we getting a sailboat?" Claire said, unfazed by Grant's excitement.

"There was a big, tarp-covered, 25-foot aluminum boat down the road. We would have to fabricate a little structure for sleeping, make some benches, fasten the mast, attach the boom, and make some sails, but I think that's our answer."

"What would you suggest that we use as sails?" Claire asked.

"Well, we're going to have to sew them," Grant said, looking at Brooklyn and Claire. "The dimensions would have to be huge. Thirty feet by 20 feet, maybe," Grant guessed. "There's still some bugs to work out."

"We would need to have perfect timing," Claire said. "We're not even sure the river will completely thaw this summer. Have you thought about icebergs?"

"I think the boat is small enough to navigate between any hazards. We would be restricted to sailing during the day, though," Grant said.

"Where would we build the boat?" Cody asked.

"Remember the arena at the community centre down the street? We could build in there during the winter and launch once the ice breaks up in summer," Grant suggested.

"If we're going to stay here and follow through with this plan of yours, we're going to need to set some traps, go hunting, and use that new auger to do some ice fishing," Claire said, looking at Cody and Brooklyn.

"I think it's possible," Grant said.

"We're going to build a boat?" Brooklyn asked.

"I think so," Grant said. "But we need to get busy if we're going to be ready by summer. It's already November, I think."

"I'll set traps and lines tomorrow," Cody enthusiastically said.

"Brooklyn and I can start on the sail whenever. We just need the measurements."

"Remember the Pythagorean theorem?" Grant asked.

"Not at all," Claire quickly responded.

"This is exciting," Grant said, leaving down the basement stairs. "So much to do!" he said.

Grant worked well into the night. He made a long list of things he would need in the coming weeks. Taking his time, he drew a blueprint of the boat and its rigging. He worked diligently at inventorying the number of bolts, screws, cleats, and various hinges and fasteners he would need, plus extra. After all the planning, one thing was sure: he would need a lot of wood, hardware, and tools. Luckily for him, walls within the various houses had plenty of wood, and there was more than enough hardware in the garages throughout Churchill Falls.

Grant thought about what he would need to do the next day. He would create a comfortable, manageable working space in the arena garage. He would need to install a fireplace and workbenches inside the garage, which housed a Zamboni, the arena ice resurfacing machine. He would also need to organize the tools that he would need. He was excited about the challenge of building a seaworthy boat but was starting to feel slightly overwhelmed.

Cody came down the basement stairs and saw his dad writing a list titled 'hardware'. Grant turned his head and saw his son with a sullen look.

"Hey, Dad, what are you doing?" Cody asked.

"Just going through everything we will need tomorrow," Grant responded. "This boat will need a lot of rigging, rope, and hardware."

Cody sat on the bottom step and put his head in his hands. Grant looked towards his son and put his pencil down after noticing his son's melancholy state.

"What's wrong, kiddo?" the concerned father asked.

There was a pause as Cody searched for words. "What's a nuclear bomb?"

"Well, that's a complicated question. It's a bomb that uses the plutonium and uranium elements. It splits the atom, releasing an incredibly deadly force that was meant to exterminate everything in its path. It was almost 100 years ago when it was first invented. The American army first used the bomb in World War II against the Japanese. It was catastrophic. Why do you ask, Cody?" Grant questioned.

"I just don't understand why anyone would want to kill all those people in Goose Bay. What happened in this world, Dad?"

"There was a war of some sort, son. Everything escalated after the earthquakes and volcanoes, especially after the Yellowstone eruption. There were food and gas shortages; the hydroelectric grid went down, communications failed, everything just froze, and people started getting crazy and brutal. Neighbours were killing neighbours, people were starving to death, and governments tried to intervene, but everything backfired. It seems everyone around Labrador was called to Goose Bay, and then, they were incinerated by the deadly blast."

"Why did we survive? Why were we so lucky?" Cody asked.

"If Grandpa hadn't built the cabin, we would have been stuck in the city with nowhere to go," Grant said. "At the outset of the chaos in Montréal, we took you kiddos and drove as far as we could. We hacked through the woods for a week after our car ran out of gas. Finally, we made it to Grandpa's cabin. We were near starving and beaten down, but we had shelter. We listened to the emergency broadcast radio signal for the first few weeks, but it eventually went down. I think that was when Goose Bay was hit. After that, nothing. It was just the four of us, Cody, so now we focus on getting out before we are buried beneath the snow and ice. The ocean is our best bet. It has plenty of fish and all sorts of delicious sea creatures."

Cody gave a little chuckle. "Tell me about the big cities, Dad," Cody asked. "What were they like?"

"Well, there were trains that ran above ground on rails and some that ran below ground in tunnels called subways. There were restaurants where people would eat fancy steaks and drink fine wines. Theatres were offering live shows with music and dancing. There were bookstores, laundromats, and different types of smells and sights. Bakeries would flood the streets with aromas of freshly baked bagels and sourdough bread, charcoal smoke simmered along the sidewalks as hot dogs and hamburgers were barbecued, and fresh coffee and espresso could be found on every street corner. Musicians played in parks, moms pushed strollers, and businessmen hurried along sidewalks to make the next big deal. Cities were full of bright lights and people, but you had to be careful. Criminals were always sniffing out advantages, traffic was dangerous, and people could be nasty to each other. Life moved so fast in cities."

"Doesn't sound like I would have liked the cities," Cody reflected.

"I think you would have. You would have loved school. Hundreds of kids read books, solved math problems, and played outside together. They would play soccer at recess and go on field trips together. Teachers would teach the students physics, geography, history, science, and literature. Homework was always a guarantee for students in school."

"What's homework?" Cody asked.

"It's studying and work that the teacher assigns for the students to do at home; it's the worst," Grant said with a smile.

"I definitely would hate homework," Cody said in agreement.

Both father and son shared a laugh in the basement of Solace 2 while Brooklyn and Claire sat upstairs making some small-game snares that they were going to set in the morning. On their journey from Churchill Falls to Goose Bay, they had seen plenty of snowshoe hare tracks, so they were confident they could eat fresh meat within the week. On a map of the area, Claire showed Brooklyn the trapline they would use. The forested path meandered through the thick bush north of Churchill Falls. The family would need to do some maintenance so they could easily access the different traps.

"Great job, Brooklyn," the proud mother encouraged. "You've made more than me."

"Can we set the snares tomorrow?" Brooklyn asked.

"Sure, sweetie." Claire finished looping the wire and set it down on their working table. "I have something for you, Brooklyn," she said, taking a small, leatherbound book from a kitchen drawer. "This is a blank journal I found down the street. I want you to start writing in this each day. Record what we do, write down your thoughts, and anything else you think may be important."

"OK, I will try. I haven't done a lot of writing," Brooklyn said.

"I think it is essential to stay organized and committed to the tasks we accomplish in the coming months. In the future, you might look at these days with intrigue. You should write about the progress of the boat, the things you catch, the things you build, and how you feel, whether it is sad, happy, angry, confused…"

Brooklyn interjected. "Do you have a pencil?"

"I found a box of pencils. You will need to sharpen your pencil regularly," Claire said, handing her a pencil and sharpener.

"How does this work?" Brooklyn asked, analyzing the sharpener.

"Just stick the pencil in and twist," Claire responded.

Brooklyn twisted the pencil inside the sharpener, and a big smile appeared.

"Just like that," Claire said.

That evening, after weeks on the frozen Churchill River and seeing the destroyed city of Goose Bay, the Cardinals had optimistic feelings about their future. They would spend the harsh winter with specific goals in mind. They had plenty of food, with plans to acquire more; they had all the supplies they needed, and they had each other's company.

After dinner, Grant went outside in the frigid conditions and started chopping wood as the snow fell in a thick, white blanket. He thought to himself that this might be the harshest winter yet. It was late fall, and everything was frozen solid and covered in several feet of snow. In these next few weeks, he would need to dig out that aluminum boat and trailer and secure as much firewood as possible.

After some mighty swings with his axe, he paused to breathe, looked up into the falling snow, and thought about the stars he had not seen in years. He remembered his dad telling him stories of the constellations and how we lived in the time of Pisces and would soon be living in the age of Aquarius. He hoped that one day, Brooklyn and Cody might see the wonder and grandeur of the stars above.

Inside Solace 2, Brooklyn and Cody sat at the kitchen table while Claire cleaned and stoked the fire for the night.

"What is that?" Cody asked Brooklyn.

"It's a new journal Mom found for me," she responded.

"Do you even know how to write?" Cody said with a snarky accent.

"Better than you," she fired back.

Brooklyn sat at the kitchen table and wrote her first entry in the leatherbound book:

Brooklyn's Journal
November 1st

Mom got me a journal. We went to Goose Bay. It was gone. It was a giant bomb. We are going to build a big boat—lots to do. Mom and I are making a huge sail. Cody and Dad are setting up the boat build tomorrow at the arena. I am tired but happy. Going to bed now.

Brooklyn took her time printing each word as carefully as she could. She would ask how words were spelled and, as a result, made only the odd mistake, which she would quickly erase. Cody watched on with quiet intrigue while Claire guided her writing.

The following day, the Cardinals had got to work early. Grant and Cody arrived at the house down the road and began the arduous task of digging out the boat and trailer. They brought axes and shovels and were eventually able to dislodge the trailer and move it and the boat to the top of the frozen ground. The task took hours but was ultimately rewarding once they could move the boat.

Foot by foot, they dragged the trailer to the arena garage with two straps they had fastened to the front of the trailer. They again started digging around the bay door of the arena garage door in the cold blowing snow. Eventually, they opened the door and pulled the boat and trailer inside the large holding bay.

The Zamboni, still parked in the corner, caught Cody's attention.

"What is that?" Cody asked.

"That is a Zamboni," Grant answered as he shut the bay door with the hanging chain around the door's pulley.

"What does it do?" Cody was fascinated.

"Well, it smooths out the ice for skaters. It carried hot water and spread it out over the ice. People would strap blades to their feet and skate on frozen surfaces. They played and danced, battled in hockey and curling; it was fun for everyone."

"People strapped blades to their feet?" Cody questioned.

"It is enjoyable if you can do it but extremely frustrating and painful if you're no good," Grant said, looking at the Zamboni. He wondered if it might start, but he highly doubted it and quickly dismissed the thought. His focus was now solely on the boat.

It was a long 25-foot metal boat with plenty of potential. It was sturdy and would be perfect for a long journey in treacherous waters with the weight of four people. It had a smooth, sturdy hull and an ideal mounting area for the keel and rudder. They would need to build the rudder and keel, reorganize the seating, create a tiller and steering console, construct insulated sleeping quarters, and make a 25-foot main mast. It was a monster job, but Grant looked forward to the challenge.

"Seems like a lot of work," Cody said.

"Well, you're not wrong," Grant said. "We just need to plug away daily, set our goals, and stick to them."

"I'm tired," Cody said, sitting on the workbench.

"High five!" Grant said, holding up his hand. "Let's build a boat!"

Cody slapped his father's hand with little enthusiasm as all the chiselling and shovelling had zapped his energy.

The space was cold, and Grant knew the next order of business was to heat it to ensure comfortable working conditions.

"Come with me," Grant said, walking towards the arena's interior.

"Where are we going?" Cody said, following his dad.

They went through a set of double doors and into the arena.

"This is where families would skate, boys and girls played hockey, and in the summer, they would play lacrosse," Grant said.

"Neat," Cody answered.

The father and son walked throughout the arena, looking for anything of use or value to their situation. Grant stumbled upon a large steel-drum garbage can and thought about how much heat it could produce.

"Cody, come help me with this garbage can!" Grant yelled to his son, who was looking at all the minor hockey pictures on the walls.

Grant and Cody spent the rest of the day fabricating the old garbage can into a rudimentary fireplace. At the same time, Brooklyn and Claire gathered anything that would help create the sails. They scavenged anything made of canvas, polyester, and nylon.

November 4th

Me and Mom got materials for the sail—very cold and snowy outside. Dad and Cody set up the arena garage for the boat. They made a fireplace out of a garbage can. We had white rice for the first time. It was good and tasty. Mom showed me different ways to stitch fabric.

November 6th

Dad and Cody finished making the chimney pipe. I got the first fire going at the workshop. It got warm fast. Dad says the fireplace is great. Mom and I went to find more fabric. Shovelled lots of snow with Cody. Arms tired. We had pumpkin pie. It was so tasty. Mom said it was old. But I could not tell.

November 10th

Cody and I set out traplines and went ice fishing. The ice was very thick. We'll need to cover holes to keep them from freezing. No fish today, but I remain hopeful. Dad has begun moving tools and equipment to the garage to work on the boat.

November 13th

There are no catches on the trapline. I caught the first fish, and Dad said it was a rainbow trout. It was delicious. We had it with rice. Dad is still working on the demolition of the boat. I helped load the garage workshop with firewood.

November 17th

I am reading a book called Lord of the Rings. It's very interesting so far with the elves, dwarves, and hobbits— the author has a neat imagination. Better fishing last couple of days. We cover up holes with sticks to keep them from freezing thick. Mom is making what she calls a quilt sail. It is patches of different fabrics. Mom taught me the zig-zag stitch, which we will use on the sails.

November 22nd

Dad finished making the removable keel. He is now working on the rudder. Mom is working on the jib sail that will be at the front or bow of the boat. She and I will begin working together on the sails. The stitching of sails seems tricky but looks fun. My fingers are getting calluses. Cody and I cut and moved lots more firewood into the workshop this week. Fishing is good. Traplines still aren't producing anything except for one snowshoe hare.

November 24th

Had rabbit tonight for dinner. It was so tasty. Mom and I are looking for a chain for an anchor.

November 26th

Snow continues to fall. It seems like I am shovelling every day for hours. Cody and I are looking for rope for the sails. Dad says we will need hundreds of feet.

December 1ˢᵗ

Finding rope with Cody over the past few days. All sorts. We have been braiding, tying, and weaving different materials to make long pieces that hold the jib and mainsail. Dad began gutting a nearby house for dimensional lumber. He says he needs 2x4s and plywood to build sleeping quarters, benches, and a base for the main mast.

December 7ᵗʰ

Cody and I are still looking for rope. Dad says we need extra for emergencies. Mom is still stitching the mainsail. It is huge. It's much bigger than the jib sail. Dad has plenty of lumber for the sleeping quarters. Halfway through Lord of the Rings now. It is so good. I love the characters, even Sauron. I hope Frodo and Sam make it.

December 11ᵗʰ

Dad finished the base mount for the main mast and began construction on the sleeping quarters. Dad says he is going on a hunt for a boom and mast. Cody had a great day of fishing. He caught three trout. We ate very well tonight. Mom is still working on sails.

December 14ᵗʰ

We finally gathered over 200 feet of rope. It took us forever to find enough. Glad it is done. Found chain for the anchor. Trapped two snowshoe hares today. Will make stew tomorrow. Mom has been stitching for weeks and always shows me new tricks. She has begun reinforcing all the seams and corners with sturdy canvas and metal clasps. She says the edges need to be rip-proof.

December 18th

Finished Lord of the Rings and loved it. It was a long book. It was over 1000 pages. I am now reading a book called Call of the Wild by Jack London. It is much shorter. There's a dog called Buck. I didn't know dogs lived with humans. The only dogs I've seen have been wolves and the odd Arctic fox.

December 20th

Dad finished sleeping quarters on the boat. The mast will come through the roof and lodge into the base; then, it will be fastened down. Cody and Dad dragged a huge tree from the bush into the workshop. They are going to use it to make the main mast.

December 22nd

Dad and I shot a massive bull moose on the Labrador highway today. It is rare to see such a huge, magnificent creature these days. We sat in the cold for hours. We pulled it back on our sled to the arena workshop and began processing it. The process took up the whole day. We shared a big meal tonight and could not move afterwards. We played a game called Monopoly tonight, and I won using the race car as my game piece.

December 24th

Very busy recently. Tomorrow is Christmas. Mom and Dad told me it was a hectic, family-oriented time of year with presents and lots of food. They told Cody and me the myth of Santa Claws, who lives near the North Pole. Apparently, he was a fat man dressed in red and had eight reindeer that drove him around. Seems ridiculous to me. Cody and I don't need presents. There is a lot to be grateful for.

January 2nd

Our homemade calendar said the new year has begun. The mast and boom have been de-barked and smoothed down. We should have it fitted in the base tomorrow. Mom is putting the final touches on the mainsail.

January 8th

Temperatures dropped to minus seventies. Can hardly be outside for any length of time. Everything freezes instantly: eyes, cheeks, nose. Dad and Mom built a mudroom as an entryway to keep our doors from freezing in the cold. Dad has trouble working with his hands in the cold.

January 14th

Mainmast fits perfectly through the sleeping quarters and into the base. Sleeping at night will be a tight fit, but we can manage. Mom says our body heat will help keep us warm. Dad said we must still treat the mast and boom with something before assembling the hardware.

January 18th

Began gathering all the bits and pieces for the rigging of the sails. Cody also began carving four oars for the boat. Two can be attached to the boat, and we'll have two spares if we lose or break the others. Dad also began looking for something that could act as an anchor. The chain we found will reach depths up to 100 feet.

January 25th

The boat is coming together. It is starting to look like the drawings Dad made. Mom made a mixture of old cooking oils, grease, fat, and old deck stain we found in a basement. She heated it, mixed it and put it in a large bucket. It stinks, but she seems to think it will work.

January 28th
Sleeping quarters, mast, and boom are all painted with the stinky stain. Cody shovelled off the roof of Solace 2 today. Snow was building up. When he came inside, he was freezing. Mom has started making us facemasks with built-in goggles for the extreme weather. They look funny.

February 3rd
Deep cold. Still in the minus seventies. Dad has fastened most of the rigging to the mast, jib, and gunwale. Mom also started working in the arena with Dad on a few things. Mom carved a tiller that controls the rudder. Dad made a pulpit in the bow of the boat to help drop the anchor and provide protection for the nose of the ship.

February 8th
Rigging hardware is done. Forestay and backstay ropes are measured and ready to be fastened to the sail and mast. Mom and I did such a neat job making the sails. They are so colourful and unique. I can't wait to see them full of wind on the water.

February 17th
Cody and I fastened the oar locks to the boat today. Dad thinks we are about four months away from a potential launch. After all this hard work, I look forward to launching this thing to see if it floats.

February 26th

Mom and Dad both seem tired and rundown. They don't complain, but I can sense it. We have worked very hard. The past few months have gone fast. We have been very conservative with our food, though we are not starving. The cold continues to punish us, but our house is kept warm.

March 4th

Dad was able to start up the Zamboni today for the first time. He found a new battery still in the box in a basement on the far side of town. He warmed it up, and it worked. He was so happy. Now, we can tow the heavy boat to the launch down by the river. Dad says we pull the boat out of the garage, then attach the mast because it won't fit under the garage door.

March 10th

We all brought the mainsail and jib and spread them out along the mainmast, which fit perfectly. We were all so proud. Eating lots of fish. Cody and I tried pineapple for the first time. It was so sweet and delicious.

March 19th

Putting all the final touches on the boat. Mom and Dad say that I should come up with a name for the boat. It may take us a while to find one. Mom thinks it's a girl, and so do I.

March 25th

Caught three more snowshoe hares in the last few days. Cody caught more trout as well. Mom and Dad are doing better since most of the boat has been finished. They were able to talk more and rest. We are now starting to make preparations for everything we need to take.

April 1ˢᵗ

Temperatures are around minus forty, which seems warm considering all the nasty weather we have been getting. Cody finished carving and treating the oars. We put them in the oar locks, and they fit perfectly. I can't wait to try them.

April 2ⁿᵈ

I helped Dad put a hitch on the Zamboni. He says there are only a few gallons of gas, so we must be smart about using the machine. We might only get one shot at the launching of the boat.

April 10ᵗʰ

Dad made a small ladder to throw over the side of the boat. Cody found a large iron sculpture of an eagle that we will use as an anchor. It is perfect because it's spreading its wings. Dad says he will get it red hot, then puncture a hole through it for the chain to go through.

April 15ᵗʰ

Getting closer to launch. Cody and I assembled a fishing tackle box with everything we might need on our journey. Mom made fried fish. It was so delicious. Mom also readied the tackle box with all the fruit and vegetable seeds.

April 21ˢᵗ

Dad put another coat of stain on the mast and sleeping quarters. The boat looks great and finely polished. We decided on the name of the boat. We are calling her 'Anastasia'. It means 'new life.' We all love it.

April 27th

Mom and Dad have been smoking lots of fish and another caribou we shot last week. We washed each other's hair tonight. The hot water felt so good on my head. It must have been two weeks since I washed my hair. Temperature is at minus 30.

May 4th

Mom and Dad keep calling today, Star Wars Day. I don't get it; neither does Cody. I've been practicing my archery lately and am hitting my targets consistently. Tonight we all played the board game called Life. It was so bizarre the way people used to live and love things.

May 13th

Temperatures at minus 20 degrees today, and it was glorious. There is still a lot of shovelling. Snow falls all the time and is up to the level of the windows of our house. Some houses are completely buried.

May 19th

Today is Cody's birthday, and Mom made a small chocolate cake out of flour, sugar, and baking soda. It was delicious. You are supposed to blow out the candles and make a wish. It seems silly to me, but you can't tell anyone, or the wish won't come true.

May 23rd

The temperature was minus 5 degrees today and rising. Mom and Dad are getting nervous and excited about the upcoming launch. Miss our cabin. We are not sure if we will ever go back.

May 28th

Dad found a bunch of maps of North America and the Maritimes. At dinner, he showed us the route we would take out of the Churchill River into the Atlantic Ocean. It was so interesting to see all the different cities that once were. Mom told us about New York and Los Angeles. Dad said we might pass New York and see all the other buildings. I am so excited. I was named after a part of New York called Brooklyn.

June 3rd

The first day of above-zero temperatures. Things are beginning to melt. The river down below looks slushy.

June 7th

The Churchill River is beginning to break up. Huge ice chunks are separating and floating down the river. It is not safe to sail.

June 11th

Water is beginning to flow at the sides of the river, and endless chunks are breaking off and floating down the river. We are so close. Bags are packed, and we're ready to go.

June 17th

Almost all of the ice is now gone. Some little ice chunks are still floating past us. Maybe in a few days, we launch. I am nervous about the Anastasia's capabilities.

June 22nd

Temperatures steady at 7 degrees. Mom and Dad say it is a go for a launch tomorrow. Yes! I will try to write in this journal soon.

Chapter 8 - The Anastasia

The Cardinals were thoughtful about what they were taking with them. They needed to travel light yet include various gear should the situation require it. They had a first-aid kit, dry sacks filled with clothes and food, extra oars, fishing gear, a toolbox, old lifejackets, and a few water jugs. They had gone over the lists, double-checked the rigging and sails, looked for any signs of weakness in the hull, and packed the boat for launch.

It had taken almost nine months to convert the aluminum boat into the now proud Anastasia. The Churchill River would be complex and challenging to navigate because of its swift-moving current and rocky bottom. Going downriver, the family would not need to do much except for steering the boat and lining up routes to avoid rocks and fallen timbers. Once at Muskrat Falls, over 250 kilometres away, they would need to guide the boat around the breaker wall onto shore, push it down the sandy embankment, around the dam, and relaunch in the river below. This worried Grant the most because they would need to offload all their gear, beach the boat, and then roll it downhill on a few logs. The entire process would likely take them a whole day.

Grant woke everyone up long before the light appeared. They ate a hearty meal of ten-year-old oatmeal and smoked trout. While eating, they could sense each other's nervous excitement. Except for their food and water, the Cardinals had moved everything to the boat at the arena the night before. The family triple-checked everything. Grant boarded up Solace 2, covered the windows and doors, and triple-checked everything.

They made their way down the dirt road to the arena. Grant opened the garage door and started the Zamboni. He slowly and carefully pulled the boat into the parking lot. It took all four family members to hoist the mainmast into place and bolt it down. They then drove the boat down the rocky road toward the crumbling concrete boat launch, Grant was constantly looking over his shoulders to ensure the boat was secure. Claire, Brooklyn, and Cody walked beside the boat, doing their best to keep it stable. So far, so good.

When they arrived at the ramp to the Churchill River, Grant looped around, put the Zamboni in reverse, and backed up until the trailer and boat entered the water. Brooklyn and Claire got into the boat, and Cody began loosening the crank to free up the boat. Slowly, the boat was launched into the water and released from the trailer. Cody held tight to the rope attached to the pulpit on the boat's bow. The Anastasia was in the water and floating.

Grant drove the Zamboni back up the road to the arena, parked, shut down the garage, and returned to the river, where Cody was still holding tight onto the boat.

"Nice driving, Dad!" Cody yelled as Grant came down the ramp.

"Thanks, we had just enough gas. It started to stall as soon as I was back in the garage," Grant said, wiping his brow.

"You ready?" Claire yelled from the Anastasia.

Grant nodded at his son. "You ready?"

"Let's do it," Cody answered.

They both got in the boat, waved goodbye to the town of Churchill Falls, and then slowly disembarked down the 100-foot-wide river. The water was cold and moving quickly.

"Shiver me, timbers!" Grant yelled.

"What does that mean?" Cody asked.

"It's an old sailor saying, meaning let my boat break into pieces," Grant explained.

"That doesn't sound good," Brooklyn said skeptically.

"If so and so happens, then let my boat break into pieces," Grant added. "Kind of like letting the Great Spirit guide me."

Grant steered the boat at the stern with his newly fastened tiller and rudder while Cody and Brooklyn were each on an oar. Claire was on the pulpit looking for any signs of danger, like fallen trees, submerged rock formations, or shallow sandbars where they might get stuck. Grant was confident the river was deep enough and free from most debris to allow for a smooth journey, but he couldn't be sure.

The three-degree, overcast morning was bitter. Their new insulated raingear kept them dry, but the wind along the river was still chilling to the bone. Grant guided the boat in the middle of the river while Claire closely watched the water ahead.

"So far, so good, snowflake!" Grant yelled toward the bow of the boat.

"Straight ahead!" Claire yelled back to the stern.

Cody and Brooklyn looked at each other and laughed at their parents. The boat was staying afloat, bringing a smile to Grant's face. The Anastasia wasn't taking on water and felt stable, even with all the weight. Grant had worried the boat might be top-heavy with the weight of the mast, but it was holding steady.

"I can't believe this river," Brooklyn said.

"We are really moving," Cody responded.

"It's so pretty out here," Brooklyn added.

"I've never seen anything like it." Cody was in awe of the sights and sounds of the raging river.

The river's first bend approached and made Grant and Claire slightly nervous. There could be rapids, rocky outcroppings or even waterfalls ahead, and they wouldn't be able to see it until the very last second. Grant and Claire had carefully reviewed the instructions and responsibilities with Cody and Brooklyn before they launched. They outlined the importance of listening carefully while on the water. They were told the different types of strokes and had practiced for a few weeks leading up to today. Grant also clearly told them the importance of not questioning his orders while on the boat.

"Brooklyn, Cody, ready on your oars!" Grant yelled.

As the boat rounded the bend, the river revealed a few white caps in the middle of the river. Claire squinted to get a better look.

"It doesn't look bad! Hit it straight on!" Claire yelled from the bow of the boat.

The Anastasia picked up speed and hit the mild rapids without a bump. She was heavy and able to take the slightly turbulent water.

"Woo-hoo!" Grant yelled.

"Smooth sailing!" Claire responded.

"No problem!" Brooklyn said, smiling at her brother.

The Cardinals continued downriver throughout the morning without any incident. The river widened, and the family could enjoy the views and surrounding wildlife. They spotted a mother moose and her calf, which was a great sign that mammals were still procreating and migrating this far north. They also saw plenty of fish jumping, birds hunting, and a mink scuttling along the rocky bank of the river.

Grant was especially happy that they covered so much ground without expending energy. The first day on the river reminded Grant and Claire how enjoyable life could be without worrying about the weather, food, shelter, and looming danger.

As they approached early evening, they had travelled well over 60 kilometres, according to the map Claire had examined. The Cardinal family decided it was a good first day on the water, and they ran the boat ashore on a sandy bank of the Churchill River. It was the perfect spot: easy to launch, flat ground, and plenty of room to set up a small campsite.

Once they tied off and anchored the boat to a nearby tree, they deliberated tasks and got to work. Cody gathered firewood, Brooklyn dug a fire pit, Claire set up the small tent they brought, and Grant ensured the boat and everything in it was secure.

Even though it was almost July, the weather was cool at around 5 degrees, and there were still patches of snow on the ground. Claire had never seen snow in July, which was why the water levels in the river were so high and easy to navigate. Though it was bitter cold at night and uncertainty lay ahead, Claire felt confident in her family's ability to persist and overcome controversy.

As Grant scouted the area for any immediate danger, he realized no bugs were in the air. Bugs were usually thick at this time of year. However, the cold temperatures were, in all likelihood, keeping the larvae dormant. No mosquitos, black flies, deer flies, nothing.

Claire set the pegs with her hatchet while Brooklyn used her trusty flint rod to start a fire with the grass and twigs gathered. Cody was busy sawing several dead fallen pine trees to keep the fire going throughout the night. Before long, the Cardinal children got the fire raging.

Cody and Grant grabbed the fishing rods and cast their lines from the riverbank. Freshly caught trout would be a nice reward after a long day on the water.

"Notice anything?" Grant asked his son.

"No, what?" Cody responded.

"No bugs…anywhere," Grant said.

"You're right, Dad. Isn't it a good thing that there are no bugs?" Cody asked.

"It's good for us, but I don't know about the birds, fish, and wildlife. Bugs are essential to the food chain. All species are connected. If the bugs disappear, other species will follow suit," Grant answered.

Cody contemplated the interconnectedness of the animal kingdoms as he continued to cast his line into the flowing Churchill River.

"So, how did you like your first day on the water?" Grant asked his son, changing the topic of conversation.

"I can't believe how much ground we are covering," Cody answered. "It's a lot different than walking."

"We certainly are moving. We'll be at Muskrat Falls before long." Grant felt a jerk on his line. He pulled hard and set the hook. "Bingo!" he yelled. "Fish on!"

"Reel it in! Land the sucker!" Cody yelled.

Grant reeled in the fish while Cody ran and grabbed the fishing net hooked on the side of the sleeping quarters in the boat. The fish came to the surface, a massive rainbow trout.

"At least 12 pounds! Get the net under it!" Grant yelled to Cody.

Cody placed the net under the fish and scooped it out.

"Yes!" Grant yelled. "Well done, Cody!"

Claire placed the grill on top of the fire and began cooking a small pot of rice while Grant began processing the monster fish by the side of the river. Cody came running up the bank to the campsite.

"We caught a monster!" Cody said gleefully.

"Excellent. Fresh dinner." Claire smiled as she loaded more pieces of wood on the fire.

The first day on the river was a resoundingly successful one. The Anastasia had proven seaworthy and could handle the weight of four people and a couple hundred pounds of cargo. They hadn't used any food except for a cup of rice; the river was still full of fish, there were no injuries, and the boat was holding firm. Grant and Claire both felt optimistic and assured about the days to come.

Grant had looked at the river map and calculated that it would take at least four days to get to their ultimate goal, the Atlantic Ocean. That night, they sang songs around the dying campfire; they talked about sailing, pirates, and the golden age of exploration. The Cardinal family eventually got into their tent and drifted to sleep beside the roaring Churchill River.

Chapter 9 - Muskrat Falls

The next few days were much the same on the river. They covered about 60-70 kilometres daily and camped at night, eating fresh fish for dinner. The Cardinals knew they were close to Muskrat Falls and the city of Goose Bay. As they approached the city, rain began to trickle overhead. So far, the river had been very kind to the young family. The hull had no leaks; they caught plenty of fish and were strong, healthy, and ready for anything coming their way.

Brooklyn started to recognize some landmarks and outcroppings, signalling they were just a few minutes from the massive dam at Muskrat Falls.

"Look there!" Brooklyn yelled, pointing to a unique pile of boulders. "We're close!"

Cody and Brooklyn were having the time of their life, except when they first got off the boat and felt the effects of sea legs. The two children were on an adventure of a lifetime and had no idea what lay ahead. They had never seen the world before or looked at the ocean and its vastness. The uncertainty and surprises of the trip fueled their drive and motivation.

Ahead in the distance, Claire spotted Muskrat Falls. Grant and Claire had planned where to run aground. It was a safe, small stone shore along the river's north bank. After taking the boat out of the water, they would start the process of log rolling their boat around the dyke and falls and down to the lower rapids. They also knew it would take a while, so they would take their time, triple-check their log placements, avoid injury and exhaustion, and launch the following day.

Grant shouted, "Row, row!" he urged his children on. Brooklyn and Cody stroked their oars together in unison as the hull scraped along the stony shore. "Well done!" the proud father shouted. "You did it!"

Claire hopped ashore with a tow rope and guided the boat further inshore. "We made it!" she yelled to her family.

Grant raised the rudder and got out of the boat. "Okay, you know the plan. We must offload everything from the boat and find some good rolling logs. After we eat a good lunch, we'll start pushing the boat."

"Kids, set up the tent and off-load the gear; we're going to start clearing the path," Claire said.

"Sure, Mom!" Cody said with enthusiasm.

"I'll go scout some decent logs," Grant said as he removed the axe and saw from the tool bag.

Claire scouted ahead and moved anything along the sandy bank, blocking a clear path to the river below. She realized getting a fire started might be difficult as the rain continued to fall. This was not going to be an easy day. She cleared branches and big rocks from the path down to the water, ensuring a clean, spacious path for the Anastasia. Though it was only a hundred feet down to the lower river, it was exhausting work. She watched her footing carefully on the slippery rocks. The last thing she needed was a sprained or broken ankle.

As Claire cleared a path down the Churchill River's bank, Grant found and chopped four straight spruce trees, delimbed, and debarked them. About ten feet long, they would span the boat's width and provide a surface for the boat to roll along on as the Cardinals pushed and pulled the Anastasia.

Grant brought the logs to the boat and found Brooklyn boiling water on a fire she had just lit. Cody had already off-loaded all the gear from the boat. The Cardinals were working together like a well-oiled machine. They took great pride in their responsibilities and together they seamlessly navigated one of the world's most turbulent rivers. Before long, Claire returned covered in sweat and spruce needles.

"You look like a Christmas tree," Grant said.

"Very funny," Claire said, putting down the axe and saw.

Grant brushed all the needles and debris from her face. "Is our path clear?" he asked.

"All clear. I certainly worked up an appetite," Claire said as she warmed her hands by the fire.

The drizzling rain continued, but the fire burned hot as they cooked some rice and trout at the breaker wall of the Muskrat Falls dam. They had all worked up an appetite and downed lunch quickly.

The Cardinals discussed the plan; Cody and Brooklyn would move each log as the boat traversed the shore while Claire and Grant stabilized the boat with a rope tied on the cleats near the bow. The boat was heavy with all the additional construction—at least a few hundred pounds of metal and lumber.

"Alright, you ready to do this?" Grant asked his family.

"As ready as I'll ever be," Claire responded.

"Remember to be careful with your footing and watch your fingers don't get caught underneath. The Anastasia is 500 pounds and will crush and pin you if you aren't extra careful."

Considering the steep decline down to the river below, Grant knew this was dangerous for everyone.

The Cardinals all rose to their feet and began the arduous task of rolling the boat. Cody and Brooklyn laid out the four logs, and Claire and Grant pulled the boat on top of the first log. It began to roll as the boat moved up the bank. Log by log, the boat moved along the shore with relative ease. Brooklyn and Cody grabbed the last log together and brought it to the front of the boat. The Cardinals were slow, systematic, and methodical. They knew that it wasn't a race. There was too much at stake.

Foot after foot, the Anastasia crept forward. They had reached the edge of the bank where the descent began. They paused for a break to gather their strength and drink some water.

Claire was so proud of how well Brooklyn and Cody were working together. They were communicating and being extra careful with each other's safety. "Drink plenty of water. This will be the most exhausting part of this job," the proud mother said.

Grant and Claire held tight to the rope as they descended one inch at a time. Brooklyn and Cody moved each log and held it in place until the boat's weight was on top of it. The boat wanted to take off down the bank and crash into the river, but Claire and Grant held firm. They both could feel blisters forming as they breathed heavily.

"Deep breaths, snowflake!" Grant yelled. "We're doing it!"

Claire and Grant's feet were firmly planted as the boat descended the final few feet to the shore. Their arms and hands burned as they finally let go of the rope.

"Yes!" Claire yelled.

"We did it!" Grant said, hugging his wife.

Brooklyn and Cody hugged each other, too.

"Well done, kids," Claire said.

"Now, let's get our gear and set up for the night," Grant announced.

The four family members marched back up the steep incline, gathered their gear, and brought it to the boat. They also brought some hot coals in a shovel down to the water's edge and set up camp next to the Anastasia. They pitched a tent, had a hardy supper and settled in for the night.

As Claire lay in the tent, she thought about the town of Goose Bay, which had been obliterated just over the ridge from where they were camping. She remembered World War II history and the pictures she saw of Hiroshima and Nagasaki and the aftermath. Had there been fallout, she wondered. Who would have launched the bomb? Were there more bombs? Was it another country? Was it a radical regime? Was it retaliatory? Was artificial intelligence behind the attacks? Claire had many questions and was eager for answers. As exhaustion set in, she slowly drifted off to sleep.

Chapter 10 - The Test

Brooklyn was the first one awake. She slipped out of the tent into the cool morning air and admired the Muskrat Falls dam. She splashed some water on her face and hair and pondered what life would have been like had she lived in Montréal. Until now, the world was the cabin: fishing, hunting, skinning, and stitching. Now, she felt awakened. She remembered all the artwork in the community centre in Churchill Falls. She thought about all the other kids and people that once dotted the planet. She contemplated machines farming the great prairies, massive boats steaming across the oceans, schools, malls, and different apartment buildings. War was also a new reality for Brooklyn. People had killed one another. They bombed each other from airplanes. It was a lot to think about, but like her Mom and Dad taught her, she tried to stay in the moment.

Cody exited the tent and sat beside Brooklyn on the riverbank.

"What are you doing?" Cody asked.

Brooklyn didn't answer as she stared out onto the river.

"Pretty neat invention, don't you think?" Cody said, looking out to the dam where Brooklyn was gazing.

She still didn't reply.

"What's the matter? What are you thinking about?" Cody persisted.

There was a long pause, and then Brooklyn spoke. "Do you think Mom and Dad did the right thing? Hiding everything from us?" she asked.

"They kept us safe, Brooklyn," Cody said. "We would be dead without them."

"They didn't mention anything. The only world we knew was shooting and skinning animals at the cabin." Brooklyn was torn between the two thoughts.

"The world was ending. They protected us. They raised us to survive. Remember, they did teach us how to read and write." Cody did his best to support his parents and reassure Brooklyn of their good intentions.

"I've been thinking all morning, Cody. This world lived together in peace and harmony for so long, then a shift in weather, and it all fell apart. Everyone turned on each other, and there was a full catastrophic breakdown. There were 10 billion people on earth. Do you know how many people that is? How could all those people not get it together and solve the issues? Right now, there are major cities out there, and we know nothing about them or their well-being," Brooklyn said.

"What would you have done?" Cody asked.

"I don't know," Brooklyn responded. "Try to stop people from killing each other."

"Easier said than done," Cody said. "We are just kids, Brooklyn."

"I know, I know. I guess I feel let down. Like somebody played a trick on me," Brooklyn said, throwing a stone in the river.

Claire and Grant exited the tent and smiled at their kids near the water's edge.

"Want to get a fire started?" Grant asked. "I could sure go for a morning tea."

"Sure, Dad," Cody said, standing up. "I'll get some wood."

As Cody left, Grant sat down beside his daughter. "What are you looking at, sweetie?"

"Nothing, just the falls."

"Are you okay? You seem a little vacant and lost in contemplation," Grant asked.

"I'm just worried about this world. Everything was completely different before we left the cabin. I want to go back to the way it was." A tear came to Brooklyn's eye.

"I know things have changed. But we are in search of answers. Together, we are going to find out the truth."

Claire noticed her troubled daughter and sat down on the other side of her. "Hey there, warrior girl. You doing alright?"

"I think this new world, this new perspective of things, is a little too much at once for our youngest. Let's show her Lake Melville in the afternoon," Grant said. "It might change her spirit."

"Oh, she's going to love it," Claire added.

"What's Lake Melville?" Brooklyn asked.

"It's the biggest freshwater lake you will ever see," Grant answered. "Your grandfather came to Lake Melville to fish the rich waters."

"Grandfather used to fish in Lake Melville? Where is it?" Brooklyn's mood shifted.

"Once we get past Goose Bay, a few miles downriver, it opens into Lake Melville. Grandpa used to hunt and trap all along the Churchill River and spent his off months fishing Lake

Melville and the surrounding rivers." Grant understood Brooklyn was still going through the emotions of understanding what the world once was.

Brooklyn was coming of age, and her moods would have ups and downs, but Grant and Claire would do their best to understand and accept anything she felt.

"I'm kind of hungry," Brooklyn said.

"Let's get a fire going," Grant said, standing up.

Claire held out her hand to Brooklyn. "Come on, let's prepare breakfast and get ready for launch. Maybe get our fishing gear ready, just like your grandfather did."

After breakfast, the Cardinal family rolled the Anastasia into the frigid lower Churchill River below Muskrat Falls. The food was secure and in dry bags. The tools and other bags were tied with ropes. They double-checked all the knots: the cleat knots, the clove hitches, and the double sheet bends that tied the sails to the mast and boom. Everything was secure, and they felt confident as Grant pushed off with an oar. Brooklyn and Cody rowed to the middle of the river and began drifting downstream.

A short while later, they approached Goose Bay, where the family had been about nine months ago. It was a quiet, ominous stretch of the river as they remembered the crater and fallout from an unknown war. Grant and Claire had discussed potential scenarios, but it was still a complete mystery. As they floated by the road leading into Goose Bay, the Cardinals were glad to be moving past such a place of devastation and tragedy. Goose Bay also represented a significant disappointment for the Cardinals, as they spent almost a month getting there, only to find it completely disintegrated.

As they floated on, in the distance, they finally saw the river widen into Lake Melville. It was one of the world's largest freshwater lakes, and Grant figured it would take about three days to cross, depending on the wind. The lake would provide the perfect opportunity to test Anastasia's sailing capabilities before they entered the more turbulent, unpredictable Atlantic Ocean.

The air cooled as pressure dropped, and rain began to drizzle. Grant considered the next major puzzle piece: attaching the keel underneath the boat. The keel would be crucial in stabilizing the boat in the strong currents and the harsh winds of the northern ocean, which worried Grant and Claire the most. Grant and Claire figured they would need to wait until they were out of Lake Melville because of the shallow banks, rising and lowering tides, and the tricky-to-navigate channels. They also decided to camp along the Atlantic Ocean shoreline for a day or two before braving the ocean and its elements. While camping there, they would carefully monitor the tides, attach the ever-so-important keel to the bottom of the hull, and then wait for the perfect time to launch.

Cody and Brooklyn rowed harder toward Lake Melville as they saw their goal right before them. The wind was perfect, not too strong or light, and coming right behind them. Brooklyn and Cody had been rowing for about an hour, but they didn't mind because it kept their bodies warm.

"There's Lake Melville," Cody said to Brooklyn. "Just like Mom and Dad said."

"Yes!" Brooklyn replied.

Aboard the Anastasia, the Cardinals made their way into the grand lake. Grant stood up and yelled: "Let's let out the jib!"

The family had practiced letting out the sails and reeling them back in, but never on the water with wind.

"Prepare to jib!" Grant yelled to Claire.

"Aye, aye!" she happily responded. Claire then released the preventer lock and started cranking the release. Inch-by-inch, the jib began to rise at the front of the boat, exposing the hand-sewn, multi-coloured mosaic of a sail. The wind gathered in the sail as Claire continued to reel the crank. Eventually, the jib reached its destination, and Claire tied it down to the starboard side cleat.

Everyone immediately felt the change of pace. The boat began to pick up speed as Brooklyn and Cody took their oars out of the water. Grant looked at the tell-tails on the jib and adjusted the tiller to maximize the wind in the sail. The Anastasia took off with a slight turn of the tiller and the rudder. They were sailing. A rush of pride filled the entire Cardinal family.

"Tack the jib line!" Grant yelled.

"Aye!" Claire yelled. She flung the jib rope a few more times around the cleat and sat back down.

"Steady as she goes!" Grant yelled.

The Anastasia was moving at a nice clip. It was peaceful for everyone, as they could relax and enjoy the gigantic lake passing by. It allowed Claire to look at the maps they had brought along for the journey. She removed the Lake Melville map she had found in Churchill Falls and examined their approximate position. She was looking for a specific cove that would be a great place to anchor for the night. The Cardinals had not slept aboard the boat yet, but they were looking forward to their first opportunity.

The winds on the lake continued to drive the boat onward into the afternoon. Grant and Claire looked at each other and smiled at the success of their first voyage on open water. They had traversed the Churchill River, but this felt completely different. They had spent a year preparing for this moment; they engineered, persisted, and were now conquering and harnessing nature and all its elements.

"Claire! Should we let out the mainsheet?" Grant yelled over the splashing water and blowing winds.

"No time like the present!" Claire answered.

"Okay, let's prepare the mainsail!" Grant said. "Brooklyn, Cody, untie the mainsail on the boom!"

"Aye, aye!" Cody and Brooklyn said simultaneously.

Brooklyn and Cody untied the half dozen ties and removed the tarp protecting the sail on the boom. The boom was secured to cleats atop the sleeping quarters.

"Raising the mainsail!" Claire said as she began to crank.

The main sheet began to ripple in the wind as Claire continued to turn the crank. The quilted canvas mainsail began to reveal itself to the Cardinals, and they all looked on with joy and satisfaction. Brooklyn was incredibly proud, as she and her mom had their hands in almost every stitch. It reminded Claire of a colourful rainbow she hadn't seen in years. She also realized that her children had likely never seen a rainbow.

"It's beautiful, Mom!" Brooklyn said.

"Mainsail up!" Claire yelled.

The mainsail was filled with wind, and Grant trimmed it to stop the luffing in the sail. Claire released the boom vang and mainsheet, allowing the boom to move freely. As she adjusted the boom's position, the mainsail fully filled with wind. Now, the mainsail and the jib were working in unison, and the boat was moving quickly. Quickly enough, that a small wake was created at the stern of the boat.

"We're moving now!" Cody said with a smile.

The significance of the moment deepened as their first nautical adventure began.

The air was cool on their faces, but they didn't mind at all. The wind rushed past them at an exhilarating speed—the fastest Cody and Brooklyn had ever remembered traveling.

Grant noted that the only thing missing was the sun. He remembered fishing with his father on beautiful summer days, and the waters were crystal clear, highlighted by the bright sun in the sky. Though the children didn't remember the sun, Grant knew they inherently missed it; the vitamins, the pain relief, and the ability to heal, cure, and reduce depression were all crucial components of living in a healthy world.

The cool wind rushed across Claire's face as she leaned back and examined the map of Lake Melville. A few miles ahead, a cove appeared, sheltered from the wind and an ideal, scenic spot to drop anchor. Claire moved cautiously, ducking under the boom, and showed Grant the map while he steered the boat.

"Looks perfect," Grant affirmed while Claire returned to the bow. "Prepare to drop mainsail!" he yelled to Brooklyn and Cody.

As the Anastasia approached the cove, the Cardinals dropped the mainsail and jib, tied off the jibstay and mainstay and rowed the rest of the way. It was only a few strokes, and they were in the calm bay. Immediately upon arrival, the winds died down, and Claire threw the iron eagle anchor overboard and watched as it dropped to the bottom of the lake.

"About thirty feet!" Claire said.

"Perfect," Grant said.

The Cardinals were thrilled the boat had worked just as intended. They were all dedicated to keeping the boat clean and organized. There were a lot of ropes aboard, so it was essential to stay disciplined, or things could get tangled quickly, literally and figuratively.

They ate supper and settled in the cramped but cozy sleeping quarters, with the mainmast protruding through the middle of the space. Though they were shoulder to shoulder, it was warm and comfortable as the Lake Melville waves gently rocked them to sleep.

Newfoundland & Labrador

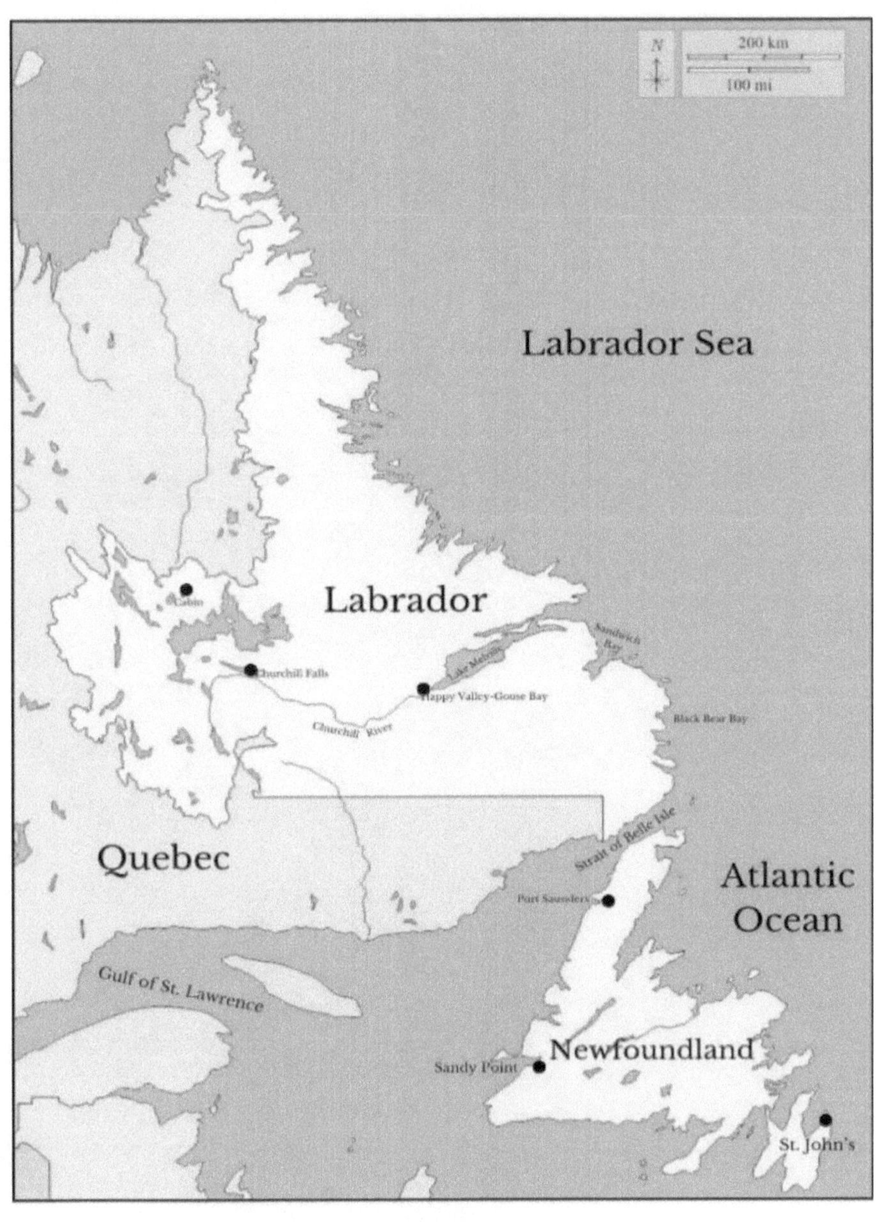

Chapter 11 - The Gateway

Brooklyn's Journal:

June 28th
We slept on the boat for the first time. It was so warm. The boat rocks at night, so it took some time to get used to it. We have been eating lots of fresh fish. Me and Cody are in charge of rowing most of the time. Mom is the navigator, and Dad steers the boat. We are all in great spirits.

June 29th
It was our second night aboard the Anastasia, and we all slept great. The mainmast is holding firm, and the sails are holding wind. Dad says we must treat the sails with wax or oil at some point. I pulled up our eagle anchor today. It was so heavy.

After a few days on the massive Lake Melville, the Anastasia approached the shallow tributaries of the tidal-fluctuating inlet that led into the Atlantic Ocean. They brought the sails down and carefully rowed the meandering channels, passing the dying spruce groves and rocky shores of northern Labrador.

The land was mostly barren and devoid of life as they drifted downstream; even the summer grasses were brown. Grant steered the boat as the tides were high, and they were on their way out. Grant knew they would need perfect timing in anchoring their boat at low tide to mount and bolt the metal keel at the bottom of the boat. It would be a dangerous job. He would need to get in frigid water and perform a tricky task without light or direction.

Brooklyn and Cody rowed slowly and steadily through the calm, flowing waters. They weaved back and forth through the channels and eventually found the final stretch, allowing entry into the Atlantic Ocean.

Once they were on the open ocean, everyone was looking for a spot along the coast where the tides had retreated, and they could still work underneath the boat close to shore.

Claire pointed to a small bay with a small stream pouring into it. "Look! That channel might work!" she said, pointing to the inlet.

"Beautiful," Grant said. "Cody, Brooklyn, you see that?" he said, pointing.

Grant steered toward the bay as Brooklyn and Cody rowed toward the small channel. They scouted the small stream inlet, and it was perfect. Grant ran the boat ashore, and everyone offloaded the gear they would need for the night, including the tent and food for dinner. Cody and Brooklyn jumped out immediately and crossed the vast waterlogged beach onto the land, searching for anything they could burn. The entire family was hungry and looking to start dinner soon.

Grant wouldn't get in the frigid water until a raging fire was going. Hypothermia would only take about ten minutes, so the timing must be perfect. He and Claire off-loaded the massive keel, and all the metal hardware needed to mount it. Grant looked across the beach and smiled with pride as he noticed his children had already started the fire.

"OK, I think it's now or never," Grant said to Claire.

"You're crazy," Claire responded, dipping her feet in the water.

"Yes, I am," he said, laughing. "Just hand me the tools when I call for them."

Grant had his tools, had the keel, and was getting up the nerve to brave the conditions. He stripped naked and pushed the boat out a few feet, deep enough to get the keel underneath. He huffed and puffed to get his body acclimated. Claire did her best to stabilize the boat with the anchor chain. Grant dragged the heavy keel to the water's edge, threw a small satchel around his neck with all the nuts and bolts, looked at Claire and smiled.

"Here we go," Grant said.

He took a few long breaths, went under the boat, and moved the keel onto the bolt mounts. He used the nuts to attach the keel loosely and then went back up for air. As he emerged, he let out a scream that spooked a flock of gulls off a nearby beach.

"It's on!" the shocked Grant yelled.

The water felt like pins and needles against his skin. But he needed to hurry. Claire handed him the wrench; he took another couple of deep breaths and then went back under. He found the bolts, tightened the first two nuts, and went up for another breath. It was cold but getting more tolerable. He took another deep breath, went under and tightened the final two bolts. He double-checked the stability and found it was sturdy and not moving.

Grant popped up from the water and ran onto the beach towards the fire. Claire threw him a towel as he rushed off hooting and hollering. He screamed the whole way there as it helped the blood flow. Claire and the kids laughed the entire time. The sight of their skinny, vulnerable, naked father screaming and yelling was something they had never seen before, and it cracked them right up.

"It's not funny!" Grant said, running wildly.

He plopped down at the fire and exhaled with a massive sense of relief. His lips were blue, and he was paler than usual.

"Did you get the keel on?" Cody asked.

"All done!" Grant said, shivering and drying his pale body. "We'll just need to tie the Anastasia down, so we all don't have to swim out in the morning. I'll tie a rope around her when I can feel my legs again."

The hatches were battened down, the fire was stoked, and the open ocean lay before the Cardinals as they cooked and warmed themselves. It had taken about two weeks to traverse the Churchill River and Lake Melville. The Cardinals had some great practice, each learning the varied complexities of sailing. They took turns steering, tying knots, and hoisting the jib and mainsail. Each now felt confident they could manage any role they might have to take on.

Seeing the ocean for the first time brought a sense of calm to Brooklyn and Cody. They looked to the horizon as the waves crashed and gulls flew overhead. Though they didn't realize it until now, the ocean had been something they had sorely missed.

Grant rubbed his arms and chest as the warmth and feeling began to return. He took a few bites of freshly caught trout and drank warm tea by the fireside.

"Well, are you ready for the ocean tomorrow, kids?" Claire asked.

"I think we'll be ready," Brooklyn said.

"How far are we going tomorrow?" Cody asked.

"As far as the wind will take us," Grant answered. "But we are looking for Sandwich Bay. It will be a place to anchor for the night where the water is calm."

"We should get in around eight hours each day on the water," Claire said. "Sailing at night is far too dangerous for a boat this small. If we were in a schooner, we would head into the open ocean, but we must stick to the coastline in case anything happens."

As Grant warmed himself, the plunge into the frigid water had reminded him of the dangers of the ocean. It would only take five to ten minutes for hypothermia to set in. If someone were to fall overboard, they would need immediate rescue. "The ocean is much different than a lake or river. It is harsh, unpredictable, unforgiving, and colder than you can imagine," Grant said, rubbing his shoulders.

"And don't forget about jellyfish and sharks," Claire added.

"What's a jellyfish?" Brooklyn asked.

"Well, it's like a clear, plastic bag floating in the ocean. They don't have eyes, brains, hearts or bones, and they sting like a son of a gun," Claire answered.

"Hey kids, do you want to go oyster and clam scavenging?" Grant asked.

"That sounds fun," Brooklyn said. "What's an oyster?"

"It's like a clam. A shell that needs some prying. Kids, I just realized you've never had oysters or clams, have you?" Grant asked.

"No," Brooklyn and Cody said.

"They are so delicious," Claire added. "A little salt and pep, maybe a dab of tabasco sauce. Mmm."

"Let's go see if we can scavenge some before the high tide comes roaring in," Grant said as he got up and dressed. He noticed the temperature drop as evening was setting in.

It was midsummer, and temperatures were still cold, sometimes below zero at night. The earth was slowly plunging into a deep freeze. All the trees around them in Labrador were dying, and the animals were disappearing. Though it was cold and grey daily, Grant was happy to be on the ocean, where food and options for anchoring would be abundant.

Grant and Claire's plan in the coming weeks was to scan the coast for signs of life, stop when needed, and take their time. Has the sun stopped shining everywhere? Were there people in Halifax? What about Boston and New York? Was anyone doing well? All were questions they wanted answers to. South was the destination, but answers were their ultimate goal.

The Cardinals strolled the beach, looking for signs of clams, oysters, or anything else they could find. Brooklyn and Cody carried the bail buckets and chatted while Claire and Grant plucked clams off the wet beach. As they strolled, they came across a rocky formation and began to find dozens of oysters hidden and tucked away amongst the cracks and crevices.

"What is that?!" Brooklyn yelled.

Grant and Claire turned to see Brooklyn pointing down on an eight-inch crab. Both parents laughed at Brooklyn and how she looked at the alien-looking creature.

"That is a rock crab," Grant said, picking it up behind the hind quarters. "They're delicious. You just have to be careful of their pincers. They hurt like the Dickens."

"Too bad we don't have some butter to melt," Claire said to Grant.

"We have never had butter," Cody said.

"It's made from cow's cream. It's whipped, salted and served on everything from potatoes to fresh buns to crab and lobster," Claire said, licking her lips.

"What's lobster?" Cody said.

"They're kind of like crabs; they're just shaped a bit differently and have bigger claws," Grant said. "Your mom and I, on our first anniversary, went to a Montréal restaurant, and both had filet mignon and lobster tail dinners. Freshly melted butter makes all the difference on lobster, asparagus and mashed potatoes. Yum yum, what a night it was."

"That was one of the best meals of my life. Remember that 96' Burgundy?" Claire said with a wink.

"Let's find a few more oysters, and we'll have ourselves a meal," Grant said.

The Cardinal family scoured the beach and found dozens of oysters and a couple more small crabs. They only took what they needed but were reminded how bountiful the ocean was. They only needed to look or drop their lines in the water to be rewarded.

As darkness set and the tides came in, they took the bounty of clams, oysters, and live crabs back to the camp. As Grant pulled the Anastasia towards the shore, Brooklyn and Cody stoked the dying fire with driftwood and twigs. He knew the tides were coming in and wouldn't retreat until the late morning, so the boat would be safe and sound, tethered and anchored.

Claire began cooking the seafood meal, sending mouth-watering aromas through their seaside camp. The Cardinals dined generously by the fireside as the tide came in. It was late, and they felt it was time for bed.

Claire and the children entered the tent while Grant ensured everything was cleaned and secure. They were in unknown territory, and predators roamed, especially after cooking an aromatic meal on the fire. He discarded all the shells and remnants of the meal into the ocean and stoked the fire one last time.

Grant wasn't a religious man but found himself looking up to the sky. "Ancestors give me and my family strength on the ocean tomorrow. Share with us good wind and calm waters. Please look after my wife and children." Grant prayed under night's darkness, especially to his parents, whom he knew were watching over him. "Mother, Father, I am trying to be a good parent, like you were, but I need a sign that we are on the right path."

He closed his eyes and waited for anything. Deep in the distance, he heard a lone wolf howling. It was far from where they were, but it still struck Grant in a very spiritual way. He had always been a practical realist, but he now realized he would need more than his knowledge to traverse the unpredictable ocean. He would need his ancestors, the spirit world, and perhaps a little luck.

Grant entered the tent and found his family sound asleep, their bellies full and hearts warm. He laid down, closed his eyes, and smiled at the thought of the howling wolf.

Chapter 12 - The Ocean

The Cardinals had broken camp, loaded the boat, and set sail early in the morning. Their sailing skills were improving, their confidence was growing, and their optimism was at an all-time high. They took turns in various positions on the boat: rigger, navigator, lookout, and deckhand. They kept everything organized, encouraged one another, and picked up each other's slack when needed.

After several hours on the water, a few miles from the coast and having travelled approximately 20 miles, the skies quickly began to darken, and the winds started to pick up. According to the map, they had hoped to reach Sandwich Bay by mid-afternoon. As they navigated the increasingly turbulent seas, Grant was careful not to be blown off course and to stay close to shore. If anything were to happen, he wanted the last resort to be the ability to swim to shore should the boat capsize.

"Winds are picking up!" Claire yelled, looking at the dark sky. "The rain is coming!"

"Claire, bring down the sails!" Grant yelled back.

"Aye, aye!" Claire scrambled and started to crank down the sails.

"Brooklyn, Cody, secure the deck!" Grant yelled.

Cody and Brooklyn tied the jib and mainsail down and secured the anchor and the different bags inside the sleeping quarters. The rain began to fall as the boat rocked up and down. Brooklyn and Cody struggled to keep their balance as they tied everything down in such a tight space. Frigid water began to splash over the edges of the boat as it violently rocked in the turbulent seas.

"Cody, grab a bucket!" Grant yelled. "We're going to have to start bailing. Claire, on the other oar with Brooklyn!"

The weather had turned so quickly that they almost didn't have time to react. Now that the sails were down, Grant instructed them to row with the waves to prevent the boat from capsizing. The sea was turbulent and cold, a stark reminder that they would not always be in control. As rookie sailors, they all understood the importance of not taking anything for granted and being prepared for anything. This was a valuable learning experience for the Cardinals, teaching them to remain attentive and focused on the task at hand. It was louder than usual, adding a new dimension to the crashing waves and strong Arctic winds.

After a few rough, cold, and anxiety-ridden hours at sea, Claire eventually spotted the rocky point leading into Sandwich Bay. Grant turned the boat toward the coast and carefully maneuvered into the bay. The waters calmed, the winds died, and the noise lessened in the peaceful bay.

Everyone was relieved that the rains had slowed, especially Cody, who didn't need to continue to bail out the Anastasia, at least for now. Brooklyn and Claire slumped over, relieved the gruelling crawl to the bay was over.

Claire turned to Grant. "It might be a smart idea to stay on the boat tonight and keep an eye on things."

"Sounds like a good idea. That way, we can deal with things immediately," Grant responded as he threw the anchor overboard.

It continued to downpour, but the family stayed relatively dry inside the sleeping quarters despite the damp conditions. The boat gently swayed back and forth, with the sounds of the waves providing a soothing ambiance.

Cody caught a glimpse of something massive outside as they ate some smoked caribou. He emerged from the sleeping quarters in awe. Brooklyn noticed her brother's stoic, shocked expression.

"What is it?" Brooklyn asked.

"I don't know," Cody answered.

Brooklyn sprang up and joined Cody on the deck.

"What are you two looking at?" Claire asked curiously.

Grant and Claire joined their children on the deck, observing a gigantic ice mass floating off the coast. It appeared as a solitary diamond against a backdrop of grey and dullness. The closer it got to the Cardinals, they realized how massive and brilliant it really was. The spectrum of colour moved from bright blue at the top of the ice to a dark emerald-green as it submerged into the ocean. Towering a hundred metres above the ocean, the almost supernatural ice mass drifted by the anchored Anastasia.

"What is that?" Brooklyn asked, still staring at the glacial mass.

"It is an iceberg," Claire said.

"But it is floating north," Grant said.

"That's not supposed to happen," Claire responded.

"It could be from somewhere south; maybe it is rejoining its family in the Arctic," Grant guessed.

"Only 10 percent of the iceberg is visible above water," Claire explained. "90 percent is below the water, making them super mysterious and dangerous."

Brooklyn and Cody were captivated by the creature's immense size. They continued to gaze as the giant ice floe drifted north towards the expanding ice cap at the top of the world. As it vanished over the horizon, day turned to night while they discussed the challenges they had faced throughout the day.

The day was exhausting, both mentally and physically. They had some food and chatted briefly; everyone eventually drifted off to sleep relatively early. In the middle of the night, Grant awoke from a deep slumber after a coughing fit and horrific nightmare. He dreamt that he and the boat were sinking to the bottom of the ocean while, on the shore, his family watched him slowly disappear beneath the waves. He got up, stepped outside, and took some long, deep breaths of the fresh ocean air. Relieved that the rain had stopped, Grant stood rubbing his sore throat and hoping for better conditions the next day.

Once the stress and anxiety left Grant as he stood on the deck of the Anastasia, he returned to the sleeping quarters and wrapped his arms around Claire, squeezing her tightly and feeling the warmth radiating from her. She moaned and nestled closer to him, and soon Grant drifted off to sleep.

When Cody and Brooklyn woke up the following day, they both declared it had been one of the best sleeps of their lives. Grant and Claire experienced a different morning, as their nerves were somewhat frayed after an exhausting and taxing day. It was difficult for them to stay asleep for long, as they were both constantly worried about the looming threats of the ocean.

Their destination for the day was to anchor in Black Bear Bay, roughly 30 or 40 miles down the rocky Labrador coast. The rain turned into freezing sleet, and the waves were just as turbulent as they had been the day before. Cody bailed while Grant did his best to keep the boat moving straight and steady.

Grant felt confident in the boat as they soared across the frigid waters. They were moving faster than ever before. The Cardinals were becoming skilled sailors and gaining newfound confidence in the tempestuous conditions.

"Brooklyn, Cody, both of you, sit port side. We need your weight to keep her straight," Grant yelled.

"Aye, aye!" the kids responded.

The kids' weight helped balance the boat and kept it steering true towards Black Bear Bay.

"Great job!" Grant yelled.

Claire sat at the bow, looking back at her children with a smile.

That night, they arrived at the relatively tranquil Black Bear Bay. They anchored the boat in the bay's center, aware that the tides were receding. The Cardinals enjoyed some smoked caribou and trout for dinner while making plans for the next day. The Strait of Belle Isle would be the next leg of their journey.

The Strait of Belle Isle, the waterway between Labrador and the Island of Newfoundland, was unknown to Claire and Grant, and they had no way to predict what conditions might be like. They had charted this route into the Gulf of St. Lawrence to avoid the turbulent waters off the coast and hoped to do some fishing along the way if the opportunity arose.

The following day, the Anastasia entered the Strait of Belle Isle. Grant and Claire knew they would begin to see the remnants of civilization along the coastline. They wouldn't come across cities or skyscrapers but would see small fishing villages with a few homes, docks, and boats. The two parents weren't entirely sure what to expect. Would there be anyone alive? Would they be friendly? Although it felt ominous, they remained hopeful that they might find a small village where they could gain some insight into the state of the world.

The Strait of Belle Isle was relatively calm as they sailed, admiring the coasts of Newfoundland and Labrador. The first sign of civilization was a road that began to run along the coast. There were toppled telephone poles, collapsed bridges, and washed-out sections of the two-lane highway. Cody spotted the first white building, but no vehicles were travelling the roads, nor was there any sign of human activity.

"Look there!" Cody yelled, pointing at the small house.

"Let's get a closer look," Grant said, steering the rudder toward the house.

As they approached the single-storey dwelling, they noticed it was abandoned entirely, featuring a collapsed roof and overgrown moss and vines. The paint was flaking off the siding, and a telephone pole had toppled onto the front of the garage.

As they sailed through the Strait of Belle Isle, every home stood derelict and corroding. The salty ocean air took a toll on buildings, regardless of their materials. No signs of life existed except the moss and vines overtaking the walls.

"I want everyone to keep an eye out for smoke as well. It might guide us in the right direction," Grant said.

Cody also noticed a large, unusual-looking object. "What is that?" he asked.

Grant looked in the direction Cody was pointing. "That, my boy, is a transport truck." Grant didn't laugh or smile, but he got a kick out of the expression on his son's face. "Those things used to haul massive trailers of goods all around the world."

"It's huge!" Cody said in awe.

"They're called transport trucks, or lorries, as the old-timers referred to them," Grant said.

"Where is everyone?" Brooklyn asked.

"I'm not sure," Claire said. "Maybe it's similar to Goose Bay, where everyone was recalled to a city centre or military base."

"This keeps getting stranger and stranger," Grant added. "I thought we would have seen someone by now."

"It's Newfoundland, snowflake; not many people lived here in the first place," Claire joked.

After a few hours, they pulled into an inlet called Port Saunders on the west coast of Newfoundland. As they rowed into the bay, the Cardinals discovered an old, abandoned dockyard with massive concrete docks where they could row right up. They tossed the boat bumpers over the side and secured the Anastasia's bow and stern. Everyone was glad to get off the boat and stretch their weary legs. It had been a few days since they last set foot on solid ground, and each family member had a slight wobble in their initial steps.

As they strolled along the dock, they couldn't help but notice the numerous disintegrating boats scattered along the paths of the once-thriving fishing community. Fallen vessels, rusted trailers, old fishing buoys, and dilapidated trucks lined the 100-metre parking lot.

Cody gazed at a large fishing trawler that had tipped onto its side. "What's a DILIGAFF?" he asked his parents, gesturing towards the name on the boat.

Claire and Grant exchanged looks and smiled. "I don't know, son," Grant replied.

"I think maybe it's a flower," Claire suggested, winking at her husband.

"Or perhaps the name of a town in Ireland," Grant added.

"Strange," Cody said with a puzzled expression.

They walked along the dockyards, searching for signs of life, but it felt like a ghost town. Nothing civilized had inhabited this place for a decade. The slow decay of time had taken its toll on Labrador and Newfoundland. Snow and ice wreaked havoc on roofs; salty air corroded antennas and vehicles, and the ocean was reclaiming what was once hers.

"Maybe we should get a fire started and have some supper," Claire suggested.

"Great idea. Cody, you and me, let's get some wood," Grant responded.

The late afternoon and early evening in Port Saunders allowed Claire and Grant to finish work while quickly getting on and off the boat. Claire and Brooklyn washed some clothes while Cody and Grant performed general maintenance on the boat. After they finished their chores and had some supper, the four family members strolled down the road to explore the local community and find a stream to fill their water jugs.

Port Saunders was a small community with a few buildings in the central part of town. At one point, its highest population was 700 people. Some surrounding homes collapsed like those in Churchill Falls, and a few barely stood. Most were boarded up; a few were exposed entirely through broken windows and open doors. They continued to stroll down the overgrown road until they reached an old gas station. Grant looked through the front window and saw that almost everything had been taken off the shelves, but he noticed a few scattered items.

Grant and Claire exchanged glances and nodded in agreement. Claire dropped the water jugs and picked up a nearby rock and threw it through the front window. The glass shattered with a sharp crack and fell to the ground with a loud clatter. Claire and Grant shared a smile. After clearing the glass away, they carefully stepped inside the store. They gathered some cans of expired food and put them in their packs. Cody went behind the counter and found a couple of Bic lighters.

“What "What are these?” Cody asked.

“Lighters. Just spin the wheel with your thumb,” Claire replied.

Cody struggled with the Bic lighter but eventually managed to get it working. "Hey!" exclaimed the excited Cody as he looked at his mom and dad.

“That’s how they used to do it,” Grant said. “Lighter fluid, plastic, a few components, and bang, you’re in business."

“So cool," Cody remarked, staring at the flame.

Grant reached the back of the store and spotted a shelf with a few bottles of liquor. He turned and smiled at Claire.

“What is it?” she asked.

“Brown liquor,” Grant replied.

“Excellent, grab a couple of bottles. Only for special occasions, though,” Claire said modestly. Grant and Claire had brewed alcohol in the past, but it was a painstaking process without the proper equipment. It was truly incredible to find a couple of unopened 12-year-old Canadian whiskies.

Brooklyn discovered a box of Nerds, a colourful candy that puzzled her. “What are these?” she asked.

“Those are Nerds. Wow, I haven’t seen those in ages,” Claire said, reminiscing about her childhood.

Grant chuckled softly at the candy. “You’re going to want to take all of those with you.”

“Why?” Brooklyn asked.

“Those Nerds throw a heck of a mouth party,” Grant answered.

All four family members loaded up with various items. Cody found some fishing line and a few lures, Brooklyn grabbed all the Nerds and uncovered a sealed can of peanuts, Grant took a couple of bottles of Canadian whisky and a sealed can of tobacco, and Claire secured some Kraft Dinner boxes, a few cans of beans, and several boxes of Redbird matches. It was a significant find and hopefully a good omen for their upcoming journey into the unknown.

The gas station was a significant discovery. After they finished searching the town and filling their water jugs in a nearby stream, the Cardinals made their way back to the Anastasia as dusk settled in. They built a fire and cooked beans, rice, and salmon that Cody had caught earlier in the morning.

The Cardinals considered sleeping in a tent on shore but opted to remain in the sleeping quarters on the boat. Although it was snug, it was warm and incredibly peaceful being rocked to sleep by the sound of water splashing against the hull.

As they wound down after a long day, Brooklyn and Cody lay on their backs, staring at the ceiling of the sleeping quarters. Brooklyn revealed a box of Nerds, and the kids enjoyed their first taste of candy since the bubble gum they found a year ago. Both of their lips puckered as they squinted at the sharp sweetness and foreign flavour. They exchanged glances, and their eyes widened.

"It hurts," Brooklyn said.

"My teeth are burning, but I like it," Cody added.

"That stuff will rot your teeth," Grant said, laughing.

"Remember to brush your teeth," Claire said, pointing her finger.

"A long time ago, people lost their teeth after eating that stuff," Grant remarked.

Just then, Brooklyn opened the door and tossed the box of Nerds over the side of the hull.

"Wait!" Cody shouted as everyone burst into laughter together.

Chapter 13 – Open Water

Claire was the first one up the following day. She stretched and walked along the concrete docks, watching the fish leap in the bay of Port Saunders. Claire felt content, but she missed all the little comforts of her cabin back home. She loved sewing, hunting, trapping, and cooking on a large flat stove. She reminisced about the past and contemplated the future for her and her children in such a barren, empty landscape.

Claire was reasonably sure there were more people out there, but what would they be like? Would they be aggressive, desperate, or violent? Or was there a safe, secure community somewhere? While she was content living in the moment and her family was eating and sleeping well, she needed to remain vigilant and focused on protecting them from potential disaster.

The mother's life journey had been challenging. She came from an abusive home, which she never shared with anyone except Grant. She left home at 16 and moved to Montréal in search of work. Eventually, she found a job at a small diner and struggled to make ends meet. Although she earned tips as a waitress, she often turned to drugs and alcohol to cope with her lost childhood and fractured family. During her darkest days, she waited on a young engineer named Grant Cardinal.

Claire reminisced about Grant's charm, intelligence, and how he looked at her for the first time. They started a conversation while he ate eggs and bacon and sipped black coffee. She was gathering the courage to ask him for a date when he beat her to it. He asked if she wanted to meet after work and stroll in Old Montréal. The rest was history. Claire smiled at the memory. She missed certain aspects of civilization—the smell of bagels baking uptown, early-morning bundled newspapers, and old moustached men sipping espressos on the sidewalks. However, there were elements she did not miss: the greed, manipulation, deception, poverty, addictions, and despair. Part of Claire was glad that she would likely never again witness that side of humanity. She held onto hope that if humankind were to escape this global disaster, they would never take anything for granted again.

Brooklyn exited the boat and saw her mother strolling along the water's edge.

"Mom!" Brooklyn yelled.

"Good morning, sweetie," Claire responded.

"What are you doing?" Brooklyn asked.

"Just thinking," she responded.

"About what?" Brooklyn asked.

"Just about the world, how it used to be and what it might look like," Claire replied. "It was a wild world, filled with so many people and agendas."

"What do you mean?"

"Well, the world was a lot more complicated. Money, power, and greed ruled the day. Ten years ago, many people struggled to make ends meet. Systems weren't working, agendas were divisive, and countries were at each other's throats. Then, suddenly, the world changed, and the bombs started falling."

"Who dropped the bombs?" Brooklyn asked.

"Well, we don't know that yet. All we know is that they were dropped," Claire said, looking at her daughter.

"I think I prefer this world to the old one," Brooklyn said.

Claire smiled at her daughter. "Me too, Brooklyn."

Once Grant and Cody woke up and everyone had breakfast with tea, they untied the cleats and sailed back out towards the Strait of Belle Isle. The waters were fairly calm, and the northerly wind was ideal as it filled the mainsail. Cody swung the boom around while Brooklyn ducked underneath to secure it to the starboard cleat.

"Steady as she goes!" Grant shouted, as he erupted in a coughing fit.

"Aye, aye," Brooklyn responded.

Claire noticed Grant's deteriorating health. "Are you feeling alright?" she asked.

"Just a bug in my throat. Probably from putting on the keel in the ocean," he responded. "I'll be fine!"

The Anastasia was cruising south swiftly along the west coast of Newfoundland when, in just 20 minutes, the temperature plunged below zero, and snow began to fall. It was July and snowing—a first for any of the Cardinals.

They bundled up in their winter gear—parkas, gloves, and hats. The biting winds reduced visibility in the swirling snowflakes. It was such an unusual sight, but it reminded Claire and Grant of the overarching purpose of their journey: the earth was cooling; the sun wasn't warming the atmosphere; plant life was withering; animals were starving, and humans faced desperate times.

The entire day had been frigid and a struggle. Grant, shivering, and Claire, with eyes watering, pulled into a cove called Sandy Point. It was a wide bay, perfect enough to drop anchor, get warm, and catch some much-needed shut-eye.

Cody and Brooklyn were about to head off into the sleeping quarters when they both noticed a large red and white structure near the bank of the shore.

"What's that?" Cody asked, pointing at the structure.

"That, my boy, is a lighthouse," Grant replied.

"What's that for?"

"It helps navigators see where the land is at night," Grant answered. "There used to be large ships that would travel all night long and had to be careful around areas where they could run aground."

"It looks so neat," Brooklyn said, gazing at the alien-looking building.

"There might have been a man who lived there, operating the light and warning oncoming ship captains through a CB radio," Grant mentioned.

"Cool place to live," Brooklyn remarked.

Grant and Claire were grateful for a chance to stop and warm up. The day had been long and exhausting on the cold, windy ocean.

The following day was tough for Grant. He woke up feeling nauseous. His throat hurt, his head pounded, and he could barely move. "Snowflake, I won't be able to do much today," he said to Claire. "I feel like death warmed over."

"What's wrong?" she asked.

"Some kind of flu or cold. It has been creeping in over the past few days," Grant whispered. "My throat is burning."

"Looks like it's just me and the kids on deck today," Claire said. "Stay snug in the sleeping quarters."

While Grant rested in the sleeping quarters, the family faced new challenges: Claire as captain at the tiller to steer, and Brooklyn and Cody as deckhands.

The weather remained grim and frigid. Dark clouds loomed over the eastern horizon, and the winds were biting and sharp. Cody pulled up the anchor at the boat's bow and cranked the jib sail while Brooklyn helped secure it to the cleats. They would leave the mainsail unattended until they returned to the Strait of Belle Isle.

Though their speed was sluggish, they were still making progress. Claire felt confident as the acting helmsman. She had steered before and was well-acquainted with the rigging of the Anastasia. She smiled as they entered the open ocean.

"Alright, Brooklyn, let out the mainsail!" Claire shouted.

"Aye!" Brooklyn responded enthusiastically.

Brooklyn untied all the clasp ties, swung the boom around, secured it, and began cranking the mainsail. The colourful sheet rose and instantly filled with wind as the boat gained speed beneath the dark sky.

Before long, Newfoundland faded into the distance, and the Anastasia headed toward Cape Breton, Nova Scotia. The temperatures dropped the further they drifted from land. This would be the longest stretch of sailing they would undertake in the open ocean. Claire hoped to reach Cape Breton by early evening despite the frigid conditions, lack of navigational tools, and her husband's illness.

Snow began to fall around noon, and the waves grew rougher than they had ever encountered. Inside the sleeping quarters, Grant felt nauseous but quickly took a couple of deep breaths and managed to recover. He couldn't remember the last time he felt this sick but realized it must have been the harsh winter winds on the water and his dip in the ocean, combined with his lack of nutrients.

Grant pondered the refreshing and thirst-quenching qualities of oranges and lemons, craving a tall glass of juice to soothe his sore throat. The Cardinals obtained most of their vitamin intake from herbs and spruce needles, but with trees and foliage dying everywhere, they would eventually need vitamin C in their diet. His cough was hoarse, and his breathing was shallow as he bobbed up and down on the rough waters.

Cody and Brooklyn were dressed from head to toe in rain gear, huddling together as the boat pitched violently on the massive waves. Meanwhile, Claire held tightly to the rudder, which threatened to slip away from her grasp, but she clung on with both hands. The wind, snow, and cold were pushing the limits of the Anastasia, yet she remained resilient. All the hard work Claire, Brooklyn, Cody, and Grant had invested in her was paying off.

Brooklyn started bailing water while Cody did his best to keep his weight forward on the boat's bow. The Anastasia leaped from wave to wave, sending loud splashes into the air with each swell. Claire gazed out over the rolling whitecaps and prayed to her ancestors. She knew the channel they were crossing stretched about 40 miles, and they were roughly halfway there. This had to be the worst of it, she thought.

The biting wind lashed against Claire's squinting face. The waves lessened after a strenuous, exhausting hour of steering, and the winds eased. Brooklyn could take a break from bailing, while Cody could lean back and relax as the boat settled on the ocean. Even Grant felt a bit better once things calmed down. Though he lay horizontal in the sleeping quarters, he knew they would soon be approaching Cape Breton.

The channel was a stark reminder that venturing into the open ocean would be treacherous. The small, hand-built sailboat was ill-prepared for massive storms and turbulent waters. They all hoped this would be the worst it got aboard the Anastasia.

"Land ho!" Cody shouted.

"Aye, aye, sailor!" Claire yelled back.

The Anastasia limped her way into Cape Breton, Nova Scotia. Claire ducked her head into the sleeping quarters. "We're heading into the Port of Sydney, Cape Breton, Nova Scotia, snowflake!"

"That's great, babe," Grant replied weakly.

The kids lowered and tacked down the sails, then put the oars on their mounts and began rowing towards a large pier. Claire squinted at what appeared to be a big cruise ship docked at the central ferry terminal in Sydney. She had never been here, but she assumed these were the ferry docks that shipped people to Newfoundland.

Claire carefully steered into the dock while Brooklyn and Cody secured everything. The proud mother opened the sleeping quarters door and told Grant they would look around.

Once the boat was tied off, Claire, Brooklyn, and Cody walked cautiously along the pier but didn't spot a soul. Rundown boats and outbuildings littered the area, yet Claire wanted to check out the cruise ship that was still afloat after all these years.

"Kids, I need you to start a fire in one of these outbuildings. There must be one with a fireplace. Once you've got one going, bring your father and some blankets to keep him warm." Hoping to help her husband avoid serious illness, Claire believed a good sweat lodge would likely help her husband.

"Sure, Mom," Cody replied.

Cody and Brooklyn set off to find a suitable building for their father while Claire approached the gigantic cruise ship. She pondered over medicine, food, equipment, a radio, and anything else to assist their journey.

The stair platform to the boat was rusted out, and Claire was cautious with each step. Just before the door, her final step broke through the rotting, decaying bridge, but she managed to reach for the handle and pull herself inside. It was a near miss, and it reminded her to constantly check her footing, as no one was around to assist.

Once on the port side deck, she walked along, searching for any signs of life. She ventured into the cruise ship's depths and began exploring the rooms individually. Most of the small rooms were empty, save for the tossed mattresses and blankets scattered everywhere. No signs of life could be found.

Claire made her way into the main dining room of the massive cruise ship. "Hello?" she called, her voice echoing eerily.

Chairs and tables were overturned all over the place. Claire cautiously weaved through the chaos. "Hello?" she repeated. No answer.

She navigated toward what she assumed was the kitchen door. As it swung open, an awful smell of decomposition hit her. As she stepped through the doorway, she saw three severely decomposed bodies. The sight was startling, as these were the first humans she had seen in a decade.

The corpses must have been there for years, as they almost appeared as skeletons. Claire moved to inspect the bodies closely. They were all tied at the wrists and ankles and chained to the stainless-steel counter. They must have been left for dead. Claire thought how excruciating it must have been to die in such a way. These were the first humans Claire had seen in ten years, and it again reminded her of what people were capable of when they were desperate.

Claire almost didn't want to know what happened to these people. Were there pirates, terrorists, or mercenaries aboard? She couldn't be sure. The explosion at Goose Bay, the eerie vacantness at Churchill Falls, and now dead captives aboard a cruise ship led her to believe that people started turning on each other.

"Hello?" she yelled one more time.

Claire stood up from the grim scene and made her way through the ship's corridor. She checked closets, offices, and storage rooms but found little of interest. Anything valuable had long since disappeared, indicating that this boat had been scavenged ages ago. She believed that the capital city of Nova Scotia, Halifax, would offer more answers as she planned to investigate the business and government district. There would undoubtedly be some answers there.

Feeling disheartened, Claire decided to leave the cruise ship. As she headed back to the portside exit, she stumbled upon a javelin harpoon that might prove helpful in the weeks ahead. Just when she felt defeated, this discovery vindicated her risky excursion.

Meanwhile, Cody and Brooklyn had discovered a small marine shack that had been ransacked but featured a small fireplace. The children found old wooden skids and started a fire in the shack. They helped their father inside and laid him on blankets beside the roaring fire.

Grant felt weak and nauseous, and his throat burned. He drank some water that Brooklyn offered from her canteen.

"We're in Sydney, Cape Breton, Dad. We crossed the harbour." Brooklyn slowly tilted the canteen as Grant struggled to drink and keep his eyes open.

Cody hated seeing him like this and hoped the sickness would pass soon.

"Where's Mom?" Grant asked quietly.

"She's exploring a massive cruise ship; you should see its size," Cody responded. "It's got to be 200 metres long."

"Rest now, Dad," Brooklyn said. "Mom will be back shortly."

"She went by herself?" Grant inquired, trying to infuse urgency into his voice.

"Don't worry, she'll be fine," Brooklyn reassured him.

Grant fell asleep almost immediately. Brooklyn made some tea by the fireplace as Cody secured the hatches of the Anastasia. While he was arranging the sleeping quarters, Claire returned with the harpoon and noticed her son.

"Cody, here," Claire said, handing him the harpoon, "This might come in handy."

"What is it?" he asked.

"It's a harpoon. I found it on the cruise ship."

"Cool. What else did you find?" Cody inquired.

Claire paused and reflected on the bodies she had just seen. "Nothing. The whole place was empty. Even the cutlery was missing."

"Too bad," Cody replied.

"Well, at least we got a sweet harpoon," Claire said with a smile. "How's your dad?"

"He's pretty sick. His forehead is burning up," Cody answered.

"I think we should stay here until his fever breaks. It won't do him any good to be out on the cold water. Come on, let's get supper started," she suggested.

"Sounds good,' Cody said.

Claire and Cody strolled back to the shack and found Brooklyn sipping tea while Grant was sound asleep, wrapped in blankets beside the fireplace. Though she hated seeing her husband in such a condition, she was relieved they were safe. It would likely be a few days before they could continue their voyage.

Chapter 14 - The Mend

Grant finally regained strength after three days of being incapacitated next to the fireplace. Unfortunately, just as he was improving, both children came down with the same illness. Brooklyn and Cody were coughing, sneezing, and occasionally spitting phlegm and blood. It was dreadful for Claire, who had managed to stay healthy throughout the week and hoped to leave this awful place.

Claire had boiled dozens of pots of spruce-needle tea and prepared hot fish soup for several meals. Over the past few days, Claire had kept what she saw on the cruise ship to herself; she didn't want a sick husband or her children to panic at the thought of decaying corpses.

Grant made his way outside on shaky legs. Feeling weak and still nauseous, he stepped onto the pier overlooking the decaying city of Sydney, Nova Scotia. The weather felt cold to Grant, but he understood that once his strength and stamina returned, he would feel much better. Claire emerged from the shack, leaving the kids sleeping on the floor.

"It's good to see you up and about, sugar bean," Claire said. "I was worried we might have lost you."

"Oh man, those were some tough days," Grant coughed and spat on the ground.

"You coughed up blood a couple of times; it was pretty grim," Claire noted.

"I felt so useless, and now the kids are sick. How did you manage to stay healthy?" Grant asked.

"Well, it must be my family's genes. I honestly can't remember the last time I was sick," Claire reflected.

"Have you checked the town? Any signs of trouble?" Grant inquired.

"We've meandered around a bit—nothing but empty buildings. No food. No clues. But I did stumble upon three dead bodies on the cruise ship."

"You found three dead bodies?" Grant was shocked as he spun to look at Claire.

"They must have been there for at least a few years. Severely decomposed, bound at the hands and feet, and seemingly left for dead," Claire described. "The ship had been stripped of everything except the mattresses and dining room furniture."

"What the hell is happening here?" Grant asked rhetorically.

"I think humanity turned on one another. No laws, no government; everything went to the wolves. Which reminds me, there's a giant pack of wolves roaming the shoreline. We saw them a couple of days ago, across the inlet, at least 30 strong in the pack," Claire said.

"Thirty? Damn. We need to keep moving. I don't want to find myself or my kids surrounded by those rabid bastards." Grant hated wolves. "They hunt and kill for sport, eat our caribou and moose, set off our traps, they stink, and are as elusive as hell."

"The kids' fevers broke this morning. Hopefully, they'll be better tomorrow, and we can be on our way," Claire said.

Grant kept scanning the water and shores for any signs of wolf activity. "Is there any food around? I'm starving."

"There's some fish and rice soup on the fire."

A few hours later, the kids began to stir, and everyone shared a meal by the fire. It was now August, and as darkness settled in, snow began to fall, causing temperatures to drop. The surge of Arctic air and the falling snow created a sense of urgency in Claire and Grant's minds. It was midsummer, yet they had travelled hundreds of miles south, and it was still frigid. They assumed everything around them would soon freeze, including the Atlantic Ocean.

The following day, Grant awoke to something stirring outside the marina shack. He peered through the window at the snow-covered ground and spotted the footprints of several animals. He opened the door, glanced left and right, and saw a lone black wolf staring back at him from 20 yards away. The wolf was enormous and showed no fear towards Grant. This was unusual, as any wolf he had encountered in the past would have disappeared within seconds. Instead, this wolf seemed more curious than afraid.

The large, sleek black wolf with bright hazel eyes tilted its head at Grant, turned its body, and continued to follow the rest of the pack that had already moved on. Dozens of tracks crisscrossed the snow, and Grant felt relieved he would avoid confronting them.

Grant thought this might be the first generation of wolves that had never encountered humans. If those wolves were under ten years old, they likely hadn't seen an upright humanoid before. Humans were on the brink of extinction, and animals were reclaiming what was rightfully theirs. He shut the door and turned to Claire. "Okay, time to get moving," he said.

"Time to get up," Claire replied. "Brookie, Cody, we need to get moving."

The family bundled up in their warmest sailing gear, loaded the Anastasia, boarded, untied the cleats, and began rowing out of the inlet toward the ocean. As they approached the mouth of the inlet, Cody spotted the wolves atop a rocky outcropping. Thirty grey, black, and brown wolves gazed curiously at the family aboard the Anastasia.

"Look!" Cody exclaimed, pointing at the pack. Everyone turned to glance at the ridge, taking in the sight of so many wolves. As they passed, the alpha wolf raised his head and howled, filling the silence with a loud 'goodbye' to the unexpected visitors. The other wolves followed their leader, and all thirty soon howled in unison.

The howls reminded Grant of the sign he was shown as they first entered the ocean. Though he hated wolves, he smiled at the pack. Perhaps they were watching out for the Cardinals, he thought.

The Anastasia left the Sydney Inlet, and the Cardinals sailed off the coast again, heading south towards Halifax. The boat was holding up well; the ropes were sturdy, the sails were catching the wind, and both the hull and keel were smooth and reliable.

That evening, they anchored in a cove near Port Hawkesbury and slept aboard the Anastasia. It was a cold night, but they stayed warm by cuddling close under multiple blankets.

The following day, everyone felt weak but found the motivation to keep persevering. They continued south, approaching the capital of Nova Scotia, the beautiful city of Halifax.

Halifax was once a bustling port city with a population of 500,000, brimming with military personnel, businesspeople, fishermen, farmers, and humble Maritime Canadians. The city would give Grant and Claire a clear indication of what had transpired in Canada and where everyone had gone. If Halifax were deserted, it would imply that the military had been decimated, given that it was once a key installation housing around 20,000 military personnel.

Cody and Brooklyn struggled to keep warm as they were still recovering from their illness. They remained seated throughout most of the day, wrapped in blankets at the stern of the boat. Grant let Brooklyn steer while Cody assisted with tying the occasional rope, though nothing too strenuous.

The Anastasia turned west towards Halifax, and everyone quickly noticed the remnants of a significant battle. Destroyed condominium buildings, fallen churches, sunken ships, scorched vehicles, and the slow decay of time reminded Grant and Claire of the aftermath of World War II.

"Doomsday," Grant remarked as he reeled in the mainsail.

"It's like Poland after the Great War," Claire replied.

The harbours lay in ruin, and the bridges had collapsed, including the Angus MacDonald Bridge and the Murray McKay Bridge, the two major cross-harbour routes. It was a grim sight. No signs of life were evident. All the trees stood dead or had utterly fallen. A few inches of snow blanketed the apocalyptic landscape as Cody turned the Anastasia around in front of the sunken McKay Bridge.

Grant and Claire rowed, searching for anything. They looked for any signs of life or civilization.

"Dad, are we docking somewhere?" Brooklyn asked.

Grant glanced at Claire, who shook her head.

"No, I don't think so," Grant replied to the kids. "Let's head back out to sea."

The eerie silence and destruction enveloped the Cardinals as they rowed from Halifax Harbour. It was clear that a war had taken place in Halifax, and the Cardinals felt relieved to leave without witnessing decomposed bodies and carnage lining the streets.

Claire leaned over the side of the Anastasia, gazing at the dozens of sunken ships—some military, others civilian. "All sorts of boats down there," she remarked, peering downwards.

"Probably a mass graveyard," Grant said, his eyes fixed on the horizon.

Cody turned to Brooklyn. "There must have been a significant war."

"About what?" she asked.

"After the Yellowstone eruption, people panicked. Dad mentioned martial law in the early days, and one thing led to another," Cody explained.

"So, people started killing each other for food?" Brooklyn inquired.

"There were millions of people. Look at the buildings they constructed. Houses piled atop houses. Old folks, young ones— everyone for themselves." Cody marvelled at the vastness of Halifax, remaining lost in contemplation of the world that existed before his birth.

"Why don't we stop?" Brooklyn asked. "We can have lunch and stretch our legs."

"Because death is everywhere," Cody answered.

Brooklyn was still kind of naive about the global chaos. Had she seen or experienced the bloodshed, the trauma would have certainly affected her differently. "What do you think kids our age did for fun?" she asked her brother.

"Dad told me about television and video games and their popularity. He also mentioned the internet and the creation of artificial intelligence."

"What's that?"

"It's like a robot that thinks for itself," Cody responded.

"I see. What's the internet?" Brooklyn asked.

"I guess it's how everyone communicated. There are things called satellites high up in the sky relaying messages to everyone's computers. Remember the homes and desks in Churchill? They had powerful computers."

"Oh yeah, computers. They didn't leave the house much, did they?" Brooklyn snickered.

"They certainly didn't check traplines or go fishing like we do, that's for sure," Cody said.

"Do you think kids could sew and tan hides?" Brooklyn kept the questions coming.

"Not likely. They were too busy interneting, I guess," Cody responded.

Both Brooklyn and Cody still contemplated what life would have been like before the disaster. They knew essential pieces were missing from their life. They both started to realize the importance of community, something they had never experienced. The Cardinal children wondered about school, the gaps in their learning, the books they missed, the sports, the excursions, and all the different friends they could have had.

The reminiscing and contemplating saddened the two Cardinal children. They had worked tirelessly throughout their lives. They had skinned animals, made beaver traps, built shelters, and started countless fires, but now Brooklyn and Cody wanted security, shelter, food, friends, and a place of belonging.

Claire and Grant knew their children were coming of age, and as they started to build an identity, they needed companionship, intimacy, and friendships. They would become fiercely independent and begin asking a thousand questions.

Both parents sat at the front of the boat as they sailed toward the Maine coast. Hours passed as they continued to let Brooklyn and Cody steer the boat in the cold, turbulent ocean off the coast of the United States.

"After knowing nothing but the Labrador wilderness, this might seem a little overwhelming for them," Claire said, far from earshot of Brooklyn and Cody. "I hope that one day they will both forgive us."

"What else could we have done?" Grant answered. "Ruined their elementary years with grim tales of nuclear war and apocalyptic nightmares?"

"Well, all is out in the open now. I hope they don't resent us and hold a lifelong grudge," Claire said.

Grant took Claire in his arms as they sailed along the snowy coast of Maine. The August snow was light, fluffy, and tolerable compared to the midwinter winds of Labrador and the -50°C weather.

"If we didn't go to Grandpa's cabin in the beginning, we would have perished along with everyone else. We are survivors, snowflake," Grant said as he kissed Claire's rosy cheek.

"Better than being tied up and left for dead," Claire said cheekily.

That night, they sailed alongside a dilapidated dock in Maine. They couldn't get out and walk, but at least they were protected from the crashing waves. They ate the last of the smoked caribou and nestled inside the sleeping quarters for the night.

The following day, the Cardinals awoke feeling refreshed after a long sleep. They had all recovered from their sicknesses and were now ready to sail towards Boston and New York, two places Grant and Claire were both extremely curious about.

The Atlantic Seaboard

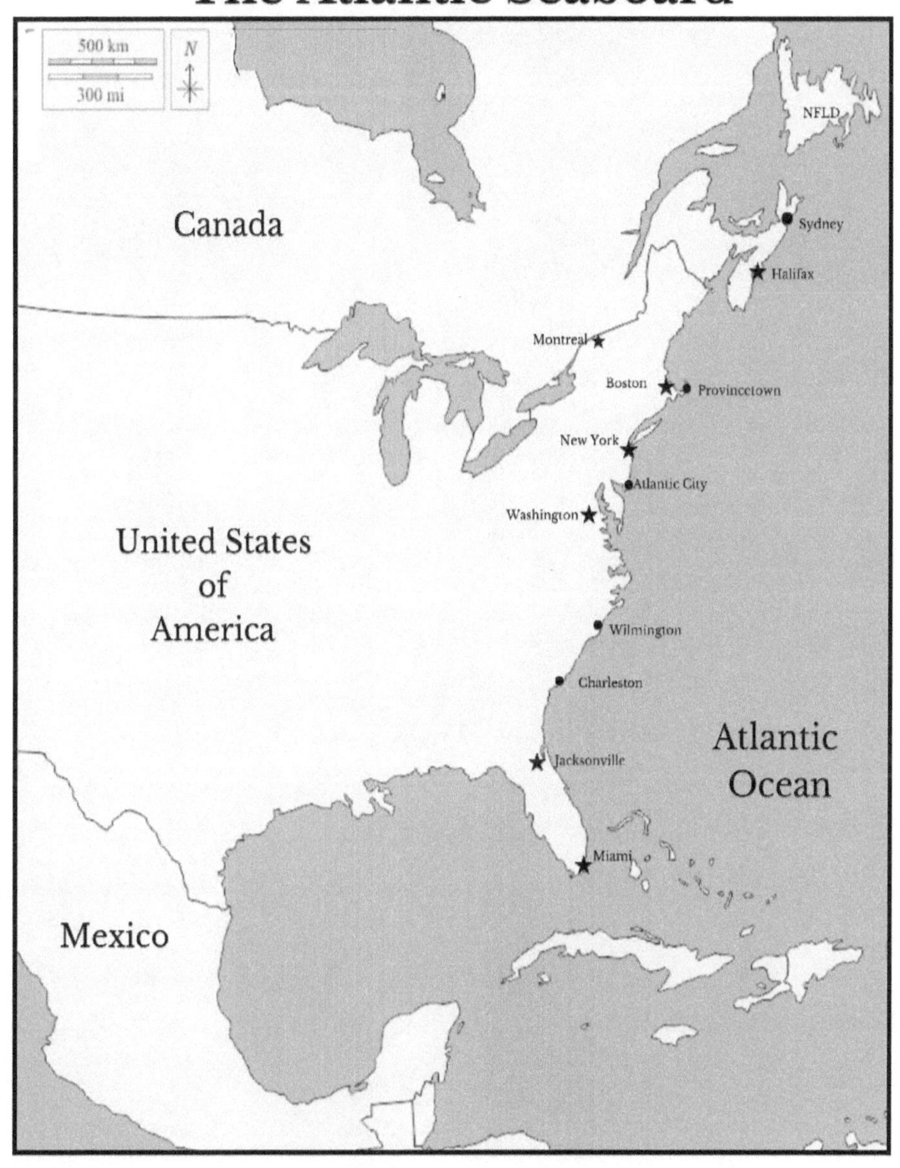

Chapter 15 – Déjà vu

After a couple of turbulent days on the sea, they arrived in the calmer Boston Harbour. It was yet another major city in ruins. They docked at the University of Massachusetts, one of the last remaining accessible docks among the half-sunken ships and debris. All four family members armed themselves, locked down the Anastasia, and set foot on shore for the first time in over a week.

The Cardinals all had sea legs after a long voyage. They stretched and wobbled as they took their first few steps. Claire and Grant prioritized finding food, as they were running low on non-perishables. The dull grey, snowy sky cast an ominous shadow over the Boston University campus.

"Okay, kids, I have to warn you, you may see some dreadful things in this city," Claire said.

"If you get scared, just cover your eyes and hold me or your mother's hand," Grant added.

"Are we going to see dead bodies?" Brooklyn asked.

"Definitely," Cody joked.

The Cardinals entered the front of University Hall through one of the broken windows. There were no signs of life, only random papers blown into the corner of the room, like a pile of raked leaves. They wandered the halls together, finding nothing other than a couple of broken televisions and chairs strewn across the floor.

They toured other campus buildings, finding much of the same. Discovering the campus cafeteria, they rummaged through every drawer and cupboard but found nothing they could use. The utensils, pots, and pans were still there, just no food. It signalled to Grant and Claire that people had been trying to survive in the final days.

"Kids! Did you find anything?" Grant asked from the opposite end of the cafeteria.

"Nothing, just pots and pans," Cody responded.

"Let's head out," Claire said.

They went outside, past the sports fields and into the city centre. They walked up Mount Vernon Avenue and eventually saw the remnants of the I-93 highway. Entire sections of the overpass had collapsed to the ground, other sections overgrown with snowy patches of grass and rusted-out automobiles everywhere.

Cody spotted a supermarket, and they all decided to test their luck. The front of the building was boarded up, but they managed to pry open a section and crawl through on hands and knees. The store was totally empty. Aisle after aisle, they checked every shelf and bin and found nothing. Grant checked behind the deli counter and bakery and only found piles of rodent droppings. Claire checked the checkout lines for anything of use, but no luck. Cody and Brooklyn walked through the back storage toward the loading dock and found a single unopened box of fruit cans. It was an incredible find for the youngsters.

"Mom! Dad! Come back here!" Brooklyn yelled. "Fruit salad," she read.

Grant and Claire came running to see the find.

"Fruit salad!" Cody yelled.

"Terrific!" Grant yelled.

"Let's load up and get out of here," Claire said. "Those cans are a lucky find. This place has been picked clean."

They each loaded the cans into their packs and returned to the streets. Buildings had fallen all around them. Houses were collapsing, apartment buildings were blown up, and things were charred black. Eventually, they came to Columbus Park, where the Cardinals abruptly stopped.

All four family members stood near the edge of another giant crater at least 90 kilometres wide. Everything had been levelled except for the edges of town where the University was— another major nuclear disaster. It was a shocking sight. All of Cambridge, Somerville, and Back Bay were evaporated by a deadly explosion. Had the whole world been lost to nuclear war, they wondered.

"I'm beginning to think this was the Russians or a unified alliance with nuclear capabilities. India? Maybe Pakistan? China? North Korea?" Grant said, still staring at the vast crater.

"Millions of people would have died in this blast." Claire was clearly upset. "Can we get going?" she said.

"Who set off all these bombs?" Cody asked.

"I don't know, son," Grant answered. "But it was someone with an arsenal of nuclear weapons."

"Did anyone fight back?" Cody persisted.

"I'm just as confused as you are, Cody," Grant said.

"I'm with mom, can we get going?" Brooklyn asked.

"Sure, sweetie," Grant said, taking his daughter by the hand and squeezed tight. "Let's get out of here."

The Cardinals turned and walked back along the quiet, decomposing streets of Boston toward the peer at the University of Massachusetts. Though they found very little, they now understood there were multiple nuclear weapons detonated across North America.

"Were citizens called back to Boston, like they were in Goose Bay?" Claire asked Grant, away from earshot of the children.

"I'm not sure. It is either systematic eradication or a retaliation for a first strike," Grant answered. "But even then, I can't be sure."

"All this death and destruction; I never could have imagined. I knew things were not good over the past ten years, but this is beyond what I expected," Claire said.

"I know," Grant said, taking a hold of Claire's hand. "We still don't have enough information. Hopefully going south will provide some more answers."

Eventually they arrived at their boat. They climbed aboard the Anastasia and opened a can of fruit they found at the supermarket. Though the outside of the cans had begun to rust, they didn't care. Inside, the can seemed fine enough. They took the first bites, and the sweetness made them shudder—chewy, sweet bites of expired pineapple, mango, pear, tangerine, and cherry. Cody and Brooklyn had never had fruit like this: sweet, fibrous, and exotic to their senses.

"This is so delicious," Brooklyn said, slurping another mouthful.

"We'll have it as a treat from time to time," Claire said, feeling awful having children who hadn't enjoyed the joys of fruit salad.

Grant untied the rope from the crumbling peer and pushed off. Claire cranked the jib sail, and they slowly exited Boston Harbour. They had decided to sail across Cape Cod Bay and land at Provincetown, where the Mayflower once landed in 1620. They would fish along the way and build a makeshift smokehouse to help restock their provisions before continuing south.

Provincetown was a perfect place to camp, as it was on the furthest point of Cape Cod, and its harbour would provide shelter from the often-violent Atlantic Ocean. It was also renowned for having some of the best fishing waters in the world.

The Cardinals arrived at the old historic district of Provincetown and were able to sail the boat alongside the break-wall. The town seemed in relatively good condition as Cody and Brooklyn tied off the cleats. As the children were wrapping the ropes around the cleats, Claire spotted something in the water. It was a creature, but she couldn't be sure. She squinted and moved herself to the boat's starboard side to look closer.

In the dark harbour waters, she realized it was a seal, and in the far distance, she realized there were hundreds of them.

"Grant, look!" Claire yelled, pointing at the oncoming seal.

Grant spun around and saw the massive creature. "Grab the harpoon!" he yelled to Claire.

Claire grabbed the harpoon she found on the cruise ship and loaded the weapon. She drew back the action and cocked the harpoon into firing position.

"Cody! Come here and tie this off!" Claire said.

Cody tied off the end of the rope to the cleat at the stern of the Anastasia.

"Get clear!" Claire yelled.

Claire leaned her lower body against the starboard side of the boat, raised the harpoon gun, took aim, and fired. The harpoon fired and stuck straight into the back of the 250-pound sea mammal. Blood began trailing the seal as it dove underwater. Foot by foot, the rope started unravelling and eventually ended with a thud against the boat cleat. Shocked by the speed and excitement of the hunt, they all scanned the water for signs of success. A couple of suspenseful minutes later, the dead seal floated to the top of the water, and everyone smiled at the prize.

Grant pulled the seal to the side of the boat and turned to Claire and Cody. "Great job, you two. It's like you've done this before."

That evening, in a desolate, frigid parking lot of Provincetown, Claire and Grant showed Brooklyn and Cody how to process a seal in the tradition of the Inuit and northern Cree. Cody and Brooklyn had heard stories of seals, but this was their first experience.

Claire and Brooklyn cleaned and rinsed the skin of blood and fat and then hung the hide from an old concrete barrier, as Grant and Cody built a rudimentary rack to stretch and tie the dried skin to. The next day they would boil the tallow and smoke portions of the meat.

As day turned to night, Claire had almost processed the entire seal. She was sure to leave the bones in the meat for flavour and nutrition. She boiled a large pot of seal meat and created a healthy broth for everyone to enjoy. The Cardinals sat around the warm fire in the barren parking lot of the Provincetown harbour and enjoyed the hearty, delicious meal.

"The meat falls off the bone," Cody said, taking a healthy bite from a seal rib.

Grant looked at Claire. "This is exactly what we needed."

"It's so fresh and juicy," Brooklyn said, wiping the grease from her mouth.

It had been weeks since they had such a large, healthy, filling meal. The wholesome, much-needed seal meat seemed to revitalize the family, who were coming off a few depressing weeks of sickness, death, destruction, and uncertainty.

"Brooklyn, I'm going to show you how to chew seal skin," Claire said to her daughter.

"What do you mean?" Brooklyn responded.

"Well, the Inuit women would chew the seal skin to soften it after it had a chance to dry. The jaws of the Cree and Inuit women are like the jaws of black bears," Claire said, smiling.

"I think we should stay here for a few days and hunt some more seals," Cody said.

"What do you think, snowflake?" Grant asked Claire.

"I think that may be a good idea." Claire happily agreed.

"We can scout this small town in the morning and maybe find a more comfortable place to camp for a few nights," Grant told his family.

The Cardinals fell asleep with full bellies and warm hearts that evening. They felt secure for the time being on Cape Cod off the coast of Massachusetts.

The following day, all four of the Cardinals secured their camp and explored the small village of Provincetown. At the centre of the seaside town was the Pilgrim monument commemorating the landing of the Mayflower in 1620. It was a tall, slender stone structure, the only thing raised above the town's two-storey standard.

At one-point, Commercial Street was the main business area; now, it was barren, destroyed, and ominous. The buildings were all unique and contained hundreds of years of stories within the walls. The narrow streets reminded Claire and Grant of Montréal and Québec City. Most of the building's windows had been smashed, and a few businesses were boarded up. The odd business had been burned to the ground and some left the way they were ten years ago. There was nothing new or out of the ordinary about Provincetown that gave the Cardinals any more clues as to what happened. It was yet another town, where people had left to go somewhere.

As they carefully inspected the town, Brooklyn found a bookstore that had been taken over by nature, but her curiosity brought her to take a closer look.

"Can I go inside?" Brooklyn asked.

"Sure, just be careful," Claire answered.

Brooklyn stepped inside and found books thrown everywhere. Shelves had been knocked over, and things were decomposing from exposure to the salty ocean air. Brooklyn reached for a book about World War II and explored the pages within. She was shocked at the images of the war, the bloody conflict, the concentration camps, and masses of war-torn citizens. There were so many people on earth, she thought.

She flipped to a page with the Hiroshima bomb explosion in 1945. It gave Brooklyn a pause as she tried to grasp the size of the explosion. She hadn't realized the scale of destruction of these nuclear blasts. She flipped to the next page, seeing its devastating effects on the Japanese. The pictures brought tears to her eyes.

Brooklyn had always felt she was one of the only people on earth. Her parents had raised her to be a trapper, fisher, warrior, and self-reliant nomad in the far north of Canada, but now she was dealing with the fact that her parents hid the history of man from them throughout childhood. Human history was savage, bloody, and unrelenting, Brooklyn thought. It was emotional for the young girl, as she flipped pages and saw pictures of people with burns and radiation sickness. The world had cast aside all morals and systems of tolerance and started killing people in massive waves without remorse or regret.

Part of Brooklyn was angry and upset, and another part was glad her parents didn't expose them to a world that was tearing apart. Her parents protected and sheltered them from the ruthless barbarians at the gate. She reflected on her earliest memories of ice-fishing and her mom teaching her how to sew at the cabin. She was beginning to empathize with her parents' decision to keep them in the dark throughout the past decade.

Cody came in through the broken door. "Hey, what are you looking at?" he asked.

"War books," Brooklyn said, with her head buried in the pages.

Cody picked up a book about terrorism and began scrolling the pages. To Brooklyn, Cody didn't seem as torn or affected by the new world as she was. He was taking it all in stride.

"Take a look at this," Cody said, holding up a picture of the smoking Twin Towers at The World Trade Center. "Terrorists flew planes into buildings full of people."

Brooklyn held up a picture of an emancipated group of Jewish concentration camp survivors at the liberation of Auschwitz. "Humans did this to other humans," she said. "The world was eating itself from within."

"This new world exposure, which started after we left the cabin at Churchill Falls, makes me feel sad inside." Cody was opening up to his sister. "I want to go back to the way I felt before."

"I understand completely. But would you rather Mom and Dad keep hiding the truth from us?"

"Part of me does," Cody said.

Brooklyn and Cody explored the bookstore and looked at the few books that were still readable. They could have spent the whole day there until Grant called them to come outside.

Brooklyn and Cody came out of the bookstore to see their parents standing in the middle of the street with their bows drawn. About 100 metres down Commercial Street was a black bear.

"Get behind us and head back to the peer," Grant said.

The bear let out a loud growl as everyone backed away slowly. As they walked backwards, the bear followed.

"Stand fast," Grant said. "Kids, keep moving to the pier."

Grant and Claire stood their ground as the bear began to trot towards them. Grant loosed an arrow, and it flew past the bear. Claire fired an arrow and missed, too. Grant and Claire reached for another arrow in their quiver and nocked their next arrow. The husband and wife drew back their bowstrings.

"Deep breath," Claire said.

Grant let loose his arrow and caught the bear in the shoulder, and it let out a yelp. Claire drew back a little more and let loose another pointed arrow. It was a perfect shot to the chest of the bear. Its legs gave out, dropping to the ground with a thud.

Grant turned to Claire. "Nice shot, snowflake!"

The bear let out its last breath, and Claire approached the beast. It was an enormous black bear, bigger than any Grant had seen in the past. It had probably been dining on harbour seals, he thought.

"Kids!" Grant yelled.

Brooklyn and Cody came running from around the corner to see their parents standing over the bear.

"Kids, we're going to skin and quarter this beast. We're going to start drying a few hides out. This place has abundant game, but we need to travel together. This big bear was probably looking for a good meal." Grant was a realist but happy they had dropped such a massive animal with excellent meat, fats, and a hide that might come in handy.

Over the next few days at Provincetown, the Cardinals were super productive. They hunted another seal, smoked various slices of meat, and dried the bear and seal skins in frames fashioned together with two-by-fours Grant ripped out of a nearby house. Claire taught Cody and Brooklyn how to chew seal skin. They were also able to make some clothes using all the needles and thread that Claire had carefully packed in Churchill Falls. Grant also found a dilapidated boat with a large steel mast that they fashioned to fit the Anastasia, replacing the old wood mast that had been beaten up over the past weeks at sea.

Cape Cod and Provincetown were a blessing for the Cardinals, but the temperatures were dropping as autumn approached. They knew they would want to reach warmer waters to sustain themselves through the gruelling winter months.

New York was a few days away and would be Anastasia's next destination. On a snowy, mid-August morning, the Cardinals packed everything up, loaded the boat and set sail around the horn of Cape Cod toward New York City.

Chapter 16 - The Catch

After a night at anchor in one of the harbours near Martha's Vineyard, a small island off the Massachusetts and Rhode Island coast, the Cardinals made their way along, the once esteemed, Long Island. All along the beaches of Long Island, they saw nothing but burned houses and scorched dead trees.

Claire had been to New York once before as a 15-year-old. She went on a class trip and recalled all the major tourist attractions: the Empire State Building, Times Square, the U.N. building, and the unforgettable Brooklyn Bridge. Claire saw a couple of Broadway shows and loved the energy and passion in the theatre district. She was now coming face to face with the realization that none of that existed anymore. No matinee shows, chorus lines, or standing ovations, only death, destruction, and the slow decomposition of civilization.

Grant wished he could shut the eyes of his children, but he knew he couldn't hide the truth any longer. So far, along the eastern coast of North America, there were no signs of human life anywhere. How could it be that no one survived, he questioned. There must be some survivors somewhere.

"Survivors must have either headed south or inland. The whole eastern seaboard is scorched," Grant said.

The Anastasia turned north at Brighton Beach and headed up the famous Hudson River. More snow began to fall as evening approached. Before long, they sailed underneath the still-standing Narrows Bridge and caught sight of the crumbling New York skyline. The reality became more apparent, the closer they got to Manhattan.

Most of Manhattan was underwater. Only a few burnt buildings remained. They passed Governor's Island and realized they were heading into another massive crater, similar to those at Goose Bay and Boston, but most of it was underwater. Greenwich Village was gone, and the Empire State Building and everything south of Central Park was demolished.

Though it didn't surprise Grant or Claire at this point, it was still a shock to see another massive devastation that killed over ten million people in seconds. Who had control of that many bombs? Would the U.S. bomb itself? Was there an outbreak? Was it a terrorist cell? Was there espionage involved, a takeover, or a coup d'état? The massive earthquakes and volcanoes were terrible enough, but why did the world incinerate itself with nuclear weapons? It was all so grim for the Cardinals as they sailed along the Hudson River.

Until now, the journey and the significant burden of sailing from northern Labrador hadn't felt like a failure to Grant. Now, a defeated feeling swept over him like a cruel joke. It could be there wasn't a destination, nobody else alive, and nothing his family could strive to achieve.

Claire noticed the look on Grant's face and nudged him on the shoulder. "You alright?" she asked.

"Oh yeah," Grant said. "So, do you want to look around?" he asked.

"Not particularly," Claire answered.

"Well, if we head south, we will hit Sandy Hook. I'm assuming it's got protection from the waves and good fishing." Grant didn't want to see any more destruction today. He turned the boat around and headed south towards Sandy Hook.

"I'm glad we are getting out of here," Grant said.

"Brooklyn, this used to be the place called New York," Claire said to her daughter. "Just over there, is Brooklyn, the neighbourhood that you were named after."

"Cool. I guess it is gone now, but I'm glad I got to see it," Brooklyn said with a frown.

"It had the coolest music and theatre scene. People hung out in parks and shopped in outdoor markets. Different blocks had people from all over, Puerto Ricans, Dominicans, Jewish, African American, Polish, German. It was such a wild place, and the food was incredible!" Claire said with a beaming smile.

The open water between New York and New Jersey became turbulent as waves crashed over the sides of the Anastasia. Cody and Brooklyn knew the routine and began bailing without being asked.

"Should I let the jib sail down?" Claire yelled back to Grant.

"Yeah, sure!" Grant yelled back.

Claire began cranking at the jib stay and down came the sail. The boat slowed but didn't stop the water from crashing over the sides. The sailing was challenging, and both Grant and Claire knew that hurricane season was on its way, and they needed to be extra careful on such open waters.

Snow came down hard as the boat finally entered Sandy Hook Bay. The waves calmed, and so did the Cardinals' adrenaline. They had all managed to stay somewhat dry despite the waves and falling precipitation. Cody and Brooklyn tossed their fishing lines in with little expectation. After a few minutes of trawling, Brooklyn hooked into something huge.

"Help me!" Brooklyn yelled. "Fish on!"

Grant took hold of the fishing rod. "Cody, grab the tiller! Get behind me! Brooklyn, grab the net!"

It was a monster from the deep. Grant used all his might to reel, pulling back and forth on the rod. He was thankful he found the professional trolling rod while scavenging the homes in Churchill Falls. While there, Grant had spun a 50-pound test line on the reel, so he was pretty confident he could land whatever was on the end of the line. The fish was powerful and took a lot of line. Grant tried to battle back. He would pull and reel in a few times. Grant began to feel the fish tiring after a good 30 minutes of battling.

"Is it still on?" Claire yelled.

"Yep!" Grant yelled back.

"I hope it is a shark," Brooklyn said to Cody. "I saw one in a book in Provincetown."

"Row toward shore! Any place to dock you can find." Grant was determined to land whatever kind of behemoth this was.

Brooklyn and Claire took the oars and rowed the boat as Cody steered the Anastasia.

"This is a big fish! I'm going to have to land it on shore! Get me to a dock!" Grant was excited. "My arms are burning."

Cody saw a concrete pier in the distance. Brooklyn and Claire rowed hard until they could pull alongside the pier. With the rod in hand, Grant jumped out and continued to drag the line and fish along the side of the pier. He then stepped down to the rocky beach and reeled in the line.

"There must be 500 feet of line out there!" Grant said as his family joined him on the beach. "Cody, grab the spear from the boat."

Cody ran, grabbed the spear, and returned to the beach, anticipating what was on the end of the line. Finally, after 30 minutes of tirelessly battling, the fish emerged from the shallow sea. Cody ran into the shallow water and plunged the spear into the head of the half-exposed fish.

"Yes!" Grant said. "Well done! We got her!"

"It's a goddamn tuna fish!" Claire shouted.

"Tuna fish?" Brooklyn said.

"It must be 150-200 pounds!"

"This is the biggest fish I have ever seen," Cody said enthusiastically.

Grant's arms and entire upper body were exhausted from the fight. The whole family dragged the giant tuna ashore, and Grant fell backwards onto his back. Everyone chuckled at his comedic fall.

"What is it?" Brooklyn asked.

"It's a goddamn tuna fish," Cody said, imitating his mother.

"Well, it looks like fish for dinner," Claire joked.

That evening, on the New Jersey shore, the Cardinals processed the tuna and ate a massive meal. As darkness set in, they nestled in the sleeping quarters aboard the Anastasia with full bellies and warm thoughts.

Grant and Claire felt much better, with their stomachs full of rich protein. It reminded them of the importance of their departure from the dark, bleak, anxiety-ridden far northern reaches of Labrador. Though they hadn't seen sunny daylight in 10 years and human extinction was a distinct possibility, they found time for positive feelings. Temperatures were balmy compared to those in Newfoundland, the ocean was bountiful, and Brooklyn and Cody were taking the worldwide disaster in stride. Cody and Brooklyn were often too busy with tasks to stop and feel depressed about a life that could have been.

The tuna was a great catch. They ate some of it raw, cooked a few large filets, and smoked a significant portion to preserve. After the giant meal and darkness settled in, both children struggled to keep their eyes open in the Bay of Sandy Hook.

"Mom, Dad, what happened right before you brought us to Labrador?" Brooklyn asked.

Grant paused for a second. "Your mom and I were living in Montréal, remember? The earthquake off the coast of California rocked North America and triggered a chain of volcanic events, leading to the massive Yellowstone eruption a few days later."

"I remember the first reports of tsunamis all around the Pacific rim," Claire added. "Millions died in the first few minutes."

"After Mount St. Helens, Mount Baker, and the rest of volcanoes erupted, forest fires ignited everywhere in the dry summer season. The skies turned grey and ash fell across North America. News stations started going haywire about mass migrations from California, Arizona, Texas, and everything west of the Mississippi River. That's when the panic started, highways clogged, and everyone started rioting and turning on one another."

"What's rioting?" Brooklyn asked.

"People started smashing and breaking into buildings, gathering anything they could find: grocery stores, malls, warehouses. Reports about staying home with provisions for 3 or 4 days started coming in. That didn't help, as it caused more panic. Governments worldwide started implementing martial law, and casualty lists started coming in. That's when governments lost control, and rogue factions started organizing. That's when me and your mom, loaded up with provisions, put you in your car seats, and we drove to Grandpa's cabin." Grant turned his head, looked at Claire, and smiled.

"We packed all the essentials, drove through the night, and made it to northern Québec and eventually Labrador, but we ran out of gas. We couldn't find an open gas station after Goose Bay. The car ran out of gas and we ditched it, strapped you to our backs, and started walking through the bush towards Grandpa's cabin."

"We slept on the ground for a couple weeks, with both of you tucked in our sleeping bags. We fed you hot oatmeal cooked over small fires, day after day. You two would wake up wide-eyed and rosy-cheeked. After weeks in the bush, we found the Labrador highway, crossed it and found Grandpa's cabin a few days later."

"How far did you walk?" Cody asked.

"We did the math and found it was over 400 kilometres. Not much later, the skies blackened, and we saw the sun for the last time." Claire said.

"What's the sun like?" Brooklyn asked.

Claire smiled at the thought. "It lights up the world. Colours are more vibrant, smells are sweeter, and there's no other feeling when it hits your face. It touches your soul, puts you at ease, and relaxes your entire body."

"You were little toddlers when we arrived. You could hardly walk. We built little bunk beds for you. Foraged for anything we could find, we organized, systemized, and prioritized anything and everything. Grandpa's cabin saved us. It had pots, pans, tools, and a tin roof to keep us warm and dry. The last time we saw humanity was when we left Montréal." Grant was beginning to tear up as he told the story. "You two had no idea what was happening. You just thought it was another day with Mommy and Daddy."

"You kids grew up so strong. Running, hiking, climbing trees, but you learned so much you wouldn't have learned otherwise, like trapping, carving, fishing, logging, and living off the land. You were the smartest, most durable kids we'd ever seen." Claire was also beginning to tear up.

"Why didn't you tell us earlier about all this?" Cody inquired.

"Like you, kiddos, we had no idea what was happening. We were far away from any towns or roads. If not for Grandpa's trapping cabin, we would have been swept away like everyone else." Grant was so grateful for his father and his teachings; he wished he could have seen how much his education had meant to him and his family.

"So, we would've gone to school? Had math class? Played with other kids at recess?" Cody asked.

"You would have gone to Laurier Elementary School. You would have taken math, geography, history, science and everything else in the board's curriculum," Claire said.

"I don't think I would have liked school," Cody said.

"Me either," Brooklyn added.

"I hated school," Grant said, laughing.

"Me too," Claire added.

Everyone shared a chuckle at their common bond.

That evening, the Cardinals climbed aboard the Anastasia after a long day of seafaring, fishing, cooking, and smoking a massive tuna in Sandy Hook Bay. It wasn't long until they all fell asleep with the waves lapping against the side of the boat.

Chapter 17 - Sandy Shores

The Cardinals sailed around Sandy Hook and down along the sandy shores of New Jersey. They expected to hit Atlantic City by nightfall. The eastern seaboard was frigid; it was almost September, and things were starting to freeze. Grant was surprised that even New Jersey and Delaware were experiencing snow and ice in the summer.

The Anastasia cruised into Atlantic City around dinnertime. It was yet another city that fire and nature had started to re-take. It seemed like a recurring nightmare: the demolished buildings, scorched earth, and eerie nothingness.

"What in the world is that?" Brooklyn said, pointing.

"That, my dear, is a rusted-out Ferris wheel," Claire answered.

"So cool. What does it do?" Brooklyn questioned.

"Well, they were lit up with colourful lights and spun round and round," Claire replied.

"It just spun?" Brooklyn said with a raised brow.

"But the views were always remarkable," Claire said, turning to Grant.

Before the fallout and having children, Grant and Claire had shared one of their first vacations in the glitzy tourist destination of Niagara Falls. It was atop the giant Ferris wheel where Grant proposed to Claire. It was a special moment and an experience they would never forget.

The Cardinals sailed into the canal leading into the heart of Atlantic City. They discovered the now-collapsed Brigantine Bridge that had connected the two ends of town. The boat then sailed into a major harbour in disarray bordering the famous Golden Nugget Casino. They found a suitable dock and decided to pull in for the night after another long day of sailing on the Atlantic Ocean.

"Welcome to Atlantic City, home of America's oldest boardwalk!" Grant exclaimed.

"What's a casino?" Cody asked, looking at the Golden Nugget.

"It's a place where people's dreams are shattered and where they pawn wedding rings," Grant joked.

"It's where you play cards for money, like poker and blackjack. People used to come here to Atlantic City to gamble money and drink alcohol," Claire described.

The Cardinal family carefully approached the old, dilapidated boardwalk and hiked along the once-bustling streets. The streets were virtually empty, except for the odd burned-out car, which signalled to Claire and Grant that people had evacuated. It was all so mysterious for the perplexed parents. Some cities were evacuated, and bombs or fire destroyed some.

"There must have been massive evacuations across the continent once the fires started," Claire suggested.

"I don't think we have an idea of the scale of destruction," Grant added.

"Fields and forests of ash and cinder," Claire said. "There must have been a last stand somewhere."

"I'm hoping Washington D.C. will give us some answers," Grant said.

"Can we check this place out?" Cody asked, pointing to the Golden Nugget Casino.

"Sure," Grant said.

They carefully made their way through a broken door and inside. They found themselves on the casino floor, filled with old slot machines and carpets saturated in water and mildew.

"Have a look, kids," Grant said. "Old Blue Eyes himself was a regular here."

"Who is Old Blue Eyes?" Cody asked.

"Francis Albert Sinatra: the best singer of all time," Grant said. "Everyone called him Frank, though. He had an executive suite here at the Golden Nugget. If I remember correctly, he had hand-carved marble toilets with gold-gilded seats. This place was hopping in the 1980s."

They scoured the different floors of the casino and found very little. All the rooms were tossed, and almost everything was saturated with mildew and mould. They didn't feel safe within the crumbling infrastructure, so they spent the night in the Anastasia along the quiet harbour of Atlantic City.

Throughout their journey from Labrador, they hadn't seen one human. It was a clear indication that people were dead or dying along the eastern seaboard and not thriving as they had hoped. Grant and Claire figured people either starved to death, were wiped out by military, insurrectionist or mercenary action, or had died in fires or on the frigid migration roads.

The following day, after a quick bite to eat, they again set sail and departed Atlantic City. The Anastasia was holding firm, and eventually, they sailed past the coast of Delaware and Maryland. It was only a few more miles until they would enter the Chesapeake Bay, the route to the Potomac River, which led to Washington, D.C. If a city survived the ordeal, it might be Washington, Claire and Grant thought.

Cody and Brooklyn tied down the main and jib sail as they drifted into Chesapeake Bay, the site of an abundance of American history. Brooklyn and Cody then sat and rowed to the Chesapeake Bay Bridge Tunnel. This uniquely engineered roadway allowed big boats to cross atop the tunnel section and smaller boats to navigate between the bridge sections of the roadway.

They tied the boat off around a protruding steel spike, and they lounged around the boat. The cold Atlantic air served an ideal refrigeration for their food, so they had another giant meal of tuna. After supper, they played cards on full bellies alongside the pier off the bridge.

"Should we go to Washington?" Grant asked Claire.

"At this point, it seems pretty hopeless, doesn't it?" Claire responded.

"There might be answers there," Grant said.

"There might be more death and bomb craters there," Claire countered.

"Washington might be the last place standing," Grant pleaded.

"I would rather not know and be able to outrun freezing weather than know and get our boat frozen climbing up the Potomac River," Claire said. "It will take too long to navigate upriver."

What she said made perfect sense; however, Grant wanted answers. Where had everyone in America gone? Were they relocated? Killed? Was the leadership underground somewhere?

As they lay sleeping that night, temperatures plummeted to minus ten degrees Celsius or 14 degrees Fahrenheit. Refrigerated food became frozen food, and the water was nearly ice.

As they all awoke and exposed themselves to the elements, they recognized the situation's urgency.

"We're going to have to start taking shifts," Grant said to Claire.

"Like sailing through the night?" Claire responded.

"Something like that. Temperatures are dropping too fast, and we're moving too slowly. Instead of anchoring every night, perhaps we keep pushing on," Grant suggested.

"Teams of two? Two at night, two in the daytime?" Claire hypothetically asked.

"That's what I was thinking. Me and Brooklyn at night. You and Cody in the day," Grant said.

"There's going to be an adjustment period, but I think it is what needs to be done," Claire responded.

The following 48 hours were frigid, but Anastasia pressed on night and day. Grant and Brooklyn sailed through the dark, treacherous waters without the stars or the moon as a guide. The coast was barely visible, but their eyes were able to adjust in the murky darkness. While father and daughter sailed, Claire and Cody slept, though it was difficult to stay asleep for long, with all the pitches and plunges of the rocking waves.

Sailing at night gave Grant and Brooklyn plenty of time to think—the monotony of sailing in the dark generated grim thoughts in the minds of the two weary sailors. Once the morning hazy light broke, it was a welcome relief as they exchanged roles.

Brooklyn woke her brother and mother and quickly took control of the boat after some smoked fish. Grant and Brooklyn fell asleep almost immediately. They hardly felt any seasickness as they drifted off to sleep.

After a few days of alternating between Claire and Cody sailing during the day and Grant and Brooklyn taking the helm at night, they realized they had covered a substantial distance. They had sailed past the sandy shores of North and South Carolina and were now in the waters off the coast of Georgia. The Cardinals had made a mad dash south to avoid the freezing waters and were now entering the warmer waters of the South Atlantic. Grant was reasonably confident the boat was out of any impending danger.

As the dreary morning light rose, the boat, driven by Grant and Brooklyn, approached the border of Georgia and Florida near Jacksonville. Grant had collected maps throughout the journey and found a military installation in Jacksonville. The Anastasia was now on the hunt for Blount Island along the St. John's River.

Brooklyn was happy to see no snow on the ground, but it was only a few degrees above freezing. Grant looked ahead and saw the beginnings of a massive barricade structure. Its main foundations were shipping containers and school buses. In front of the wall were miles of barbed wire and iron structures, similar to the ones found on the beaches of Normandy during D-Day. Then, the decomposed bodies began to appear.

All roads were jammed with horrendous battle scenes: dead, rotten civilians, skeletons of military personnel, eroding armoured vehicles, and scorched earth. The scene was traumatizing for Brooklyn, who had never seen such horrific things.

"What happened, Dad?" Brooklyn asked as they slowly moved up the canal.

"It looks like the government set up some sort of barricade; it was overrun, and a battle erupted." Grant was just as shocked as Brooklyn. He now discovered things were more complicated than he initially thought. He assumed mass migrations of North Americans flocked south to avoid the freezing and, presumably, starvation. Florida, along with, in all likelihood, Texas and Louisiana, were in similar situations, Grant thought.

"Can we leave this place?" Brooklyn asked, turning to her father.

"I want to check this loading dock out first. You can stay on board and look after your mother and brother." Grant slowly pulled into the harbour of Blount Island, a major cargo facility and military installation he had researched at the bookstore in Provincetown.

Grant pulled alongside the peer and tied down the Anastasia. "You stay here and keep an eye on things. If anything happens, wake your mother and blow the whistle as loud as possible. I'll come running, I promise," Grant said with an assuring smile.

Brooklyn was brave, but the environment made her nervous. She wrapped herself in a blanket and plunked down on the stern bench. As Grant walked off with his pack, bow and arrows, Brooklyn pulled out her journal and began to write.

October 2nd

Me and Dad stopped in Jacksonville. Mom and Cody are still sleeping. We have been taking shifts at night to keep the boat moving south. We have been racing away from the cold. There have been no humans on our two-month journey. There are no trees here, only blackened earth. There are dead bodies everywhere from a major battle. We have no answers, no idea about other people. All seems hopeless, except for the abundance of fish we have been eating.

Once Grant had made it to the road, he realized that people living south of the Jacksonville barricade were safe until they couldn't hold the line, which eventually broke. The ten years leading up to now were bloody, desperate, and savage. North America was a frozen, scorched wasteland with no signs of recovery.

Grant wanted answers and knew Blount Island was a base for the United States Army. Though it was mostly destroyed, Grant crept along the massive parking lots of blackened and eroding military vehicles. Judging by what he saw, this battle and carnage must have happened close to ten years ago. Bodies were decomposed to the point where only skeletons and clothing remained.

He approached what appeared to be the central headquarters at Blount Island. Above the main entrance, it read: 'Marines. The Few. The Proud.' He peered through the window and went inside the battered building. There were papers and garbage everywhere and a directory on the wall with all the different departments and locations: logistics, security, harbour master, shipping, lodging, military personnel, nurses, and weapons.

Grant thought 'military personnel' might be a great place to start finding answers. He moved in the direction of room 107. It was eerily quiet as he walked down the hallway lined with decorated marines and veterans from the various wars throughout the 20th and 21st centuries.

He peeked through the open door of room 107 and saw the various workstations inside. He looked through all the desks and filing cabinets for signs of intelligence. Then he stumbled upon Corporal Henderson's desk, Chief of Communications. He rifled through drawers and eventually found a folder with a stamp that read 'Top Secret.' He opened the folder and found the title page 'Operation Poseidon.' Grant believed he had discovered the last military operation of the American Marines.

Page by page, he scrolled through the file, learning about the military and civilian personnel, the equipment, the set dates, and the destination. As he read, he discovered the Marines sent a convoy of 20 ships and 2000 people to Guadeloupe, Dominica, Martinique, St. Lucia, and St. Vincent. The military intelligence had deemed the islands abandoned and sent a series of arks to the islands.

These 20 ships would not only carry 2000 people but also books, seeds, tools, batteries, and animals that would help domestic the small island chain. It was a last-ditch effort to save North American civilization. Blount Island would serve as the disembarkation point for the armada. Finally, Grant had some answers. He and his family had a destination and a community to potentially strive for.

The Cardinals would need to travel along the Antillas Mayores, also known as the Greater Antilles, a group of large islands in the Caribbean Sea. They would pass by the Bahamas, Cuba, the Dominican Republic, Puerto Rico, and the British Virgin Islands en route to their destination. Looking at the map, Grant knew it was a long way, about 1500 miles or about 2500 kilometres, through the hostile, southern Atlantic Ocean, but it would ultimately be worth it if they could find a civilization.

Grant put the top-secret folder and a few worn maps in his bag and exited the building. Grant smiled to himself, knowing he had found what he had come for. He was glad to leave Blount Island, as it felt like a nightmare, an abyss of chaos, death and destruction. There was no colour, birds, insects, or even grass growing on the island.

He left the building with a certain sense of pride and relief. The thought of 2000 people living together in harmony excited him. Grant weaved his way back to his family at the Anastasia through the maze of cargo containers and rundown vehicles.

Cody, Brooklyn, and Claire were all sitting on the edge of the peer, with their feet dangling off the side. Grant admired the innocence and purity of his family in the moment. They had come so far under dark, miserable conditions, and he was glad to arrive with some good news.

"Cardinal clan!" Grant shouted, walking down the peer. His family all turned their heads to look at their returning father.

Brooklyn popped up to her feet. "Dad! Why did you take so long?"

"I knew he was okay," Cody said, shoulder-checking her sister.

Grant hugged his family like he hadn't seen them in a month. "I've got some exciting news."

"What is it?" Claire asked.

Grant removed the folder from his pack. "Operation Poseidon," he said, handing Claire the folder.

Claire flipped and scanned the pages. "Is this a military operation?"

"This is the Noah's Ark mission. Operation Poseidon launched massive ships carrying 2000 staff, personnel, and family members to the Caribbean. Guadeloupe, Dominica, St. Lucia, a massive island chain they retreated to. Blount Island was their launching point." Grant looked excited in a way Claire had not seen for a decade.

"So, are we setting sail for Guadeloupe?" Claire asked.

"The Windward Islands. That's what they're called. Everyone vacated the islands during the fallout from Yellowstone; then, the U.S. planned this mission to reoccupy and recolonize. This might be a chance to join a collaborative effort." Grant pulled his two children under his arms.

"How far is it, Dad?" Brooklyn asked.

"We've come about halfway. One thousand five hundred miles to go," Grant answered.

"Well, what are we waiting for?" Claire said with a smile.

The Cardinals were happy to depart Jacksonville and Blount Island. The next stop they planned for was Miami. They wanted to spend a night triple-checking their supplies, sails, and rigging knowing they were heading into some of the world's most turbulent waters. They assumed that hurricane season would be treacherous with changing global temperatures and shifting ocean currents, so they needed to be prepared.

The waters off the east coast of Florida were rough, but the Cardinals' polished skills and sailing experience helped them navigate the tricky tides and swift currents. It took two days and two nights to reach Miami. Now that there was a definitive destination, the entire family seemed energized and enthusiastic about their journey.

Nights were spent in coastal channels that were perfect for anchoring and sleeping. Brooklyn and Cody were exposed to their first glimpses of alligators, which frightened and mystified them. Reptiles were a completely foreign concept to the children who grew up only knowing northern mammals and migrating birds.

As they sailed into Miami, Grant and Claire taught them about all the reptiles and creatures, native and invasive, in the Everglades: the panthers, armadillos, manatees, geckos, and leatherbacks. They taught them about the different fish and wildlife within the ocean around Florida: the corals, sea stars, sponges, groupers and eels. Brooklyn and Cody were inquisitive children who asked many questions about ocean life. It was utterly alien to them, and their curiosity was boundless.

Claire steered the Anastasia into the channel leading to Miami Beach. The first harbour they came across was perfect. It had breaker walls and several boats still on trailers alongside the wharf. Grant and Claire discussed searching for a spare mainsail and jib-sail better suited to the open ocean and the Caribbean waters. They contemplated finding a new boat but found it would be too difficult to move without a way to launch. They would prepare the Anastasia in the best way they could.

They pulled alongside a pier at the marina, lowered the jib and mainsail and tied them off on the boom.

"Line looks good!" Cody said.

Brooklyn grabbed the dock and tied the Anastasia down. The Cardinals set foot on the pier after three long days alongside the east coast of Florida. The weather was relatively warm at 12 degrees Celsius or about 54 degrees Fahrenheit.

"That feels good," Brooklyn said, stretching her arms and legs.

Cody jumped on the dock and did a couple of squats trying to get rid of his sea legs. "This place is awesome!" he said looking at the tall, bright, modern architecture.

"This is where some of the richest people in the world lived," Grant said. "The Hulkster lived here, for goodness' sake!"

"Who is the Hulkster?" Cody asked.

"World wrestling champion of the world," Grant said while grabbing Cody in a playful headlock. "He body-slammed Andre 'The Giant' at WrestleMania III."

"Come on Brooklyn, let's go find some new sails," Claire said, rolling her eyes.

Claire and Brooklyn walked towards the wharf where all the worn boats were stored on stilts or trailers. Grant and Cody went the opposite way towards the residential area with their weapons ready.

The boys strolled the decaying streets, looking for any signs of danger and anything useful. The streets were lined with dead-standing palm trees and some that had collapsed along the sidewalks. Telephone poles and wires littered the streets, cars were decaying, buildings were either destroyed from exposure or were on the brink of collapse, and glass was everywhere.

Cody secured a bag of white rice from a restaurant basement, and Grant found a fishing store. It had been ransacked, but he found a new fishing rod, new line, four new life preservers, and a few random lures better suited for fishing in the warmer, southern waters.

Brooklyn and Claire found a boat called the 'Amaya.' It was roughly the same size as the Anastasia and the sails were neatly folded and ready for transport inside duffle bags. It was a great find, and the sails were lighter and easier to work with than the homemade sail they had been using.

The Cardinals met back on the docks where they had a massive meal of tuna and rice. The sails would have to wait to be installed until the following day, as they were gripped by lethargy after a long day and big meal.

After a good night's sleep, they spent the morning affixing the sails to the Anastasia's mast. It was tedious work, but nobody minded, as they were staying relatively warm on dry land, opposed to the wet, confined spaces on the Anastasia.

"Let's give it a test run," Claire said after she secured the final tie strap.

"Brooklyn, Cody, raise the jib sail!" Grant said with his best captain voice.

"Aye, aye!" the kids yelled back.

The new jib sail and mainsail went up with ease. The Cardinals watched as the mainsail revealed a massive four-leaf clover.

"Looks like we picked the right one, Brooklyn-babe," Claire said.

"What is it?" Brooklyn asked, looking confusedly at the clover.

"That, my dear, is an Irish symbol of luck," Claire said.

"Just what we need," Grant added.

The next day, with all the preparations and rations for multiple days on the ocean, the Anastasia departed the marina at Miami Beach, and waved goodbye to North America.

Central America

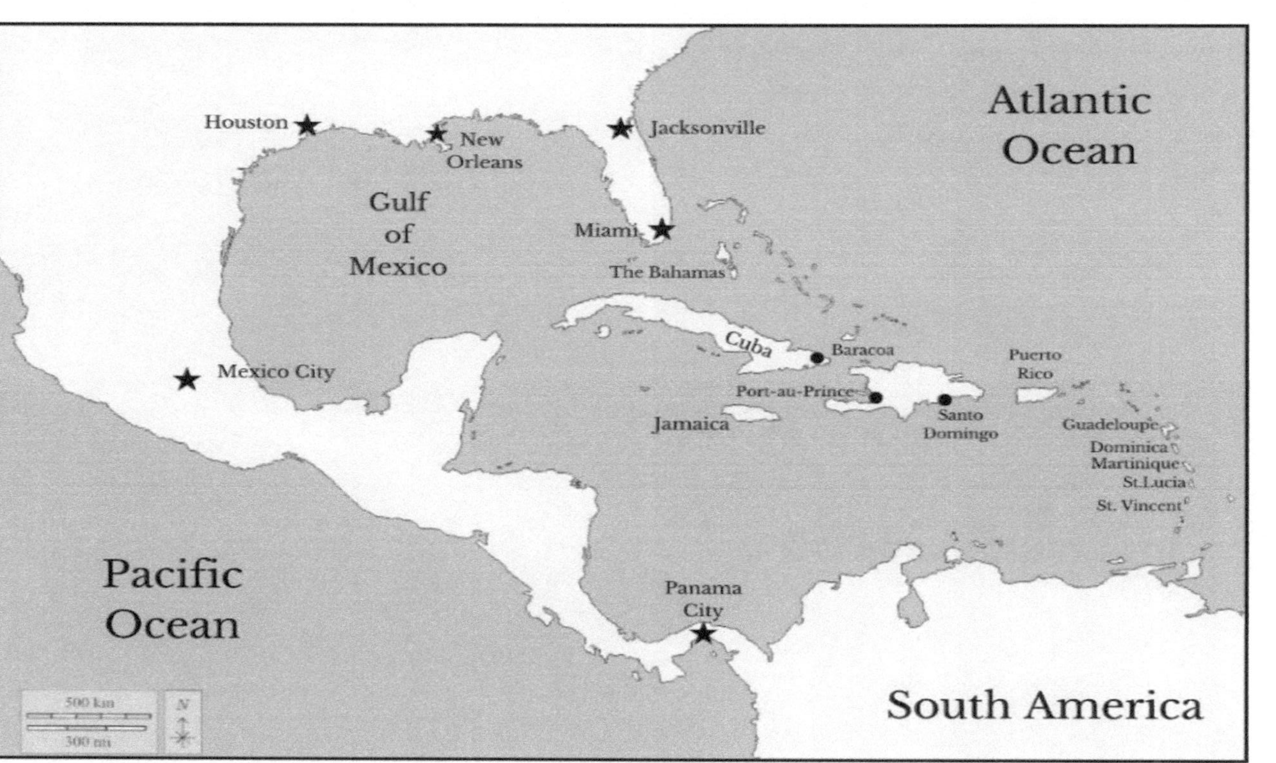

Chapter 18 - Windward Bound

Claire was looking carefully at the map of the Caribbean, plotting a course through the thousands of islands. The route that best suited them was between Cuba and the Bahamas. They left the Florida Keys, the southernmost part of Florida and headed south to reach Cuba. This stretch would be a significant test for the Cardinals, as it was an open ocean with roaring white caps and strong southerly winds.

They passed various lighthouses along the Florida Keys islands and finally turned south. Claire double-checked her handheld compass. She adjusted the boom slightly and caught a full sail of wind.

Grant was sitting on the boat's bow as the Anastasia picked up speed. He awkwardly fell backward, and Claire chuckled at his clumsy manoeuvre. Grant picked himself up, looked back at Claire and yelled: "We're moving now!"

The kids looked out on the blueish-grey waters with intrigue and curiosity. The Florida Keys drifted into the horizon off the stern of the boat, and they found themselves surrounded by an ocean desert. Winds were pulling the ship fast, so Grant anticipated being on the Cuban coast by nightfall.

About halfway through their journey, ominous black clouds appeared from the east. It worried Grant and Claire, as they knew they were in the middle of hurricane season and had no way of forecasting the weather.

"Brooklyn, Cody, bring down the jib sail!" Claire shouted, steering the tiller.

The kids hopped to the boat's bow and lowered the jib sail. Grant moved back and began lowering the mainsail.

"We're taking everything down, and we're going to ride these black clouds out," Claire said to whoever was listening.

Grant finished tying down the mainsail and tacked the boom down out of the way. "This is going to get rough," he said looking at the ominous system above.

The downpour started, and Brooklyn and Cody got their buckets and started bailing as soon as the rain began. With the rain came thunder and lightning which cast an anxious, frightened feeling amongst the Cardinals. Waves became bigger and sent Anastasia tossing back and forth fiercely. The water was cold but more tolerable than the biting northern Atlantic they felt throughout the past few months.

"Everyone, hang on and get your life jackets on!" Claire screamed over the noise of the waves, rain, and thunder. "This is just the beginning!"

Grant got the kids and himself in the newly found life vests and brought Claire hers and threw it around her shoulders and began buckling it up as she steered. The boat hit a large wave and knocked Grant off-balance, and he almost fell over the side of the boat. Claire clicked the life jacket buckle together and smiled at her husband's close call.

"You alright?" Claire asked.

"Never better," Grant responded with a sarcastic tone. "You let me know whatever you need to get us through this crap," he yelled.

"How about a pina colada?" Claire joked.

"White rum or dark?" Grant joked back.

The Anastasia moved up and down, wave after wave. Brooklyn and Cody constantly bailed as Claire did her best to steer into the waves to ensure they wouldn't tip the boat.

The whole family felt nauseous after several hours of repetitive, queasy motion. With each passing wave, their bowels would sink, and the mechanism in their inner ear would throw off their equilibrium. The black clouds covered the entire sky and didn't provide any sense of relief to the weary travellers.

Claire navigated the turbulent waters, mile after mile. Rain slammed against her face despite her best efforts to shield her eyes from the downpour. The clouds darkened, and there was no end in sight as they stretched into the horizon.

The Anastasia swayed up and down like a never-ending carnival ride. After another hour of traversing the storm, Grant spotted a break in the storm and was optimistic the waters would calm, the rains would stop, and they would be out of any impending danger. The boat calmed as the storm passed, and eventually, everything seemed quiet. Everyone laid back and relaxed as the Anastasia bobbed up and down.

"Well, that sucked," Claire said, rubbing her arms.

"Let's take a break and raise the sails later," Grant said, leaning back against the mainmast.

It had been an exhausting day. There had been very little downtime as they all needed to work together. Later in the afternoon, after a long rest, they raised sails and set course due south. They arrived off the coast of Cuba as the day became night. All in all, it took them 17 hours to make the journey. They pulled into Matanzas Bay, which provided shelter from the unpredictable Atlantic.

They anchored and slept aboard the Anastasia that night, with everything soaking wet, including their clothes and bedding. By morning, everything was relatively dry, and they were ready for the next stretch of their journey after a hearty meal of dehydrated meats and tuna. Claire figured that the next two days and nights would be along the coast of Cuba, which showed little signs of life along its overgrown shores and crumbling buildings.

On the third day of sailing along the Cuban coast, they decided to dock and camp out for the night in a place called Bahia de Baracoa. Despite the dead trees and lifeless surroundings, they were all happy to get their feet once again on solid ground.

They off-loaded their camping gear, and Brooklyn immediately started a fire with her flint-rod necklace. Grant had caught a couple of seabass and snappers throughout the day, and the Cardinals would have an old-fashioned barbeque on the beach.

Conversations were few and far between as the Cardinals became more focused and determined to land safely in Guadeloupe. To Claire and Grant, the silence of Cody and Brooklyn was a good sign. They had endured trauma and change in the past year and were becoming more comfortable in their own bodies and minds.

Claire and Grant set up the tent and made their surroundings comfortable. Cody gathered wood and piled his gatherings beside the fire. They truly worked as a team and made things easy on one another.

Claire and Grant hugged one another on the sandy beach, looked at the horizon, and imagined a sunset that wasn't there. Cody fileted the fish, and Brooklyn boiled a pot of rice to accompany the grilled seafood. The Cardinals shared a big meal oceanside and felt hopeful about the coming weeks.

Although the weather was much better near the equator, it was still chilly at night. They slept soundly and awoke to the peaceful sound of small crashing waves. They ate some leftovers, cleaned and packed up their gear and set sail for the island of Haiti and Dominican Republic.

The first night, they anchored in the Canal de la Tortue, the body of water between Haiti and the island of Tortuga. The second night, they docked in the abandoned docks of Puerto Plata. The third night was spent in Samana Bay. They were taking their time, being cautious, and eating plenty of seafood.

The entire family felt pride after how far they had come over the past two months. It was now late September, and the cool weather told Grant and Claire that anything north of New England would be frozen solid. They had planned the journey perfectly. Had they done anything different, they would have been caught and exposed to the sub-zero elements.

Though not exactly deep-ocean-seaworthy, the Anastasia had provided them with a maneuverable vessel that could weave through the shallows of the various islands, canals, and river systems surrounding North America. They planned their provisions accordingly and learned a tremendous amount along the way. If things didn't work out on the Windward Islands where the American Marines landed, they believed they had the tools and mental fortitude to start somewhere fresh, wherever that may be.

Claire and Grant wanted their children to learn and grow with kids their age, especially as they developed their identities. Claire could sense Brooklyn becoming more womanly; she could have adult conversations without losing her temper or getting upset. Cody was becoming more self-dependent, as well. Grant and Claire were especially pleased with his initiative, as they never had to ask him to do things as he was always a few steps ahead.

They sailed past Puerto Rico and south of the U.S. Virgin Islands and now were only a day away from Guadeloupe, the first of the five Windward Islands where the Marines had supposedly landed. Compared to the northern Atlantic and its Arctic winds, the journey through the Caribbean felt almost like a vacation.

That evening, they stayed on the abandoned island of Saint Martin in a marina called Fort St. Louis. The circular marina sat below a massive escarpment with a stone fort atop the hill. The French military had built the fort to defend the interests of the King sometime during the era of expansionism and colonization.

Like any other day, they set up beach camp, ate heartily, hiked to the top of the hill and sat on the fort walls that overlooked the ocean. They shared some stories of the world before the children came of age. It was still so surprising for Brooklyn and Cody to hear stories that had been deliberately hidden from them for so long. Grant spoke of his first girlfriend in elementary school, his time at McGill University, and Grandma Cardinal's homemade molasses candy in Labrador. Claire reminisced about Halloween and Christmas and the presents Santa brought and placed under the colourfully lit tree.

"So, a fat man from the North Pole, I assume he is Inuit or Cree, hops in a magic sleigh, rides around the world in one night, climbs down through the chimneys, and gives every child a present? Did I get that correct?" Cody said.

"You forgot the magic reindeer that guided his sleigh 20,000 feet above sea level," Brooklyn added.

Grant and Claire both laughed and nodded in agreement.

"Parents and kids would line up at malls for hours to get a picture with a fake Santa, an elf, and some giant plastic candy canes," Grant joked.

"Then they had Boxing Day," Claire said, looking at Grant.

"Come on, what the heck is that?" Brooklyn asked.

"It's where all the malls would put everything on sale," Grant answered.

"What's a mall?" Cody asked.

"A place with a bunch of stores," Claire answered.

"Why wouldn't they put everything on sale before Christmas when it could help everybody out?" Brooklyn innocently inquired.

"That's a great question, kiddo," Grant said, smiling at Claire.

Claire and Grant admired the innocence in their reasoning, humility, and integrity. Why wouldn't businesses help out their customers when they needed it, Grant pondered.

"Our ancestors have been asking those questions for a long time," Claire said to Brooklyn.

"Well, many of those businesses were trying to make as much money as possible without really considering the thoughts and well-being of their customers." Grant was doing his best dance.

"It was a different time, sweetie," Claire said. "People were sprawled out on drugs in our city centres; homeless people were everywhere; normal citizens couldn't afford homes; it was rather depressing. Normal people didn't look out for each other in the modern world."

"Tomorrow, we will be approaching Guadeloupe, the first of the Windward Islands. We don't know if we will be welcomed, so I don't want any hostile behaviour. They may have guns or other weapons, so we need to approach with tact and reserve. We will anchor offshore and raise a white flag of truce to let them know we mean no harm," Grant said.

"The U.S. military was once the most powerful army in the world; now we don't know. They are highly decorated soldiers who most likely fought in Iraq, Afghanistan, Somalia and other war-torn countries. If they ask us to leave, we will leave. If they ask us to jump, we will ask how high?" Claire took on a sombre tone. "I don't want to have come all this way to be killed for some silly outburst or insubordination. Let's all be as pleasant as possible. Got that?"

"Yes, Mom," Cody and Brooklyn said.

"In fact, don't speak unless you are spoken to. We don't want to set a bad first impression," Claire said.

"We will be alien to them, and they will be very suspicious of us skinny Canadians aboard a rickety old boat with a homemade rudder. Let's not give them a reason to get upset," Grant said.

The entire family slept soundly on the beach of Saint Martin. They cleaned the boat in the morning and organized things as best as possible. They also went into the frigid waters and washed their dirty, odorous bodies for the first time since they had boiled water in Miami. After the cold plunge and warming by the fire, they boarded the Anastasia and rowed out of the Fort St. Louis marina and, once again, onto the open waters of the Caribbean Sea.

In the late afternoon, they spotted a small island on the horizon that could be nothing by Guadeloupe. With their sails open and catching full wind, the Anastasia approached the Windward Island.

"Let down the sails!" Grant shouted. "We'll anchor once we are within seeing eye distance of the shore." Cody and Claire cranked the sails down and tied them off. "Cody, grab the flare gun," Grant ordered.

Cody went into the sleeping quarters and grabbed the small plastic orange box he had found in Churchill Falls. He brought it out as the Anastasia slowed down and handed it to Grant.

"Drop anchor!" Grant yelled.

They were now a couple hundred yards from the shore of Guadeloupe, and there were few signs of life. They could only make out the sandy shore with green grasses amidst the browning treeline. It was a relief for Grant and Claire to see the island was maintaining some vegetation despite the decade-long cloud cover.

"Well," Grant said, "I think it's time."

"Go for it," Claire said.

Grant took the flare gun out of the box, loaded the round, aimed to the sky, and fired. The glowing red amber shot into the sky with a trail of grey smoke behind it. It was blinding to the weary eyes of the Cardinals. Now, all they could do was wait.

Chapter 19 - A Long Time

The Cardinals bobbed up and down in their small sailboat. Having travelled halfway around the world was a remarkable venture and accomplishment. They had braved the raging rivers, traversed hostile terrains, and sailed the eastern seaboard of North America in an aluminum-hulled boat with little to no supplies.

The proud parents looked at their eager, enthusiastic children with hope and accomplishment. Though Claire and Grant had held the truth of the world from their children, they did instill a positive work ethic and resilience in their lives. Claire and Grant had successfully created a positive environment for their formative years to help overcome what would have been an anxiety-ridden childhood.

Brooklyn and Cody had grown up and developed their senses through the stimulation of hunting, trapping, fishing, and other old-world tasks. Considering they were thrown into a different world over the past year, they had adapted quickly, and their inquisitive nature broke through the vale of depression and chaos around them.

Claire and Grant talked for years about hiding the truth from their children. Seeing Brooklyn and Cody's hardened resistance on the waters of the Guadeloupe archipelago was worth the trouble of concealment and the potential for repercussions.

The flare burned out and landed in the water. Cody was looking through his telescope for any signs of life. He scanned the sandy shore and the dying coconut palms. The Cardinals sat and waited, but nothing was emerging from the jungle.

The waters were crystal clear with white sand and colourful schools of fish dancing between the corals at the bottom. Brooklyn was more attuned to the activity in the water than the treeline. Claire and Grant fixated their gaze.

"Should we raise the sails and try finding a different place? Maybe try to find a marina?" Claire suggested.

"We could try that," Grant said, losing hope.

"Wait!" Cody yelled. "Look!" he said, pointing to the shoreline.

A lone man on the beach waved a white flag at the Anastasia. The moment froze Claire and Grant. They both slowly turned to each other with looks of amazement. They then turned their gaze back to the man waving the flag.

"Excellent!" Grant said. "A white flag!"

They slowly and deliberately rowed into the bay's shallows, bit by bit. Stroke after stroke, the excited anxiety shot through the nerves of the entire Cardinal family. This would be the first contact in a decade. At first, they were worried about the man's intentions. Was he a good guy? Were his intentions evil? Was he a schemer?

The closer they got, the less threatening the man became. He was dressed in cargo shorts and a black t-shirt, and his hair and beard were long and grizzled. His face was weathered but welcoming, his eyes were forgiving, and his smile was genuine.

"Bonjour!" the man yelled. "You look three sheets to the wind!"

"Bonjour, monsieur!" Claire yelled back to the man. "Ça va?"

"Bon! Excellent! Welcome to Guadeloupe!" the man said.

This was the first human contact the Cardinals had made in a decade, bringing a rush of joy through their bodies and minds. He was a handsome, wise-looking man who was completely clean, except for his kneecaps and hands, which were covered in dirt.

"Hello, I'm Pierre! I'm the western harbour master and local crab fisherman. Pull your boat up along my dock, just around the point there," Pierre said, pointing to the rocky point. "I was just working in the garden when I saw your flare."

"I'm so glad you did. Thanks for letting us dock! We've been on the water for weeks!" Grant yelled, turning to Brooklyn and Cody. "You heard the man, let's row the boat around the point!"

"We are happy you've made it!" Pierre yelled to the Cardinals.

Cody and Brooklyn hopped on the oars and rowed to Pierre's dock. They tied off and jumped on the deck with weary legs. Pierre appeared from a rocky path above, came down, and shook hands with everyone.

"Pardon my dirty hands; I was just digging up some carrots in the garden," Pierre said.

Cody and Brooklyn observed the strange gesture of shaking hands, but they mimicked their parent's gesture and shook hands with the stranger.

"Hello, children, my name is Pierre. What are your names?" he asked with a bit of a French accent.

"I'm Brooklyn, and this is Cody."

"Oh, how lovely," Pierre said.

"I'm Grant, and this is my wife, Claire. We are the Cardinal family. We've travelled all the way from northern Labrador, Canada, to get here. It has been one remarkable journey, and we have many questions, Pierre."

"Labrador? Oh, my goodness. In that?" Pierre said, shocked at the sight of the Anastasia and her condition.

"The Anastasia held up quite nicely. A little cramped, but home sweet home," Claire said.

"You are very brave to have sailed the ocean in such a tiny vessel," Pierre said with a shocked smile. "Brave and perhaps un petit foolish."

"We didn't have many other options," Claire said with a cheeky smile.

"You are courageous," Pierre said to Brooklyn and Cody. "Come, there is much to discuss," Pierre said. "Come, let's go have some supper. We don't get guests very often!" Pierre took the hands of Brooklyn and Cody and led the two youngsters up the path toward the house.

"Sounds terrific," Claire said as she turned to Grant and smiled. The moment was emotional as tears came to Claire's eyes.

Grant put his arm around Claire, and they followed Pierre up the path.

"Aren't you excited?" Grant asked Claire.

"It's a little overwhelming," she answered.

The Cardinals followed Pierre along the jungle path to his island home. It was a relatively modern home with windows, a metal roof and a paved walkway. The carport had been converted into a rudimentary holding pen.

"Come, Brooklyn, look here," Pierre said. "This is Quasimodo, my horse. He is quite the character."

Brooklyn poked her head around the corner and saw the white and brown Mustang. She had never seen a horse before, only in the pictures she saw in the books she read in Churchill Falls and Provincetown. She was hesitant as the horse approached the newcomers.

"He is quite friendly," Pierre said. "Try feeding him some hay. He'll adore you for life."

Brooklyn grabbed a handful of hay, reached through the fence and offered it to Quasimodo. The friendly horse began to chomp Brooklyn's offering, and she grinned from ear to ear.

"He likes you," Pierre said.

"Really?" Brooklyn exclaimed.

"You can tell by the way he wags his tail," Pierre said with a wink.

Cody, Grant, and Claire looked at the smiling Brooklyn feeding Quasimodo. Brooklyn gently stroked the side of Quasimodo's cheek, and she felt herself transported to a different place. Her imagination ran wild with such an interaction with an animal.

"Maybe you can ride him after supper?" Pierre suggested.

"Ride him?" Brooklyn asked.

"That's how we get around on this island. We either walk, ride bicycles, or ride horses." Pierre was a gentleman. He was obviously caring, gentle, and socialized, but Grant and Claire were still cautious.

They went inside the modest home, and Pierre began showing them around. Out back of the house, his wife Jeannie was grilling some fish and vegetables. The sight of colourful skewered vegetables was shocking to Cody and Brooklyn.

"This is my wife, Jeannie. She is a master cook, fisher, gardener, and raiser of chickens. These, my dear, are the Cardinals. They are the family that fired a flare from their boat. They have come all the way from Northern Canada to get here," Pierre said as they all shook hands.

Jeannie wore overalls, and her hair was tied back in a black bandana. She put her BBQ tongs down. "Well, it is an absolute pleasure to meet all of you," she said, smiling at the kids. "What an incredible journey that must have been. You must be exhausted."

"It was certainly epic," Grant said. "We sailed along the east coast; stopped in Boston, Cape Cod, Atlantic City, Miami."

"Any signs of civilization?" Jeannie asked.

"Nothing. Scorched earth, decomposition, death, and darkness," Claire answered.

"What are those?" Cody asked, pointing to the grilling vegetables.

"Those are skewers of zucchini, potato, yam, and carrot," Jeannie said with a smile.

"Honey, those are vegetables. They come from plants that farmers grow," Claire added.

"These children have not seen vegetables before?" Jeannie asked. "Well, you have to try them. They are so yummy."

"We've grown vegetables before, but none so colourful. This year, we couldn't grow anything," Brooklyn said.

"It was far too short of a season in Labrador. We had snow in July; however, we brought along an assortment of seeds," Claire said. "Everything from apple to squash."

"Wonderful!" Jeannie said. "There are many things we didn't bring here."

Jeannie and Pierre looked at the Cardinals with a significant amount of sympathy. They were skinny, extra pale, and exhausted from the long journey. "We have much to discuss. I have a thousand questions," Pierre said.

"And you must have a thousand for us," Jeannie added.

Jeannie made the guest room up for the Cardinal family after having a delicious, tasty, filling, and nutritious dinner. They were so grateful to have a sit-down dinner. They hadn't used knives and forks for months and were appreciative of the civilized hospitality they were receiving. Before long, the children were sound asleep in the hammocks that hung from the ceiling rafters.

Pierre entered the dining room carrying four cups and what appeared to be a homemade bottle of wine.

"We have a couple of bottles of Canadian Whiskey on the boat. I'll go grab them!" Grant said, darting out the door.

"It's a very happy day." Claire smiled at Jeannie and Pierre.

"How did you find the island?" Jeannie asked.

"We found military intelligence in Jacksonville, Florida," Claire answered. "All seemed rather hopeless when we arrived in Florida. Boston and New York had been struck with nuclear weapons, and there wasn't a soul in sight. No fires, no footprints, nothing that hadn't been sitting there for ten years."

Grant came back into the house with the bottles of whiskey. "You're going to love this stuff," he said, sitting down at the table.

"We were just saying all seemed hopeless until we found the intelligence in Jacksonville," Claire said.

"We were lucky, too," Jeannie said.

"We came here with the military envoy. Ten years ago now. The whole United States was dead or dying. The last rogue gangs and desperate hoards broke through the barricades in Jacksonville. The fighting was ferocious, and it wasn't long after that that we launched the envoy to come here. Jeannie and I worked at the embassy in Jacksonville and were part of the military administration. We came here with the rest of them aboard the light cruisers. We brought animals, seeds and tools, everything we would need." Jeannie was doing her best to be as sensitive as possible.

"Four other islands have since been colonized, along with Guadeloupe. We have farms, a school, tradespeople, alcohol refineries," Pierre said with a wink. "We have fishers, seamstresses, loggers, masons, and a working democratic government, which I will show you in the morning. There are sugar farms, massive root gardens, freshwater streams, and a dormant volcano near the island's interior."

"You have a school and a functioning government?" Claire asked.

"Absolutely," Jeannie said. "Though ex-military, we still wanted peace and functionality."

"That is great," Grant said, pouring some whiskey into everyone's cup. "We are so thankful to be here. We truly thought this world had ended."

"When Jacksonville fell, we thought it was the end, too," Pierre said. "How long were you alone in Labrador?" Pierre said.

"We've been alone since day one. Claire and I took the kids and headed north to my father's trapping cabin," Grant answered, sipping his drink. "We lost radio contact after a month and have been alone since then. To be honest, we are still trying to figure out what happened."

Pierre looked at Jeannie with concern, then back to Claire and Grant. "Yellowstone, Mount Rainier, Mount St. Helens, just about every volcano in the Pacific Northwest erupted within a few weeks of one another. But not just your everyday eruptions; we are talking about a major purge of magma from within the earth's core, which had been building for centuries. Millions died those first few days. Then came the hurried, frantic migrations. Americans, Mexicans and Canadians flocked east away from the fallout. UNICEF, the Red Cross, humanitarians, and governments did their best to curb the tidal wave of people, but there just weren't enough resources or...compassion; it was everyone for themselves. Rioting, pillaging, and plundering came with the panic and anxiety of the mass migration. Martial law was put into effect, militaries mobilized, and more and more people started dying. Schools, arenas, hotels, everything east of the Mississippi swelled." Pierre took a drink. "That was when we lost the sun. Satellite reports of major weather shifts and cloud cover made everyone panic, not just North Americans."

"That was when the bombs started dropping," Grant mentioned.

"Nobody knows who struck first, but NORAD was knocked out, making North America vulnerable. Most of the military personnel here figure it was a rogue faction that took over a nuclear armament. Most of South America was killed through bombs and chemical weapons. Last word from Europe was that a massive tank envoy had cleared most of the continent."

"Jesus," Claire said. "Is anybody left over there?"

"We don't know. But it doesn't look good," Pierre said. "After the bombs and the grid went down, there was radio silence. I worked with the military when they put up a massive barrier along the Georgia/Florida border."

"Jacksonville and the border was an absolute mess," Grant added.

"Entire crops died that first summer. Some things survived, but very little. We did our best, but there wasn't enough to help everyone. Have you ever seen somebody starving to death? It is the most horrific thing I have ever seen," Pierre said, taking another drink. "The world was freezing and dying. The clouds didn't part; they only got darker. Washington, Boston, New York, Toronto, and Ottawa were all destroyed. Next thing we knew, we were on a military ship headed for Guadeloupe."

"So, nobody knows who fired the nukes? Could it have been the Pentagon?" Grant asked.

"I suppose it could have been. It could have been a lot of things: Russia, China, North Korea, hell, even Europe," Pierre said.

"What about artificial intelligence?" Grant suggested.

"Another distinct possibility," Pierre answered.

"No communications with anyone else?" Grant asked.

"Nothing. We lost contact with all of our allies. When we wake up tomorrow, I'll take you to headquarters inland. It's not much, but we have a council that organizes and keeps things moving in harmony. Everyone has very specific roles. Most of our forests are dying, but grasses are still popping through, so grazing animals have taken on a significant role," Jeannie said.

"We have cows, pigs, chickens, goats, but very little in terms of fruits and vegetables. We, like you, haven't seen the sun in 10 years, so our strategies have changed." Pierre was doing his best. "I know all of this may seem overwhelming with all you have been through."

"It's fine. We haven't seen or met anyone in so long. It's great to have some adults to talk to finally," Claire said.

Everyone shared a laugh.

"We waited for an occasion just like this to crack open this bottle," Grant said, grasping the bottle.

"Your family is the first to come to the island in ten years. We were losing hope that there wasn't anyone else out there," Jeannie said.

"We are so happy that you've made it. Your children are going to love the island," Pierre added.

"We are looking forward to it," Claire said, putting her head on Grant's shoulder.

Everyone settled for the night after a pleasant evening with some cards and drinks. Claire and Grant laid down on the soft mattress and were transcended. It was the first bed they had been on since their cabin, and it was glorious. Both the children slept soundly in their hammocks as Grant let out a loud yawn.

"Whisky makes Grant sleepy," he said, putting his arm around Claire.

"Are you worried at all?" Claire asked.

"About what?" he asked.

"We're in a completely foreign land, with foreign people and government. I don't know, I'm just being pragmatic and a little hesitant," she said, kissing Grant on the cheek.

"We just need to observe, listen, and be open to the lessons and rules. They're probably running a tight ship here, with the military and all." Grant was reasonably optimistic about the prospects of the island chain. "Good night, my love."

"Sweet dreams," Claire whispered.

Claire and Grant drifted to sleep to the peaceful sounds of waves crashing and insects chirping.

Chapter 20 - Community

Claire and Grant awoke peacefully and slowly recognized their foreign surroundings. It certainly wasn't the cramped quarters of the Anastasia. As they both got their bearings and rubbed the sleep from their eyes, Claire noticed Brooklyn and Cody standing in the doorway.

"Why are you up?" Claire asked her children.

"We are excited," Brooklyn announced.

"Why are you staring at us?" Grant asked.

"Because we are excited for the day," Brooklyn said.

Grant and Claire were a little foggy from the dandelion wine and Canadian rye whiskey the night before, but they too, shared Brooklyn's enthusiasm for the day. Both parents were relieved they didn't need to dry out their wet boots or start a fire or fish for breakfast. They were now on dry land; they had optimism again in the form of green grass and civilization.

The Cardinal family walked down the hall to the kitchen, where Pierre and Jeannie were wide awake and making breakfast. Grey, overcast morning light poured into the living area as the smell of the cooking bacon and eggs transported Claire and Grant into the distant past. The sounds of the crackling bacon and frying potatoes reminded them of the diner where they first met: the checkered floors, the red spinning stools, and the jukebox with all the golden oldies.

"It smells delicious in here," Grant said, reminiscing. "Remind you of anything?" he asked Claire.

"The diner where we met?" Claire answered.

Grant smiled at his wife. "I haven't smelled bacon and eggs frying in ten years," he added.

"Good morning, sleepyheads!" Pierre said, giving the bacon a flip. "I hope you like bacon, eggs, and hashbrowns. No better way to start the day."

"I don't think I've ever had bacon and eggs," Brooklyn said. "I've had wild turkey eggs once, I think."

"It sure smells good," Cody said. "We haven't had potatoes in a long time."

"We brought a few bags of potatoes to the island, and they have done really well. We've been able to propagate them and distribute them all over the island. Probably our most successful crop, with all the animal manure and black earth," Pierre said.

"What else has been successful?" Claire inquisitively asked. "I've been harbouring an entire tackle box of seeds on our voyage."

"That's terrific, Claire. Carrots, beets, parsnips, anything underground, does really well here," Jeannie answered. "Ginger, garlic, onion, turnips. Our wheat fields struggle, but we are able to harvest plenty for the island," Jeannie said, whipping the bowl of soon-to-be scrambled eggs. "If you like to get your hands dirty, you're going to love our agricultural centre and community gardens."

Claire admired Jeannie and was reminded of having some female energy around. Claire imagined how wonderful it would be to have friends to share stories and recipes with, play board games, and laugh together over the little things in life. Jeannie seemed caring, trustworthy, and lighthearted; the type she would immediately connect with.

"So, after breakfast, we'll tie the wagon up to Quasimodo, and we'll head to the island capital square," Pierre said to Brooklyn. "Sound good?"

"Yes!" Brooklyn quickly affirmed. "Are there other horses on the island? Or did you only bring two of every animal?"

Pierre chuckled. "We brought a dozen horses to the island, and they were successful in breeding, so we now have plenty and room for more." Pierre looked at Claire and Grant. "I think Brooklyn might be perfect for our animal sanctuary."

"What do they do there?" Brooklyn asked.

"Well, lots of things," Pierre said. "They train horses, milk cows, separate calves, and move animals into new paddocks."

"That sounds like fun!" Brooklyn responded.

"They also help with the newborn animals. They make sure the animals are healthy, well-fed, and are nurturing properly. We also have over 2,000 chickens on the island, so our animal specialists are very busy," Jeannie added.

Brooklyn and Cody listened intently as Jeannie and Pierre spoke. Despite not having seen or met anyone in a decade, they quickly felt a deep connection to the islanders, who felt like long-lost relatives—an aunt and uncle reunited after years apart. The Cardinal children hung on every word, captivated by their wisdom and presence.

"Come, sit down," Jeannie said, bringing everything to the table.

The fantastic hosts brought piping-hot scrambled eggs, crispy bacon, golden hash browns, and an unidentifiable jar of green sauce.

"What is this," Cody said, picking up the jar of green sauce.

"That, my friend, is my world-famous hot sauce. Now I have to warn you first. This is super spicy, and if you're brave enough to try it, try only a little dab," Pierre said with a grin.

"I'll try it," Cody said bravely.

"Son, you have never tried spicy food before," Claire said as she started to dish out food. She couldn't remember having so much food between last night's dinner and today's breakfast. She was so thankful to see her children's faces showing a little more colour. Despite the short amount of time, Claire's strength was also returning.

"This looks so delicious. Thank you so much," Claire earnestly said.

"You're very welcome," Jeannie said, smiling. "You've earned it," referring to the oceanic voyage. "I can't wait for you to see our greenhouses. We've started experimenting with fruit trees, and things are really taking off."

On his own, Cody took a heaping teaspoon of the hot sauce and put it in his mouth.

"Did you just eat a spoonful of it?" Pierre asked.

It took a moment for it to hit, but Cody's face flushed red, and he reached frantically for a glass of water.

"I told you to be careful," Claire said, laughing.

"Even I don't even eat it by the spoonful," Pierre said laughing, while watching Cody's body and mind breakdown.

"It's so hot," Cody said. "It's burning!"

"Drink some more water!" Brooklyn yelled.

Cody ran out of the room, and everyone got a good chuckle.

"Poor little fellow," Jeannie said. "Ghost peppers are the spiciest thing we have on the island."

"He's a fearless little boy," Grant said with a smile.

The dust eventually settled on the commotion created by Cody underestimating the hot sauce, and they began to eat their wholesome, nutritious breakfast. Cody eventually returned, looking nauseous and gauntly white. Nobody mentioned his foolish mistake as he slowly began pecking at his meal.

"Now, when we roll into the town square, you must realize you will be quite the celebrity to everyone here. They haven't seen any newcomers for ages, and the sight of you might be a bit shocking," Pierre said while taking a bite of food.

"I wouldn't worry. You're going to love everyone. After breakfast, you can wash up and change down in the bathroom. There are fresh towels and soap in there, too," Jeannie said.

"We have a gravity-fed shower. It's a little chilly but refreshing," Pierre added.

"That's great," Grant said. "I look forward to it."

Brooklyn and Cody silently enjoyed their meal, paying no mind to the adults around them. Eggs were foreign tasting to them, but they enjoyed them, nonetheless.

"So, you said everyone has a role on the island. You and Jeannie are fishermen?" Grant asked.

"We set traps most of the year and provide fresh crab to the people of the island. Jeannie and I are also the official harbour master's and local guides here on the island's west coast," Pierre answered. "The island is very thinly populated, so everyone has multiple jobs and responsibilities."

"How are the crabs around here?" Grant asked.

"We have a decreasing population of coconut crabs, because most tropical tree species are dead or dying. We do have an abundance of fiddle crabs, blue crabs, and our favourite, the spider crab; long legs, deep water, very tasty," Pierre responded.

"You'll love our seafood nights," Jeannie added.

"Just curious, but how far is the town square from here?" Claire asked.

"It's about 20 miles," Pierre answered. "Jeannie and I have a place in town we use and would be happy to share it with you until we figure out some plans for you folks. There are vacant homes all over the island, some in better condition than others. We are doing our best to inventory them."

After breakfast and equipping Quasimodo with his wagon harness; Jeannie, Pierre, and the Cardinals set out towards the town square. Grant and Claire admired the countryside, covered in grazing goats, cows, and horses, while Cody and Brooklyn were laughing and holding on for dear life as they bounced up and down.

"It reminds me of Ireland or Scotland," Claire said. "No trees, just green grasses."

"It is so nice to see the colour green again," Grant responded.

There were a few dilapidated houses, but most seemed in good condition. There was the odd windmill, fences lined the pastures where animals grazed, and chicken houses could be seen on nearly every property.

Quasimodo easily pulled the wooden wagon along the paved road and over rolling hills. There was a man off in the distance with a scythe, chopping down some tall grass near what was, seemingly, his modest home. Pierre waved, and the older man waved back.

"That's Franklin!" Pierre said to everyone. "He is one of our resident grazing experts and pasture managers. He lived in Oklahoma before the darkness. You are going to love him."

"He has some lovely jokes too," Jeannie shared with Brooklyn and Cody.

"He seems nice," Claire said, waving at Franklin.

"We are very friendly here," Pierre said. "Right, Quasimodo?"

Quasimodo let out a high-pitched scream, followed by a couple of grunts.

"Look!" Brooklyn said, pointing to a waterfall and stream.

"Beautiful, isn't it? We have fresh water here but recommend filtration because of all the pasture run-offs," Pierre said. "But the streams are completely safe for afternoon swims," Pierre said, smiling at Brooklyn and Cody.

"Most of the island trees have died, but we are experimenting with a variety of things in the greenhouses," Jeannie said. "It's turned mostly to pastureland around here."

The whole ride in the back of the wagon was an experience. Pierre seemed to know everyone and everything. Cody noted young carpenters working together on the foundation of a new windmill.

"Look dad!" Cody said pointing to the windmill. "What's that?"

"That's a windmill," Grant answered.

"We are starting a bunch of power-generating projects on the island," Pierre said. "We've got a few hydro-dams in the works too."

"Just like Churchill Falls and Muskrat Falls, eh dad?" Cody said.

"Yeah, just on a smaller scale," Grant answered.

The wagon trotted past a home with clothes hanging on the line to dry and Claire was reminded of her childhood in Québec. Her mother used to hang their linens and clothing out to dry on Sunday afternoons and Claire would help collect the clothespins. She smiled and shed a tear as they passed by.

Grant was looking closely at what was growing on the ground. Throughout the countryside, he noticed small dwarf wheat, clover, bluegrass, ryegrass and alfalfa. It was clear to Grant that the pastures were the island's lifeblood. The grasses fed the livestock, providing meat, milk, cream, butter, eggs, yogurt, cheese, and sour cream. It was very encouraging for everyone.

"How many people live on this island?" Grant yelled up to Jeannie and Pierre.

"About 600 now. We've just had some new babies and passed 600 last May. We started at 400 a decade ago and have been on the uprise ever since," Jeannie said.

"Is there a hospital?" Claire asked.

"We have a couple of island doctors available in their homes but no formal hospital. Maybe one day, though," Jeannie answered. "Island life has been very healthy for everybody so far, and there is little need for a hospital. The doctors do keep very detailed records of each new birth and blood relations, so we avoid any unwanted health conditions, if you catch my meaning."

The horse-drawn wagon continued past dozens of greenhouses, overgrown tennis courts and gas stations, and a few dormant commercial stores.

"Once, Guadeloupe had a population of 400,000. Now we are at 600." Pierre let out a laugh.

"What about the other islands?" Claire asked.

"Communication with the other islands comes weekly, as we exchange each other's newspaper and vital intel. As of right now, we all have similar populations and industries. Each other's newspaper shares tips about farming, homesteading, and anything you could think of," Pierre said. "We've utilized an old printing press. Paper seems abundant for now, but we're searching for alternatives."

Quasimodo and the wagon moved from the dirt road onto a black asphalt road which provided a much smoother and quicker ride. Eventually, they arrived at what once appeared to be a shopping mall in the city centre. It had the classic French architecture of the 18th century combined with all the modern amenities.

"What is this place?" Brooklyn asked.

"Looks like an old shopping mall," Claire said, looking up at the archway.

"You're going to love this place!" Pierre said as he hopped down.

Jeannie tied Quasimodo to a wooden fence alongside several other horses, their reins secured to the sturdy posts in front of the shopping mall. The Cardinals followed closely behind Jeannie and Pierre as they all made their way through the main doors.

The island had no power grid, so the skylights and a few lanterns lit up the mall space. There were dozens of people inside, moving from store to store. Each storefront had been converted and looked like a giant flea market. There were various market food stands, stores with metallurgy, tools, kitchenware, books, farm tools, fishing gear, and more.

"Here, we use the honour system rather than money. We record what we both take and bring to market. We exchange and play our respective roles within this functioning society. There are debts owed, and debts paid, but we don't take more than we need. We may, one day, find the need to create a currency, but thus far, we haven't needed to. Everyone has responsibilities." Pierre pointed to the book storefront. "Look there, Brooklyn and Cody, it is one of our libraries. You can take any book, any time. Just remember to sign it out and bring it back. You'll love Suzanne; she's our head librarian and has an inventory of every book on the island."

Brooklyn looked inside and smiled as they passed by. She desperately wanted to go in and spend the entire day sitting and reading one of the thousands of books, but they continued through the mall.

"Growing fruit and vegetables is challenging, but grasses and grain are our lifeline. We have pasture seed, wheat, soy, barley, and more. A few farmers on the island's east coast are experimenting with wind turbines and powering lights within a greenhouse; the results are slow but promising." Pierre was pleased to see the Cardinals' excitement.

"So, lots of farming collaboration. That's terrific," Claire said.

"Cody, here's our tool store—tools for any job. Borrow anything you want; bring it back in the same or better condition," Pierre said. "We've been recycling much of the metal here on the island, hoping to one day create a forge to smelt and create a new industry. Cody, you'll love Rudy; he heads a team of blacksmiths just outside the city centre."

"What's a blacksmith?" Cody asked.

"It's someone who forges metal and reshapes it using heat that ranges from 1400°F to 2000°F," Pierre answered. "Now, up here is something that will be pretty special to you two," he said to both kids.

They passed a fabric storefront, a used furniture outlet, and a wooden wheel shop. Claire and Grant had so many questions as they browsed the eclectic mall. It all seemed so peaceful, quiet and genuine. There was no panic, no hurried anxiety, only a diverse group of citizens carving out a life together on a remote island.

The darkness of the mall helped disguise the Cardinals' celebrity as they perused the different stores.

Pierre pointed ahead. "Up here on the right is our famous island university. Both of you kids will come here and learn a variety of skills. There are classes in woodworking, farming, construction, mathematics, history, fishing, boat-making, forestry, language classes, and various other electives. I think they may even play sports together sometimes."

Brooklyn and Cody's faces flushed with nervousness, and a wave of butterflies fluttered in their stomachs as they approached the massive storefront that had been transformed into a functioning classroom.

"The island children don't spend too much time in the classroom; they are usually in the field or helping with a local project. Brooklyn, you're going to love the horse palace," Pierre said, smiling.

Brooklyn quickly spun her head around and looked at her parents. "Horse palace?!"

"I guess you'll just have to wait and find out," Claire said.

"We have an island zoo, a horse palace, chicken barns, cow stables, we even have a reptile zoo," Jeannie explained.

The six new friends walked into the mall university, where a classroom of about 20 kids sat analyzing the math on the front chalkboard. It was a diverse group; some older, some young, and from seemingly everywhere on earth.

Pierre motioned to the teacher in front of the chalkboard, a woman of about 60 who came over to greet the newcomers. As she moved toward the back of the class, every student spun around to see who was at the door. They stared at the foreigners, immediately making Brooklyn and Cody nervous and slightly anxious.

"Claire, Grant, this is Sandra, our island schoolteacher." Pierre introduced everyone, and they all shook hands. "She teaches all the basics, including her most famous course: The Wonderful World of Milk."

"It's wonderful to see some fresh faces," Sandra said.

"That milk course sounds interesting," Grant said with a smile.

"It's not as boring as it sounds, I assure you," Sandra said, smiling. "It's a real pleasure to meet you," she said. "You must have come such a long way. We haven't seen anyone new in a decade."

"It certainly was a long way," Claire said. "But we are so happy our journey led us here."

"You must have come by boat," Sandra said. "Where are you coming from?"

"Well, Labrador in northern Canada," Grant answered.

"Newfoundland! Unbelievable," Sandra genuinely said. "What a journey that must have been."

Brooklyn and Cody watched the teacher with a mix of curiosity and intrigue. They had never experienced a formal classroom setting before. To the Cardinal children, Sandra appeared as a warm, caring individual with an abundance of admirable qualities.

"Sandra, I'm going to take Grant and Claire to the government building to sort out some boring details about housing, food, and transportation for the Cardinal family," Pierre said.

"Terrific," Sandra said. "Let me know if there is anything I can do."

"Well, I was wondering if you would like to look after Brooklyn and Cody for a few minutes while we figure out their situation in the coming weeks. They will be two of the brightest students on the island."

"I would be delighted," Sandra said, smiling at the Cardinal children. "It's a pleasure to meet you."

Cody and Brooklyn were terrified by the 20 sets of eyes staring at them. It felt like a herd of wolves stalking their prey during the midnight hour. Cody and Brooklyn had scaled mountains, hunted caribou, and sailed across the Atlantic, but nothing had prepared them for the chilling presence of these strange, alien children—who now seemed like the most terrifying challenge they had ever faced.

"Don't worry, kiddos, you'll be friends in no time," Grant said nonchalantly.

"We shouldn't be long," Pierre said to Sandra.

"Don't go," Cody pleaded.

"We'll be back in no time," Claire said.

Brooklyn grabbed Cody's hand and squeezed. "It will be alright," she said to her brother.

Cody swallowed hard, doing his best to ignore the sweat gathering on his palms. He couldn't remember the last time his mouth felt so dry, or his heart raced this fast.

"They're kids, just like us," Brooklyn said, trying to reassure her brother.

Grant and Claire said goodbye to Cody and Brooklyn and left them to the devices of school for the first time. The moment triggered sadness for Claire as she thought about all she had missed: dropping them off at school, going to their pageants and recitals, graduations, and parent/teacher meetings.

Pierre and Jeannie led Grant and Claire out the rear entrance of the mall and down a patchy sidewalk. The past 24 hours had been a whirlwind of emotions for the Cardinals. Yesterday, they were on the open ocean without a clue about their future. Now, they were learning the new ways of a familiar yet foreign civilization. There would be no ice fishing, hunting, long nomadic journeys, or worrying about the frigid winter conditions. Though it was a rollercoaster of emotions for Claire and Grant, it was a relief to have the assurances and dependability of a surrounding community.

"Here we are," Jeannie said as they approached a modest-looking house.

Everyone went inside to find two ladies sitting at desks sipping afternoon tea. The main floor office had a few maps of the island on the walls, a couple of filing cabinets and some bookcases with various binders and books.

"Hello, ladies," Pierre said. "This is Abigail and Brigitte, our two administrators of the island. They are incredibly lovely and very well-organized, as you can see. This is Grant and Claire. Their two children, Brooklyn and Cody are at the school."

"Grant Cardinal, it's nice to meet you both. This is my wife, Claire." Everyone shook hands and exchanged pleasantries in the dimly lit administration office.

Brigitte and Abigail were shocked at the sight of Claire and Grant. Claire and Grant were still skinny compared to the islanders and their starch-rich, high-carbohydrate diets. The Cardinals had lived on the bare minimum for years without regular fruit, dairy, and grain intakes.

"It looks like you two need some cookies and milk!" Brigitte joked.

"Maybe a carrot cake or ribeye steak," Abigail added.

"I was thinking apple pie with vanilla ice cream," Grant said cheekily.

"I was hoping for some chicken wings and pizza," Claire said with a chuckle.

"They've come from Labrador, Canada," Jeannie said.

"Oh, my goodness," Abigail said. "That's thousands of miles away."

"The four of us travelled about 4000 miles, to my best estimation," Grant said. "We made a lot of stops along the way; New York and Boston were all but gone. Lots of burnt towns and carnage. We're just so happy to see a civilization that survived."

"There is no one out there, at least along the eastern seaboard," Claire said. "Even in the small towns. We kept our eyes on the horizon, looking for other boats, billowing smoke or anything else, but nothing, not a soul."

"It's remarkable that you've found us," Brigitte said. "Where are your children now?"

"They're at the school with Sandra," Pierre interjected.

"How have they been dealing with things?" Brigitte followed up.

"They have been remarkable despite learning about the end of civilization only recently. We sheltered them for a decade, only exposing them to the northern reaches of Labrador. It wasn't until this past year that we shared the news of the catastrophe that followed the summer of 2028," Claire explained. "They were shocked at first, then upset, then finally accepting and inquisitive."

"They've both worked so hard. We couldn't have got here without their help," Grant added.

"Remarkable, isn't it?" Pierre said, pouring himself a tea out of the nearby kettle. "They have travelled all the way from Canada and in a homemade boat, no less!" Pierre exclaimed.

"It's wonderful that you've made it. Your family is the first-ever new arrival. We always wondered whether there would be any others," Abigail said. "There has been no traffic on the radios we have, no chatter, just static."

"We have someone monitoring the radio 12 hours a day. We expected to hear something by now, but nope, just dead air," Brigitte added.

"No contact from Europe or Asia?" Grant asked.

"Nothing," Abigail answered.

"Well, you should be incredibly proud that you've made it this far. What an extraordinary journey it must have been. You and your children must be utterly exhausted. Have Pierre and Jeannie been nice to you so far?" Brigitte asked cheekily.

"Well, we were on our boat for months. We stopped in several cities along the eastern seaboard, all were destroyed and barren of life." Grant was still puzzled as to what happened to everyone else. "We found this place out of sheer luck, but it has certainly restored our faith in humanity and the Great Spirit," Grant said, looking up toward the sky.

"You're both going to love Brooklyn and Cody," Pierre said to Abigail and Brigitte. "They're both brave, strong, inquisitive children and will fit in immediately. They're both in math class right now with Sandra," he added.

"A family of four; this is wonderful," Brigitte said. "How are the children? What have you been doing all these years? Could there be more of you?"

"We sheltered at my father's remote cabin in the middle of a barren, frozen wasteland," Grant answered. "There are no others that we know of. Most communities were called into Goose Bay, which was levelled by a nuclear weapon, just like Boston, New York and who knows where else."

"Goose Bay? That's NORAD," Brigitte said Abigail.

"That's why our radars and trackers went down," Abigail responded. "Do you know who hit Goose Bay?"

"No clue whatsoever," Grant answered. "But it was after the dark clouds moved in."

"We scanned every east-coast town we could and didn't find a single clue, or human for that matter, only corpses and scorched towns. There may still be people out there, but we certainly didn't see them," Claire said.

"Unbelievable. How did you find us?" Brigitte asked.

"On our way south, we stopped at Blount Island in Jacksonville and found the military base. I searched the grounds for hours and finally found your plans for the Windward Island excursion," Grant said. "It was absolute luck that we stumbled upon those plans. Right before that point, all seemed hopeless. Boston and New York were craters, and even peaceful Newfoundland had been obliterated."

"Given the rubble and chaos on Blount Island, it's miraculous that you've made it here. It's even more amazing that you've found us. It was madness in our last few days there," Abigail said. "Hundreds of thousands of people stood at our barriers, like hungry zombie hoards. The base personnel barely had enough supplies for ourselves, let alone the rabid mob. It got ugly in Jacksonville, but we were able to escape unscathed."

"Jacksonville and Blount Island was pretty grim, no signs of life at all," Grant said.

"I must say our military leaders on the other islands would love to hear your intel and any other insight you might have. We were all under the impression there was nobody else, but here you are. Ten years of checking signals, airwaves and nothing," Brigitte said. "We even sent messages in bottles."

"I know there is going to be a transition for you and your family, but we want to make it as smooth as possible. There are some lovely homes still intact. We have coastal houses, farmhouses, central island houses, big ones, and little ones. As for needs, we need help with our animal and grain farms on the island's east coast," Abigail said, pointing along the eastern road. "Does animal and grain farming appeal to you?"

"It certainly does," Claire said.

"Absolutely," Grant added.

"We'll take them out there," Jeannie said, smiling at Grant and Claire.

"Take a few days, find a home. Anywhere between 150 and 350 Lakeshore Drive," Brigitte said, pointing to the map.

"Offload anything from your boat. Get some produce and some meat. Get lots of rest, and we'll rendezvous this Friday at the community centre. We can talk about your future roles and anything else you might need. We have a big pot-luck buffet, and some musicians play some oldies," she said with sincerity.

"Here are some plots with ready-to-live-in homes," Abigail said, pointing at the map. "They should have beds and linens in the closets and stacked wood for fires and cooking."

"Thanks for everything, Brigitte and Abigail," Grant said. "This island has been the most wonderful discovery and biggest blessing. We are so grateful for your courtesy and hospitality."

"Go get some rest, Mr. and Mrs. Cardinal," Abigail said. "We'll see you soon."

Grant and Claire left the office smiling. They had always wanted to go house hunting together.

"Love you," Grant said, kissing his wife on the cheek.

"Back at you," Claire said, taking Grant's hand.

Pierre, Jeannie, Grant, and Claire departed for the mall to pick up the children and some food for the next few days. Things were moving fast. They encountered dozens of people for the first time in a decade, but Grant and Claire took it all in stride and were thankful for all that they had.

Chapter 21 - An Education

Sandra, the island's schoolteacher, stood at the front of the classroom going over various math lessons with the children. Every problem had meaning and context. They converted pounds to kilograms, centimetres to inches, and litres to gallons while Brooklyn and Cody sat at the back of the room, being as quiet as humanly possible.

The two Cardinal children were still nervous from all the boys and girls staring at them earlier, but now they were starting to relax and see the logic in Sandra's mathematics class. She provided real-world problems facing the people of New Guadeloupe. Sandra would look back to Brooklyn and Cody every few seconds to see if they were listening.

It all seemed relaxing and put both Brooklyn and Cody at ease. They were soaking in everything they could. The young boys in the class were intrigued by Brooklyn and her appearance. She was much skinnier than the rest of the class, but she was physically fit, which provided an allure of mystery to the males in the room. Cody provided mystery too, as his weathered, no-nonsense look provided an aura of a man who was experienced at hunting, fishing, trapping, and logging.

"Class, I would like to introduce you to a brave brother and sister who just arrived from Labrador, Canada. They travelled over 4000 miles, the equivalent of 6,437 kilometres, to get here. Please welcome Brooklyn and Cody Cardinal." The whole class smiled and clapped for their new classmates. "Come up here," Sandra said, beckoning the Cardinal children to the front of the class.

Cody got up, and Brooklyn reluctantly followed him to the front.

"Why don't you introduce yourselves?" Sandra said.

There was a long pause while their heartbeats started increasing, and they once again looked at all the staring eyeballs. Finally, Cody got the nerve. "Hi, everyone. We are the Cardinals from northern Labrador, Canada. We are so happy to be here. After the earthquakes, volcanoes, and the bombs dropped, our mom and dad took us to our Grandpa's trapping cabin in northern Newfoundland, where we trapped all sorts of animals; we fished, hunted, and used the natural resources to sustain our livelihood."

A young girl raised her hand. "Yes, Kate? Do you have a question for Cody?" Sandra asked the young girl.

"What did you hunt and trap?" Kate said.

Cody was taken aback by his first social interaction with somebody his age who wasn't his sister. To Cody, Kate was pretty. She triggered feelings he had never truly felt before. "Well, we would hunt whitetail deer, but they disappeared about five years ago. Then, we focussed on the caribou herds that would eat the lichen on the rocky hills. We also hunted grouse, ducks, moose, trapped rabbit, mink, squirrels, fox, all sorts of things."

Kate sat smiling at a blushing Cody. Brooklyn, readying for her introduction, turned to see a smug look from Cody.

"Hi, my name is Brooklyn. We made all our clothes from the hides of animals. We made tools from the bones and ate most of the rest," Brooklyn added. "Things got extra cold these past few years, so we decided to make a boat. Mom and I stitched the sails, and Cody and Dad built the boat. We sailed down the Churchill River and out into the Atlantic Ocean. Eventually, we ended up here."

"Fascinating," Sandra said.

"We harpooned seals and killed a black bear in Cape Cod and landed a massive tuna near Sandy Hook. We saw beluga whales near the mouth of the St. Lawrence, saw a giant iceberg, and caught sea bass in the Florida Keys. We spent a lot of time on the Anastasia," Brooklyn said.

A young boy, this time, raised his hand. "Yes, Jack?" Sandra said.

"Who's Anastasia?" Jack asked.

Brooklyn looked at Jack and smiled. "Anastasia is the name of our boat."

"Why did you call it Anastasia?" Jack followed up.

"Anastasia means resurrection or new beginning, which seemed pretty suitable, as we were looking for a new beginning among an unknown, dying world," Brooklyn said.

"You two have been on an incredible journey, and we are so happy you've made it to your new beginning here in New Guadeloupe," Sandra said.

Just as she finished speaking, Grant and Claire emerged in the doorway and saw their children at the front of the class.

"Wonderful, your parents have arrived. Grant, Claire, join us," Sandra said. "Ladies and gentlemen, this is Brooklyn and Cody's mother and father, Mr. and Mrs. Cardinal."

The class gave another enthusiastic round of applause as Grant and Claire joined their children.

"Thank you," Grant said. "We were so delighted to be welcomed here and look forward to rebuilding together."

"We admire everything you built here in the wake of such tragedy. We look forward to the community centre on Friday night and hope to see each and every one of you there," Claire added.

"We have many stories about icebergs, blizzards, and wolf packs, but you'll just have to wait," Grant said, winking.

"Thank you very much; we look forward to seeing you very soon. Everyone, say 'goodbye' to Brooklyn, Cody, and their mom and dad," Sandra said, addressing the class.

Sandra followed Cody and Brooklyn outside the doorway to have a more private conversation with Grant and Claire. The students clapped and waved goodbye as the Cardinals left the classroom.

"What an incredible journey you have been on," Sandra said to Claire and Grant.

"It was wild," Grant said. "But we gained confidence as we moved along."

"Brooklyn and Cody can return whenever they feel ready," Sandra said. "There's no pressure," she said to the Cardinal children.

Cody and Brooklyn peered through the doorway to get a last glimpse of Jack, Kate, and the rest of the class.

"I'm sure it won't be long before they're back," Claire said.

"Take care. We look forward to seeing you soon," Sandra said, shaking hands with the Cardinals.

The Cardinal family met up with Pierre and Jeannie at the wagon outside the main doors. They had loaded up on food and supplies that would last the new family a few days until they were settled and well-rested.

Everyone climbed aboard the wagon, and Quasimodo pulled away toward the island's east coast.

"I know just the spot," Jeannie said. "It has an ocean view, plenty of pasture, a small cove with a pier for your boat, and three big bedrooms."

"If you like it, whenever you're ready, we can bring a couple of you back to our place so you can sail your boat to the island's east side," Pierre said.

"You're all going to love it!" Jeannie said.

"Sounds great," Claire said.

Chapter 22 - The Chalet

Pierre drove Quasimodo and the wooden wagon down the long, winding road on the outskirts of the New Capital City. They passed a small landscape crew that was whacking down weeds with a scythe at the side of the road.

"Howdy, neighbour!" Pierre yelled. "This is the Cardinal family. New arrivals!"

"Terrific!" one worker yelled back.

"Welcome!" another followed.

Grant, Claire, Brooklyn, and Cody smiled and waved to the friendly landscape crew.

"You four are going to be the talk of the island in the coming weeks," Jeannie said.

Eventually, they arrived at a beautiful, single, modern-looking home that overlooked the ocean. Wooden posts lined the driveway, fencing in fertile green grasses carpeting the property. The house had a single garage, a few outbuildings, and a medium-sized barn.

Grant's eyes lit up at the property. It was perfect: a few acres for animal grazing, a workshop, a barn, a home that looked like it was taken care of. It was something he had been dreaming of for years.

"We put a new roof on her last year!" Pierre yelled back to the Cardinals. "We got it ready for Sandra, the teacher, but she ended up living a little closer to the school."

"It's gorgeous!" Claire yelled back.

Grant turned to Claire and smiled with a sense of relief.

"Wait till you see inside!" Jeannie yelled.

The wagon came to a halt, and they jumped off. Pierre unhitched Quasimodo and tied him inside the fence so he could feed on the six-inch grass while waiting.

"This place is a dream after living on an aluminum boat," Grant joked.

"It's spick and span outside and in," Pierre said. "There's a great rainwater collection system here. It stores it underground in a 10,000-gallon cistern. That would be about 40,000 litres. There are some solar panels on the roof if you feel adventurous enough to hook them up," Pierre said. "You'll need a battery too. Might be a good project for you and Cody in the coming weeks."

"Has anybody got a solar system up?" Grant asked.

"There have been a few who have tried. There isn't enough UV light breaking through the cloud cover," Pierre answered. "We might get enough charge to last a few hours on the CB radio, but nothing substantial yet."

"So, you've been listening on the radio with no luck?" Claire asked.

"I don't think anyone is out there," Jeannie said.

"If we made it, there has to be others too," Claire responded.

"Come inside, kids!" Peirre said. He pulled the keys from the mailbox and opened the front. "Don't lose these! We don't have a key machine on the island," he said, throwing the keys back in the mailbox. "Best to just leave the doors open."

Brooklyn and Cody ran up the steps and through the front door. Claire and Grant followed them and were immediately stunned by the ocean view from the living room window. Though dark clouds blanketed the sky, it was still a breathtaking view from their vantage point. They could see the whitecaps as they broke over the rocky shores below. There was a dining room table and chairs and a couch and loveseat in front of a central fireplace. The ceilings were high, and the whole space was relatively bright.

"It's spectacular," Claire said.

Brooklyn and Cody ran to the big bay windows overlooking the ocean for a better vantage point.

"Can we stay, Mom?" Brooklyn asked.

"Why don't you both go choose a bedroom?" Claire said as the kids immediately ran down the hall.

"This is great. It's more than we could have ever asked for," Grant said to Pierre.

"I knew you would like it. There's easy access to the shore and the pier where you can tie your boat. There's no boat house, but that could also be a future project," Jeannie said.

"There's a big, walk-out basement too!" Pierre added.

Grant walked down the hall and found the kids had established their territory in two neighbouring rooms with plenty of room and ocean views. As Grant peered in, both children sat staring at the ocean, seemingly lost in metaphysical speculation. He turned and found the main bedroom with a big metal bed frame and an upturned mattress covered in plastic. It was the biggest bedroom Grant had ever seen.

"Snowflake! Come look!" Grant yelled.

Claire came into the bedroom and was immediately shocked at the space. He put his arm around his wife and smiled.

"I love it," Claire said, her eyes tearing up.

"We'll take it!" Grant joked to Pierre and Jeannie. "Where do we sign?"

Pierre and Jeannie rode the wagon back to their house that night, leaving the Cardinals to decompress and re-energize in their new home. They made a big meal and, after dinner, explored the grounds. The evening air was cool as they strolled and discovered the different buildings.

The barn was perfect for keeping livestock; it had harnesses, a couple of saddles, tools for every type of job, and a loft for storing hay.

"This would be a perfect place to keep a couple of horses," Grant said, nudging Brooklyn.

"Can we get horses!?" she excitedly responded.

"I think that's a distinct possibility," Grant said.

"I can't wait," Brooklyn said, smiling.

They moved to the detached garage and found even more tools left behind by the previous owners; there were ratchets, hammers, saws, clamps, drills, and everything else they could need.

"What do you think, Cody?" Claire asked her boy.

"It's like a playground," he joked.

"This should keep you busy, eh?" Claire said.

"Want to go down to shore?" Grant asked.

"Yippee!" Brooklyn squeaked.

The family walked down the bumpy path to the rocky shore. The waves crashed as they made their way to the cove, which sheltered the peer from the turbulent ocean. The water was clear, and they could see schools of fish swimming near the coral. The pier was made of rocks and had a concrete surface to walk and work on.

"Look at all the fish, Dad!" Cody yelled.

"We'll have to get the boat in a few days when Pierre returns with our new horses!" Grant said.

"What!" Brooklyn immediately turned to her father. "You're not joking, are you?"

"Nope, Pierre is bringing us two mustangs. So, we need to get their stall ready and maybe build a wagon so we can start farming and bringing goods to and from the mall." Grant was finally starting to feel the pain and exhaustion roll off his shoulders. He thought of his father watching over him and smiled.

Having a community again was a huge part of life that was missing for such a long time. Collaboration, teamwork, and being able to lean on the help of others were crucial, and the Cardinals were now receiving help in their most desperate hour.

The Cardinals strolled the beach and paused at the path leading up to the house. The four family members put their arms around each other's shoulders and looked out to the ocean.

"I love you guys," Cody said.

"I love you guys, too," Brooklyn said.

Guadeloupe

New Capital City
Chalet
Pierre and Jeannie's home
Mercator
N
10 km
6 mi

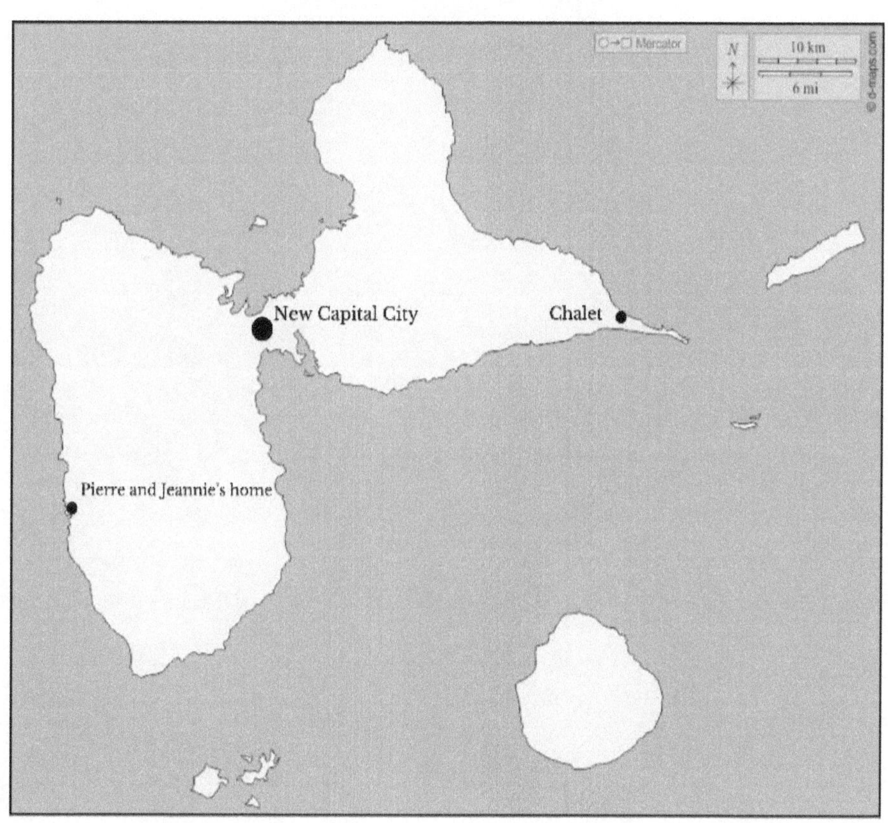

Chapter 23 - The Reveal

A couple of weeks later, after acquiring horses, a milk cow, a few sheep, and a dozen laying hens, the Cardinals had settled into a new daily routine. The early mornings, reminiscent of their days in Labrador, became the cornerstone of their lives, as there was rarely enough time in the day to get everything done.

Cody and Grant had sailed the Anastasia over and docked it at the pier. They had already used the boat a few times to go fishing and quickly realized it would play a significant role in their lives. They would need it for fishing and transportation around the island, and they might even travel to the other four islands sometime in the future. The ocean water was not great for the aluminum hull that had begun to rust, so they had started constructing a boat house near the cove's edge. It was a big project, but it would, ultimately, be necessary.

Cody and Brooklyn had set up their rooms to their liking, having found seashells and different rocks to help decorate. Brooklyn also continued writing in her journal regularly, while Cody was more practical with his journal, writing down lists of pieces, parts, and tools they needed daily.

Claire built a smokehouse in the side yard to help preserve all the fish they caught, which was a big hit at the mall with all the island's citizens. It was becoming a life of abundance where there was more than enough to go around.

Grant was on the roof working on the solar system to help power the refrigeration unit and a few lights throughout the home. He retrieved a few batteries brought over by the military, and the charge controller was already installed, so it wouldn't take much for him to connect the power.

"Okay! Flip the breaker!" Grant yelled down to Cody.

Cody ran inside and flipped the breaker, and the kitchen light came on as Claire was jarring some smoked fish.

"Hallelujah!" Claire yelled.

"We did it!" Cody said, running out the door.

"Yes!" Grant yelled back.

After another successful day, the Cardinals made their way to the Community Centre to celebrate with the other citizens on the island. It was an eclectic, diverse group with clear social ties. They ate, danced, and laughed together in ways that reminded Grant and Claire of weddings they had been to in the past.

It was a special night for Cody and Brooklyn, as they both had their first dances. Kate, the girl who asked the questions on the first day of school, asked Cody to dance. Although nervous, he said yes and did his best to mimic the other dancers' moves.

Brooklyn saw her brother dancing and didn't want to feel left out, so she got up the nerve to ask Jack, another student from class. He agreed, and they slow-danced to the string quartet that played everything from Mozart to the Old Crow Medicine Show.

Jack got up the nerve to lean in for a kiss, but Brooklyn turned her head away and smiled at the thought of kissing a boy.

Claire and Grant even hit the dance floor, celebrating their new life together. They had travelled the world together, made it through the Armageddon, raised two bright, wonderful kids, and did it together as an inseparable team. Claire laid her head on Grant's shoulder as they danced the night away.

Grant and Claire woke before light the following day and milked the cow before letting her go to the pasture to graze. They collected eggs, filled up the chicken feed, and cleaned their water trough.

They returned inside before the children were awake and began making breakfast. They scrambled some eggs and buttered some toast. As the eggs started to cook, Brooklyn came out of her room, yawning and scratching her head. Soon after, Cody came out of his room, doing the same thing. Both kids sat on the stools at the kitchen island and watched their parents prepare a delicious-smelling breakfast.

As the water boiled for tea, the eggs finished, and the smell of toast filled the Cardinal's home, a strange beam of light shot through the living room's bay windows, catching everyone's attention.

It was blinding as it pierced the air, causing the entire family to squint at the unfamiliar phenomenon. The golden glow bathed the space, bringing the colours of everything inside the house to life. It was warm and soothing, a gentle contrast to the shock of the Cardinal family. It had been a long, dark decade since they had last seen the sun, but now, at last, it had revealed itself.

Cody and Brooklyn stood frozen, unsure of what to make of the strange, beaming light. Tentatively, they took a few steps forward, allowing the light to wash over their faces. Slowly, they closed their eyes and smiled, savoring the warmth as the light embraced their joyous expressions.

9 781738 079667